Bollywood Bargain

Aliens of Extraordinary Ability

IreAnne Chambers

Published by Purple Storm Publishing, 2020.

BOLLYWOOD BARGAIN

First edition. March 1, 2020.

Copyright © 2020 IreAnne Chambers.

ISBN: 978-0996414654

Written by IreAnne Chambers.

Table of Contents

DEDICATION

To the family I love and my best friends of forever.

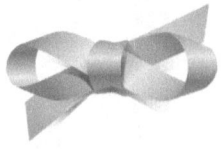

BOLLYWOOD BARGAIN

The last thing Raine O'Shea wants is an arranged marriage to Bollywood Actor, Dev Shukla. Her last chance for true love died with her husband... Right?

Raine just lost the love of her life. The last thing she wants is a new husband. Now she doesn't have a choice. If she wants to keep custody of her stepson, she needs to accept a marriage arranged by her late husband's family. But while she's willing to accept another man's proposal, she's not certain she could ever open her heart again. Surely her last chance for true love died along with her husband... Right?

Bollywood actor Devaj Shukla doesn't have any desire to marry his cousin's widow. But once his mother plays the tradition card, and reminds him of the romantic scandals in his life that would disappear if he got married, he realizes he can't refuse. Besides, he loves the little glimpses of Raine's feisty personality he sees peeking through her pain every now and then. Perhaps an arranged marriage won't be so bad after all.

Before they can consider their future together, they must first face their pasts—and the secrets that still stand between them. When all is said and done, the real question becomes whether or not this marriage will lead to happy ever after...or heartbreak...

AUTHOR'S NOTE

This is a work of fiction for the enjoyment of my readers. My family and I are long time Bollywood movie fans. Although research and care has been taken to present a story that is factual as it pertains to Indian traditions, any inaccuracies is unintentional, and if by chance offensive, my apologies in advance. My goal was to bring the feel of a Bollywood movie onto the pages of a fun, cozy, and clean romance read.

The characters and events portrayed in this book are fictitious or are used fictitiously. Any similarity to real persons, living or dead, is purely coincidental and not intended by the author.

CHAPTER ONE

"This is for you." I look at Dialah. She shrugs. The familiar orange juice in a glass is placed in front of me.

"What's this for?

"It's from him." The waitress flashes me a scheming smile and points to the bar. The man wearing a cream-colored sweater, blue jeans, and boots sits with his back facing me. I can't see his face in the mirror behind the bar, but he has thick, brown hair, and broad shoulders. I take a sip. A fuzzy navel. How did he know?

My stomach feels like it does when I'm waiting in line for the ValRavn at Cedar Point Amusement Park. No one ever chooses me. I sidle over to his side and fold my hands on the bar next to him.

"Thank you for the drink. I'm Raine." My eyes bond with his when he turns to face me.

"I'm Prem. And you're welcome."

I've never hooked up with a man who had a mustache. I've never hooked up with a man, ever. That's about to change. I know it already. "Would you like to join us? We're sitting near the dance floor." He picks up his drink and follows me to the booth where Dialah and I sit every Friday night.

I scoot in first. Prem slides in beside me. His thigh is glued to mine. I'm not moving. He doesn't either. Dialah is staring at her drink. I look at Prem. "This is my friend, Dialah."

"Hi, Prem."

Wait. What? "You two know each other?"

A dimple appears on Prem's cheek. "Dialah is friends with my sister."

"Oh." I'm not sure exactly what just happened. I sip my drink through the little black cocktail straw until the glass is empty. Sweet. I take a breath before asking what I want to know, but Prem grabs my hand.

"Let's dance." He doesn't let go, and I follow him to the dance floor. He walks us straight to the middle and circles me in front of him. I place one arm across the back of his shoulder, and he pulls me closer. We fit. Perfect. Not too tall, not too short. I place my other hand in his, in classic slow dance form. The first words to the song begin to play. "Every time our eyes meet, this feeling inside me..." I'm shaking. Can he tell?

No one ever chooses me. I'm always on the side watching, waiting for my turn. What should I talk about? Prem adjusts our clasped hands over his heart. The back of my hand warms to each beat. I smile and force myself to look him straight in the eyes. They're blue. His embrace tightens around my waist. I'm his. I already know it. I close the gap between our cheeks. Nothing more to say.

• • ⚜ • •

"I NEED TO KNOW." DIALAH ignores me while she reapplies the Thrill Seeker lipstick I gave her as a gift. Music in the ladies' room blasts each time the door opens.

"What do you need to know, exactly?" Dialah leans closer to the bathroom mirror and swipes the edge of her bottom lip with her ring finger.

"C'mon Dialah. Don't pretend you don't know what I mean. You knew Prem before I introduced you to him. It's not a coincidence. And how did he know what I drink?"

Overlapping girl conversations and flushing water make it hard to hear without yelling. Dialah pulls me out of the ladies' room to a corner down the hall. "Listen. It's true. I know his sister. We were talking the other day when I was visiting and Naz—"

"Who's Naz?"

"Prem's sister."

"Right. Go on."

"Anyway, we were talking about how it's hard to meet new people. Especially for Prem and Naz. His mom only introduces him to Indian ladies and Naz to Indian men. Prem overheard our discussion and joined in."

"Dialah, can you get to the point? I need to know before he comes back here to find us."

"Fine. He asked me if I had any friends I could set him up with. I thought of you."

"So this is a set up? And why not tell me?"

"I didn't want you to get hurt. I know how you feel about blind dates."

"Uh, yeah." I can't help the sarcasm. I'm starting to feel played and I'm not sure how I feel about that just yet.

"Prem came up with the idea that he would be here first, and if he thought you were someone he would like to meet, he would have a drink sent over."

"But we didn't even have time to sit down before the waitress brought the drink."

"I guess you have your answer then, don't you?"

"What?"

"He saw you, and he knew."

My stomach swirls. I know I like him. Everything points to him feeling the same, but the nagging disbelief it can happen to me reigns over my logic. We weave our way back to the table. Prem has ordered more drinks for the three of us. Dialah takes hers to the bar to join up with a guy she met the last time we came. I can't focus on her right now. Prem stands up to allow me to sit between him and the wall. The space between us closes, and he puts his arm around the back of my seat. It's cozy. I drain half of my drink in one sip. I need to relax.

He bends near my ear to speak. "Do you think you might want to go somewhere less crowded? Somewhere we can talk?"

His breath on my earlobe doesn't help calm the storm building inside of me. I turn to face him, only inches apart. I want to keep looking at his eyes. I make myself focus there. I want things to be different with Prem. No secrets, only truth, transparency. My gaze drops to his lips. I want him to kiss me. It feels too soon, but I don't care. "Yes."

He gives me a fast, familiar kiss on the mouth. I've never kissed a man with a mustache. It tickles. I lean forward for more, but he slides out and offers his hand to help me out.

I take it. He doesn't let go and instead interlocks our fingers together. "Let's go tell Dialah."

"Wait."

Prem stops to listen.

"I didn't drive."

"I can take you home."

My insides become a swirl of tornadic activity. Again. "I'm not sure it's a good idea to leave Dialah alone."

"I think she'll understand." Prem holds my hand all the way to where she's standing.

She probably will understand, but I still don't want to leave her.

"Are you ready to leave?" Dialah winks at me and smiles at Prem.

"Uhh..." I can't get my words out in time.

"Yeah." Prem answers for me.

"Good. Let's go." Dialah finishes her diet coke and searches her purse to pull out her keys. We walk out together, and Dialah heads for her car. Prem pulls me in the opposite direction.

"Wait, Dialah!" I let go of Prem's hand and catch up with her. "I'm not coming with you." My voice catches somewhere between "not" and "coming."

Dialah laughs. "Of course, you're not." She can be so confusing sometimes. I don't know what to say or think. She turns back to her car. "Raine, I only came out tonight for you to meet Prem. He's clearly interested. I was only waiting for him to ask you out."

"What?"

"It's what we planned. We agreed he would ask you out, and then I would meet up with Naz at his parents' house."

"Oh. My. God. Dialah? Is that why you insisted on driving tonight?" I'm really going to be sick now. I look back over my shoulder to find Prem. He's waiting right where I left him.

"Raine. Go, it's okay. You deserve this." Dialah opens the door to her car while waving her keys in the air. I wait until I see her drive away.

Prem comes up from behind me, his hand is comfortably placed in the small of my back. "Ready to go?"

I nod yes and follow his lead back toward the direction we started. He stops in front of a bronze Ford pickup truck with raised, rooftop running lights. He opens the door and helps me in. I love riding in trucks high above the pavement. I never get tired of them. I wonder what he'll say when he learns I drive one too. I start to feel excited. He hops in on the other side and drives us out.

"Stick shift? I've always wanted to drive a stick." He looks over at me, and I can tell exactly where his mind went. I pretend I don't catch on.

"Do you want to try?"

"What? Drive it?"

"No, not exactly." He lifts his hand off the gear. "Here. Put your hand there." I put my hand on the gear, and he covers it with his. "Now, pay attention to when I shift."

We drive for a while down Lake Avenue. I can tell the direction the gears go at each change. "You don't have to sit so far. Come closer. It'll be easier." I slide over until our thighs are almost touching.

6

We continue driving together like that until we reach a stop light. When Prem turns on the radio, one of my favorite songs is playing. He even listens to the same country music station I do. I'm not sure where we're going, but it doesn't matter. One route I take every opportunity to drive is Lake Road and Route 6. One of my favorite routes. I've driven it all the way through Huron to Sandusky to get to Catawba Island. It has clear views of Lake Erie and any style of house you can imagine gracing its shore. I roll my window down so I can hear the waves since it's too dark to see the water. Prem pulls into Bradstreet's Landing and parks at the fishing pier, facing the water. The pier is still lit with orange street lamps, and I can hear the lake roll in segments, crashing against the break wall.

"Can we get out and walk to the end?"

Prem doesn't answer. He hops out and comes around to open my door and help me down. I really don't need assistance, but I like his attention. When he puts his hands on each side of my waist, I can't help the shiver that follows. I fall against him, and he holds me for a second. This time I avoid eye contact. I'm afraid if I look, I will actually get what I want, so I start to walk toward the pier instead. Prem puts his arm around my shoulder as we walk.

"Do you like to fish?"

I can't believe he asks me this. If he knew the memories I have of this exact pier. I decide to tell him. "I used to come here to fish with my mom and dad... Well, I should say my stepdad, but he really was the only father I ever knew so I called him Dad."

"So you *do* like to fish?"

"Yeah, but I haven't in years. This pier and I have history. I came here when it was only steel beams and strategically placed boulders."

"Really?" I can tell I have Prem's attention now. He's easy to talk to.

"Yep. I remember they reminded me of the beams used to build skyscrapers. I followed my dad with my hands full of fishing gear and poles, balancing as I went."

"How old were you?"

"I don't remember exactly, but I was pretty young. I can't believe my mom let me walk those beams. I didn't even know how to swim. You had to step across open water in between."

"Were you afraid?"

"Not really. I knocked one of the poles into the water once. I still have a vivid picture of it fading from sight as it sank. The pole was brand new"

"It's probably still down there somewhere."

"Maybe. It's funny, I completely forgot about that. I don't even know why I'm telling you." I look down into the dark water over the edge of the pier. We're standing on the same side the pole went over. My dad's anger still scares me when I remember it. He swore and blamed me. My mom just sat in her chair behind us, propped against the oversized stones, saying nothing. I still miss them.

The wind blows hard. My hair fans across my face. Prem squeezes me close then turns me to face him. My back leans against the rail of the pier. He brushes my hair back while cupping my cheek. "How about we make a new memory to replace that one?"

I can see dark blue flecks in his eyes even under the orange lights. He bends down and kisses me full and soft on the mouth. I kiss him back. My entire body molds itself to him. The light hint of beer lingers on his tongue. It makes me want to taste more of him. He knows exactly what I want and wraps his arms tighter around me. My fingers flow free through his thick mass of hair. I don't want him to stop. I feel safe in his arms. I never feel safe. Chills prickle the sides of my arms. My decision is made. I'm not stopping unless he does.

He whispers across my lips, "You're cold."

I am cold. And warm. The wind is ravishing my back while my front is warm within the heat of Prem's embrace. I don't want to move. He doesn't have a coat to give me, but he massages my arms and back. We start to walk back to the car.

"I don't want to take you home yet."

"Where do you want to go?"

"Do you want to come to my house? I don't live far from here. It's in Lakewood."

All kinds of answers are warring to come out. I only just met him, but I can't ignore what I feel. Not this time. The same words from earlier echo in my head. *I'm not stopping unless he does.*

. . ✧ . .

"NO!" I SLAM ON THE brakes and look in my rearview mirror. Did I miss it? I can't tell. I pull to the side of Arthur Avenue and crane my head around to look. I see the wild rabbit hop across a neighbor's yard near Prem's house. I laugh and look down at my tame passenger, sitting in her pet carrier nibbling a piece of lettuce. I can't help feeling relieved that I didn't just mow down a distant cousin. Tufan has been begging to see her since I met him. I pull into Prem's driveway and see Tufan standing at the screen door. He steps out and then runs back inside.

I can hear him yelling, "Daddy! She's here!"

I walk around to the passenger side of my truck and open the door. "Come here, Honey baby."

"I thought you'd never ask." Prem wraps his arms around my waist from behind and nuzzles against the nape of my neck. I'm still not used to his mustache.

Tufan slips between us and the door. His tiny, white teeth flash brilliant against his dark skin and black curly hair. "I want to see, let me see."

I pull out Honey's pet carrier and place it on the grass in the front yard. Tufan jumps up and down, forcing us to step out of his way. I laugh, kneeling to Tufan's level before opening the pet carrier. One of Honey's ears droops.

Tufan giggles. "Swawesome! Can I hold him?"

"Absolutely. *She* loves being held. Honey is a girl rabbit."

I mouth "swawesome" as a question to Prem because I have no idea what Tufan just said.

Prem whispers the translation. "Sweet and Awesome."

Cute. I gather Honey up and out, kiss her nose, and nuzzle her cheek before I cradle her in my arms. Her bright pink eyes wink together. I gently lower Honey into Tufan's arms. "Girl rabbits are called 'does' just like female deer. C'mon, let's go sit on the porch."

I pick up the carrier and walk to the porch. Tufan skips ahead, curls blowing in the breeze. Prem frees my hand of the carrier, wraps his arm around my shoulder, and plants a kiss on my temple. I love him more each day we spend together. It doesn't feel like we've been together an entire year, the longest I've ever been with anyone.

"Raine! Hurry!"

Prem's mom, Pooja, comes out to join us on the porch. Her maroon *sari* is sleek and elegant, her hair perfectly braided and styled on top of her head. I'm still a little anxious when she's with us. I sense sometimes she doesn't approve of me for her son. Prem is very close to his mom since his father died a few years back at the Cargill salt mine in Whiskey Island. I'm not sure exactly what happened, but from what Prem tells me, there was a sizeable settlement. Other times, like now, she's smiling and happy watching her grandson play with Honey.

I sit back and rock in one of the wooden chairs lining their wraparound porch.

"Would you like a juice? Tea?" Pooja's smile reminds me of Tufan's.

"That would be wonderful. Thank you. August proves true to its reputation this year."

"I'll get it, Mom. I know what juice she likes." Prem kisses my cheek and walks in the house.

I love spending evenings with his family, relaxing in the padded wooden rocking chairs. The heavy balls of hanging ferns give it a Dixie plantation feel. The house is so large and gracious, I can imagine being on a southern plantation. The residents of Arthur Avenue made their street unique by getting the city to replace the clunky, metal streetlights with those that resemble gas-lights from the 1800's. When Prem told me, I thought it would be great if all the streets in Lakewood could be converted.

"Raine! Raine!" Tufan's scream jolts me. Pooja is laughing while trying to console her little man. "Hurry, take Honey and hide her." He wiggles past Pooja and runs to my lap holding Honey out for me to take. "She wants to cook her for Sunday dinner." His long lashes rim the top of his wide eyes.

I smile and fluff the hair on top of his head. "She's only kidding, bud. Look." I nod in Pooja's direction. She smiles, folds her arms across her chest, and rocks. "Do you know how many people joke with me about how they want to cook my rabbit?"

He shakes his head.

"Almost everyone who learns I have a pet rabbit. It's because not a lot of people have rabbits for pets. Usually they have them for food."

"Well, I'm never eating Naniji's *vindaloo* again." He leaves Honey settled on my lap.

"What's wrong?" Prem comes out and hands me a cold glass of orange juice and takes a seat in the rocker beside me. Tufan runs down the stairs and begins catching fireflies in the front yard.

"It's nothing. I was just teasing Tufan." Pooja cools herself with a fan shaped like a palm leaf. Now I really feel like we're on a southern plantation. I take a sip of my juice. Peach schnapps. I reach over to place my hand on top of Prem's while we rock in unison. My man.

. . ⚜ . .

HEAVES AND HEAVES OF nothing threaten my morning routine, again. Dialah texted she's waiting for me outside. I hurry to wash my face and brush my teeth. The flu is not fun. It feels like weeks since I actually felt good. I run outside. It's not Dialah. It's Prem. I hop up into his truck, lean over to kiss his cheek, but he turns his head. I find his lips instead. "Mornin' babe. How do you feel?"

"Still a little out of it again. What's going on? I thought Dialah was picking me up?"

He puts the truck in reverse and backs out of the driveway. "Change of plans."

"What do you mean?"

He pauses a minute before putting the truck in first gear. "I'm taking you to the doctor."

"No." I shake my head. "There is no way I'm going to the doctor with you."

"Not taking 'no' for an answer." He shifts to second.

"Prem, there's no reason for it. They can't give you anything for the flu anyway. You just have to ride out the symptoms."

"Or maybe it's not the flu. Anyway, I already made an appointment with Dr. Hill."

"Why the hell would you call my gynecologist?"

I am not happy. One of the few things Prem and I argue about is when he tries to control me.

"Gyno-what?"

13

I'm not explaining it. "If you're going to make me go to the doctor, the least you could do is pick the right kind of doctor."

I know he means well, but I'm perfectly capable of deciding when I'm going to the doctor.

"Listen. I'm sorry. Dialah made the appointment for me."

Even worse. Now he's getting my friends to help him. I roll down the window. Every time he shifts gears, I want to hurl more of the nothing left in my stomach. The cool air is soothing.

"I'm not cancelling now. You can still see her."

Dr. Hill is only twenty minutes away, but the morning rush hour makes traffic crawl in places on I-90. I'm so tired I don't have the energy to argue. We get there and I wouldn't complain if Prem carries me. My name is called, and I follow the nurse to the examination room. I don't like doctors. Period. Especially gynecologists. I'm not thrilled about seeing one for a sick visit. My queasy stomach erupts again when the nurse starts asking questions. Why can't they keep my answers in their computer system so I don't have to always answer the same questions? Now the stirrups? I giggle every time I visit because of the pot holders placed over each of them, so you don't have to put your feet on cold steel.

"Excuse me?" I'm not paying attention when the nurse asks me another question.

She repeats it. "When was your last menstrual cycle?"

Oh God. Why do they need to know that for a sick visit? "I really don't remember. Early last month. I think around Martin Luther King Day?" I remember being happy I was off work because you don't get many days off from an active construction site.

The nurse smiles. "So you're late this month."

"Late? No, I'm not late. I can't be late. I'm never late." I pull out my iPhone from my purse and check my calendar. It's not possible. I scroll the pages and count. I'm late.

• • ❦ • •

I SPREAD THE BLUEPRINTS across the table at my construction site office trailer. The designs for the next phase of the housing development proposed for next quarter will be more strategic than the first phase. I can already identify where we need to be careful and where we might get into a slip-up with city codes. Someone raps hard on the door. It must be a visitor because all my laborers know to just walk in. I open the door for two uniformed police officers.

"Raine O'Shea-Shukla?"

"Yes?"

They both remove their hats. "Can we come in?"

I scan the room for the nearest exit to make a run for it. It's something bad. I know it. Tears erupt. "No. I don't want to hear it." I back away from them, but they help me sit.

"Ma'am..." I know the expression on their face. It was the same when I was notified about my mom's accident.

CHAPTER TWO

Road rage. I've heard about it all my life. A thought passing through your mind when another driver angers you. A comment from a friend. A bulletin on the news. It happens to others. Not me. But it did happen to me.

My husband's funeral is a blur. Our wedding, a week ago, is a blur. Prem in a casket, a blur. It's raining. I sit here and listen to its rhythm. The tracks on the window match the constant stream of silent tears that mark my face. I don't wipe them away. I want the reminder of the anguish I'll never let go. Tufan is fused to my side and I to his. Pooja holds his hand on his other. I try to be calm, but I ache all over. Still no one knows. The baby nestled safe inside me is a promise. A promise to me that Prem will always be with me. A promise to Tufan he is not alone. I'm only twelve weeks. I'm not telling anyone. Not yet.

Tufan is quiet beside me. His eyes are lost in the activity surrounding us. I squeeze his hand and he squeezes back. I want him to know I will never leave him. And I won't.

• • ❧ • •

"NO. I WILL NOT ALLOW it." Pooja shakes her forefinger in front of my face. Her words are harsh and final.

"Please. I can't stay here. Everywhere I look I'm reminded of him. I need to take Tufan and move somewhere to get away. Make a fresh start."

"Tufan stays with me."

"Pooja, you know I love him. I love him like my own flesh and blood. And he loves me. He's my son in every way. Please, Pooja. I'm a mother to him." Tears reign my life these days, and today is no different. I need to move past the pain and get out, but I refuse to do it without Tufan. I'm not going to let him lose another mother. It doesn't matter if she died in childbirth and he never met her.

I sit at the table in the kitchen. The same kitchen where I said my last goodbye to the man I planned to spend the rest of my life with. I prop my forehead with my hand to hide the tears. Not that it matters. We all have our crying fits. Pooja comes and sits next to me. She takes my hand in hers.

"Daughter..." I can't look at her. The hurt is too much. I can hear the same hurt in her voice. It's unbearable. "Listen to me." She takes my chin and forces me to turn. "We will get through this together. You have lost a love, I have lost a son, and Tufan is two times my son. You know what I mean?" Pooja shakes her head back and forth. "I cannot lose him also."

I sniff. Pooja hands me a tissue. I wipe my eyes and all the mascara I finally decided to put on this morning is now smudged across my eyes. I know what she says is true. Maybe it's the hormones making it so much worse, I don't know. I still haven't told her my secret. I can't lose this family. My baby's family. I take her hands and hold them together in mine.

"I know what you say is true. It's just hard. Too hard. I don't think I can stand it sometimes."

"I know. You forget, I lost a husband too. And think of Tufan. He has lost both his parents at five years old. We can't let him lose you too. I see his love for you. I will find a way for us to go on together and stay together."

"How Pooja? How?"

"I already have a plan. You leave it to me."

. . ❦ . .

"DEVAJ SHUKLA!" I IGNORE the voice of my mom yelling from the balcony of our house in Mumbai. I walk around the exterior of my silver Maserati Spyder. No dents. No nicks. No scuffs. Neat rims. Another success. I own the speed of this ride.

"Have you been racing again?"

I shield my eyes from the sun to look up at her. "Me? Racing? What do you think, I'm stupid?" I can't let her know the truth. I can't lie to her either. She always finds out.

"No, but you think I am. Come visit me up here. I want to talk." She vanishes from my view. I know I should go to her now, but I also know if I do, I will be stuck listening to lectures on the dangers of racing. I decide to delay the visit by returning the Spyder to its garage. I need to have Giovanni give it a safety check before I take it out again. I'm glad I have an Italian mechanic. He's probably done with the Ferrari by now. I want to go over what he's done so I can drive that baby tomorrow.

An hour later, I knock on my mom's door.

"Come in."

I open the door and find her relaxing on the *jhoola*. At least she doesn't look angry. I walk to her side and kiss her cheek before sitting in the chair next to her. "So tell me, how have you spent your day?"

"The same way I spend every day, of course. Shall I ask the same of you?"

"I wish you wouldn't."

"Okay. I will not ask because we both know already." I stare at the ceiling where the rods from the jhoola connect the rings at the top. I hate when she's right. She's always right.

"When are you going to settle down, my Devaj? Have children? Your cousin is gone now too. You are all that's left of the Shukla's. And you owe it to India."

Not this again. How exactly do I owe this to India? I don't want to tell her the worst part. I swallow hard because I know I'm the last of the Shukla men, and there probably won't be any more. But there is Prem's son. "Mom, have you forgot about Prem's son?" That was the wrong thing to say.

"How can you say that?" Tears breach the edges of her eyes. "Especially after what happened to Prem? Don't you think I want my own grandchildren too? None of us know how much time we have left. You need to begin to put important things first."

I go to the edge of the jhoola and nudge her over so I can sit beside her. "Mom, please. You know I want you to have grandchildren, but how can I have a wife with my schedule?"

She turns to face me, solemn and composed now. "Devaj." I wish she would call me Dev like everyone else. She waves her hand in the direction of the balcony with its wall of windows framing the sea in the distance. "Look at this house by the sea that you own. Look at the garage where you keep useless cars worth more than one man's lifetime of work. I think you can take a break, hmm?"

A break. Bollywood doesn't take a break. She should know this after years of work in the entertainment business with my dad. I can't tell her this, though. It will only upset her more. Make her remember Dad. Make her remember my brother Jayesh. No, a break is not possible. Not now. Maybe not ever.

• • ⚘ • •

"NO WAY, NO HOW." I can't believe Pooja even considers I'd consent to it.

"Raine. I know you think it's ancient. Believe me. It's done all over India. Many families are happy because of it. Parents know what's best for their children, what's best for the family."

"Or they don't let on that they're miserable."

"Come, child. Didn't we agree we want what's best for Tufan? Eh?" Pooja places both her hands on the side of each of my cheeks. "I have come to love you like a second daughter. My own child, Naz, will have the same thing done for her." I doubt she will, but I keep that to myself. Pooja kisses my cheek on each side. "Trust me."

"I'll think about it." I can't believe Pooja wants me to marry Prem's cousin. From India. A marriage of convenience. Me.

"Don't think too long, child. Arrangements have to be confirmed. All the ladies want Devaj, but Devaj doesn't want

21

all the ladies. You'll see. Devaj is very handsome too. All the Shukla men are." *No one ever chooses me* rings in my head again. Prem did. Prem chose me. And now he's gone. Now I have to consider marrying a man who didn't choose me. Who, from the sound of it, can choose and does choose anyone he wants.

"Pooja, I said I'll think about it. Only for Tufan."

"Good. Here. Take your lunch and I will let you know what happens when you get home." She hands me my black lunch box.

"Pooja, I said—"

"Go, go, go..." She twists me around and pushes me toward the door. "Don't worry. I see it all working out."

It's going to be a long week. I wonder if continuing to live with Pooja is a good idea. Prem is the one who wanted us to live here. At least now I only get sick when I get up. I'm still not showing. No one knows. I can still move out. But without Tufan. My lawyers confirmed it. Legally, Tufan must stay with blood relatives. I'm not. It doesn't matter that I was married to his father or that we planned for me to legally adopt him. It doesn't matter that I'm about to give him his own flesh and blood brother. Or sister. It doesn't matter that I love him and care for him as my own. It just doesn't matter.

. . ❧ . .

"MOM, NO! WHAT ARE YOU thinking?" The jhoola swings forward, back, and side to side. I stop it with my hand and hover above her.

She ignores me, and I sit down next to her. "Tell me. How could you do this without asking me?"

"I did ask you. Really Devaj. It makes perfect sense. Think about it. You need a wife, and she needs a husband."

I'm so angry I have to turn around to hide my face. I lean my hand against the wall, hoping to get my composure. "Call Aunt Pooja back and tell her no."

"I won't. You don't see it yet, but you will. I know this is meant to be. This girl, Prem's widow. She doesn't want to leave Tufan, and Tufan doesn't want to leave her. We must do this for him. For the family."

The thought of my only nephew without his father throws me a gut punch the size of a wrecking ball. I still remember how I felt when Dad died. And Jayesh. Losing my dad and younger brother was hard. But I was an adult. I turn around to see my mom. She knows. She knows I'll do it. She knows I won't let Tufan lose everyone in his life. I hate that she knows. "Do I at least get to see a picture?"

"Of course. Pooja sent me wedding photos. Let's go into the office."

Wedding photos. Not the best way to envision my future bride, standing next to someone else. "I'm curious. Who came up with this idea for me to marry... What's her name?"

"Raine O'Shea-Shukla. Raine like the water that falls from the skies." My mom opens the top drawer of her desk and pulls out a large, yellow envelope. She opens it and paper photos slide down onto the desk. I want to ask why they didn't send us digital photos, but I don't. I already know the answer.

23

My mom scans each page and flips it behind the other. "Here." She finds the one she wants, turns it around, and hands it to me. "There. They are all together."

I take the stack of photos from her hands and look down at the photo of Prem with his new wife and family surrounding them. I can't tell too much from the photo because of her wedding clothes, but she's not awful to look at. I can't see the color of her eyes in this photo, but I'm guessing they're green to match the blazing color of her hair. More gut punches assault me. Tufan is so young. They're all happy in the picture. I know it is short-lived. "I can't believe they were only married a few days. Are you sure she has agreed to this? Which one of you came up with the idea?"

"Pooja and I both came up with it. I was telling her about your problems with all the actresses who lie about their relationships with you."

"Ma! Tell me you didn't talk with Aunt Pooja about them?"

"Devaj, it's public. She probably already knew."

"Probably? Please. I don't want that mess brought into our personal lives. I have a legal team to handle it. Naz handles it. Leave it there. It's what I pay her for."

"It doesn't matter. It just proves to me now is the perfect time for you to take a break, get married, have children. It's all arranged."

"All arranged? How do you mean? Shouldn't we at least meet first?"

"Of course you will meet. You leave in three days. I've already arranged things with your agent. Naz has the visa. She says you're an extraordinary man with abilities so there is no problem." I'm sure Naz didn't say it quite that way. I remember when Naz had me petition for the Alien with Extraordinary Ability visa in preparation for roles I was up for in the U.S. We laughed at the name of the form. I'm not laughing now, and this isn't a reason to use it.

"You already talked with Toni?"

"Devaj, do you forget what I did all my life with your father? None of them will say no to me. I've known Toni for years. I still carry some influence in Bollywood, and be glad I do or you wouldn't be going anywhere."

Right. Anywhere is exactly where I'd like to go right now. "Fine." I can feel my heart beating in my chest and draw in all the air I can until my lungs are full, and I let it out slow. I need space, air, and speed. I don't say it, but I dare her. I dare her to stop me. She doesn't. I text Giovanni to bring the Ferrari to the front.

.. ⚓ ..

"THREE DAYS? HOW CAN you do this? I said I would *think* about it, not agree to it. Pooja, what have you done?" I want to crawl out the window, down the stairs, get back in my car, and head straight down I-90 all the way to Catawba Island. Lately, my mind heads in that direction a lot. One day I will, I know it.

"Nothing I didn't say I would do. It's only a meeting."

"Only a meeting? The man is traveling from India, and you're telling me all he expects is a meeting?"

"Yes. Blue and I have spoken and agreed. All you need to do is meet him and see what you think."

"Blue?"

Pooja laughs at my question. "Blue is Devaj's mother. Everyone calls her that. I'm not sure where it comes from. A nickname, I think, from her husband." Pooja begins to set the dining room table. I plop down in my seat on the side. I'm not happy with her right now. I watch Tufan playing with Honey, hopping around in the living room. Hardwood floors are the best for animals. Easy to maintain and easy to clean up. For a moment, I'm returned to the day Tufan feared Honey would end up in Pooja's vindaloo. Since that day, Honey has become a member of this family. Even Pooja cuddles with her now.

"Come on, Tufan. Dinner is ready." Pooja sets the pot in the center of the table. Tufan looks over at me and leaves Honey to nibble on a piece of lettuce in the middle of the living room. He runs straight to the kitchen, washes his hands, and returns to the dining room to sit next to me.

"Raine..." His little hand takes mine in his. His voice is kind, reminding me of Prem. My heart widens so that even more love can fill it. "Uncle Dev is a good man." The steady, calm of his voice is wise beyond his years. "My dad talked to me a lot about all the things they used to do together when they were young. I miss Daddy. When Uncle Dev is here, I know I will feel better. You will too. You'll see."

I want to wrap him close to me and protect him from everything left in the world that might harm him. It's not fair. Life has not been fair to this gentle soul. I am so blessed to still have him in my life, and I know at this moment, I will do everything in my power to keep him there. Pooja opens the pot to begin serving. Vindaloo.

CHAPTER THREE

The flight from Mumbai to Cleveland is long. I hate going through customs. I barely slept. I didn't fit in the new Airbus beds in business class, and the haze of jet lag is already heavy behind my eyes. Aunt Pooja said they would be waiting for me at the baggage claim. Not exactly how I'd like to meet my future fiancée. Cleveland Hopkins International Airport is nothing compared to India's new Chhatrapati Shivaji. Not even close. I see an odd mix of people passing by. The corridors and hallways display artistic photos of places I can only guess must be local. And no paparazzi. I forgot how it feels not to be recognized.

"Ma, stop." Blue folds the collar of my shirt down and tries to flick back the hair on my forehead with her fingertips. "Stop, I said." I swing my head out of her reach. I don't want to think what the tabloids would say if any photographers grabbed a shot of that.

"You need to be presentable."

"You should have thought of that when you booked the flight three days ago." I didn't have time to prepare for anything. My hair is longer than I usually wear it, so it's in a man bun on top of my head. I'd grown it out for a movie role that only wrapped up last week. No time to cut it before we left. Now I'm stuck looking like a pretentious hipster. For now.

"Don't walk so fast. I can't keep up." Blue's short legs skip a few times to stay in line next to me.

"Do you want me to get you a wheelchair?" As soon as I say it, I know it's a mistake. Jet lag. I just need to sleep. Blue stops walking and waits in the middle of the corridor. A group of people walking behind her split to avoid crashing into her.

"Devaj, it was a long flight for both of us. I don't need you to speak to me like that."

I close my eyes for a few seconds as if that will give me all the sleep I need. "I'm sorry. You're right. I'll walk slower." What choice do I have? I should have had the Spyder shipped. Maybe I'll call Giovanni to take care of it.

"Good."

I'm sure we're walking even slower than before my wheelchair comment, and I almost want to call for a wheelchair for myself. I know Blue would not find it any more amusing so I keep quiet and walk. I'm definitely calling Giovanni.

We walk through two divided halls emptying into the room with numbered conveyor belts of circling suitcases. Not all of them are running. We find the one for our flight and wait. I look around to see if I can recognize Aunt Pooja.

"Uncle Dev!" I turn around to look for the person matching the voice. One head of curly hair slams into my legs along with the body attached to it. I bend down to Tufan's level and hug him as tight as I can while lifting him up as I stand.

"Wow! You've grown. I won't be able to lift you much longer. How did you know it was me, little man?"

Tufan smiles and laughs. "Of course I would know it was you. I've seen all your movies."

"You have?" Sometimes I forget about those when I'm with family.

"Of course I have. I tell everyone about my famous uncle."

I set him down to greet Aunt Pooja. She kisses each of my cheeks then moves to the side. Behind her, I see the girl from the photo.

"This is Raine. Raine, this is Devaj."

Raine steps forward and holds out her hand.

"Call me Dev." I don't know why I do it, but I do. Instead of shaking it, I bring her hand to my lips and kiss the top of her fingers. I look right at her the entire time. Her green eyes are glistening. I don't know if it's shock, surprise, or something else.

. . ⚓ . .

I PROMISED MYSELF I wouldn't cry. I'm not. I reach out to shake Dev's hand. He takes it immediately and raises it to his lips. What is he doing? I can feel my cheeks grow hot. I don't expect the kiss. I haven't agreed to anything. Yet. He's holding my hand way too long, and I snatch it back. The woman beside him steps toward me next.

"It's so nice to finally meet you. I'm Blue. Devaj's mother."

"Blue?"

She smiles at me and nods. After being kissed on my hand, I almost feel like I should curtsy.

Blue kisses each cheek and holds my hands out to the side. "You are beautiful. Eh, Devaj?" I can tell he doesn't agree. He looks away to grab a suitcase off the conveyer. I don't know why I'm embarrassed. I expected it. He didn't choose me.

Tufan comes to stand by me and holds my hand. He gives it a squeeze. I hold him close to my side while his uncle pulls a second suitcase from the belt. He stands each one upright and pushes in our direction.

Pooja takes Tufan's other hand in hers. "Let's go. I know you must be tired. We're parked in the parking garage, not too far. Are you hungry?"

Blue walks next to Pooja, leaving Dev to follow behind. "I'm not. I just want to sleep. Dev?"

"Thank you, Aunt. Sleep. Sleep is all I want."

Having Dev walk behind me makes me feel like a peacock on display. I can't wait to get back to work at the construction site. Taking off work to come here? Big mistake.

· · ⚬⟊⚬ · ·

SLEEP. DEEP, BED-SINKING, pillow-hugging sleep. I'm not ready to wake up. The soft satin sheets touch every part of my exposed skin. Something tickles my foot, and I kick it away. I'm not ready to wake up.

My nose tickles, but I keep my eyelids shut. Golden red splotches of color bleed through the lids of my eyes from the sun. It must be morning. I'm not ready to wake up.

Low, muffled, crunching is near the pillow where my head is positioned. I think about what it might be and decide I don't care. I'm not ready to wake up.

The tickle in my nose travels to my cheek, and I brush it away. What the...? Something furry scales the side of my hand from my pinky down. I open my eyes. One pink eye stares back. One pink eye nestled in white fur with whiskers and puffy cheeks munching on lettuce. It's sharing the same pillow with me. Three things happen next. I'm not sure what order.

I jump out of the bed to run for the door, Tufan's giggle peals the air, and Raine's horrified face appears in front of me. She looks down, then up, turns around, and leaves. No good morning. No hello. Nothing. Then I remember.

. . ✤ . .

HE'S NAKED! I CATCH myself looking. My face must be turning fifty shades of red. My brain stops thinking. I turn around and bolt downstairs. Pooja and Blue are sipping coffee in the kitchen while Pooja shells peas. I feel like I should join them and help, but how can I after what just happened? All I want to do is hide. I don't know how I will be able to see him again. Not after I've *seen* him. All of him. All his broad shoulders, ripped abs, and money maker-V. My cheeks burn hot, again. I turn the corner and head for the door.

"Raine?" Pooja calls from the kitchen. "Where are you going? It's late, almost eleven o'clock."

I need to leave the house. That's all I know. "I'm just going to sit on the porch for a while."

The screen door snaps closed, and I walk around the corner of the porch. I sink into the oversized porch swing pillows, pull out my iPhone and earbuds, and then scroll to my playlists. One Direction is perfect. I put my head back, close my eyes, and swing. I start to sing one of my absolute favorite songs. "Does it ever drive you crazy...everything that you've ever dreamed of...disappearing when you wake up ..." I can feel the tears begin to fall, but I don't care. I keep singing.

. . ⌘ . .

TUFAN IS ON HIS BACK, holding his stomach. I'm distracted from what I should do first. I glance over my shoulder and see my bare bottom staring back at me in the mirror above the dresser. The matter is settled. The first thing I do is put some clothes on. I wrap a sheet around my waist.

"Tufan. Hey, Tufan." He can't hear a word I'm saying. His only focus is hiccupping giggles of five-year-old bliss. I pick up a pillow from the bed and throw it at him. That settles him, and he throws it back. I have his attention. "I need you to take the rabbit..."

"Honey."

"What?"

"Honey. The rabbit's name is Honey."

"Okay. The rabbit...Honey, the lettuce all over the bed, and take them out of my room so I can get dressed, yes?"

Tufan picks up Honey and plucks the lettuce from the bed. "You have to admit, Uncle Dev, that is one to match you and Daddy, yes?"

"Me and Prem?" I'm still on the tail end of waking up, so I don't have a clue what he's talking about.

"You know. The jokes you played on each other? Daddy told me you played jokes on each other. I want to make you feel like home. So you'll stay." He walks out of the room with his hands full, and I ruffle his hair on his way out. Prem's smiling face flashes in my memory. That's when I know. Any thought of leaving Tufan is wiped away forever.

The joke was funny. I've no doubt Raine disagrees. I need to find her and try to explain. I'm not sure what I'll explain because I'm not the one who came into her room without knocking. I can't find what I want to wear in my suitcase, so I settle for the first thing folded on top—sweatpants and a t-shirt. I don't bother with shoes. At the bottom of the stairs, I notice it. It's not morning. It's dark out and all the lights in the house are on. Aunt Pooja and my mom are in the kitchen. I head in the direction of the counter to pour some coffee.

"I can make you traditional if you want."

"No, Aunt. I'll drink what's in the pot. What time is it?"

"Just past eleven." I slept too long. I take a sip of the black liquid. "Have you seen Raine?" Aunt Pooja points to the porch. I head in that direction.

"Wait." She opens the refrigerator door, pours a glass of orange juice, adds a shot of clear liquor sitting on the counter, and hands it to me. I start to sip it. She stops me. "No. It's for Raine. Trust me."

I walk outside onto the porch and look to one side and then the other. I can hear a soft, feminine voice singing a familiar song, but I can't remember what song it is. I walk to the corner and turn to find her leaning back with her eyes closed. One Direction. She's singing One Direction. I must have made a sound because she stops and opens her eyes.

"I'm sorry. I didn't hear you."

"I hope you don't mind if I join you. I think we need to talk." I hand her the glass of juice.

"We probably should." She takes one sip and sets it down. I can see shadows of expression change on her face from the light showing through the window.

I don't know where to start and say the first stupid thing that comes to mind. "So. One Direction?" I can tell through the darkness she's smiling. I guess that's a good sign. It takes a minute for her to respond though.

"Yes. Prem thought it was funny too. A twenty-five year-old fan of One Direction."

It is a little weird. I decide to tease her some more. "Which one are you?"

"What do you mean?" I can hear the defensive laugh in her voice.

"C'mon. You know. Which Directioner are you?"

"Oh that. Harry, of course."

"I thought for sure it would have been Zayn."

A hint of a smile begins to form. Two dimples appear on each side of her mouth. Her voice is somehow calmer now. "The truth is I think they're all very talented. Harry has a stage presence I enjoy. And of course, his hair."

"His hair?"

"Yes. I love his hair. He can rock a man bun."

I want to ask her if she thinks I do the same, but I don't. Instead, I rock in the chair and sip my coffee. I'm not sure how to move the conversation in the path I want it to go.

The chain links of the swing squawk in unison with my chair. Finally, I break the silence. "Raine, I'm really sorry about earlier."

"No." She raises her hand to stop me. "I'm sorry. I shouldn't have come in. I was looking for Honey and Tufan. I wanted to make sure they weren't getting into trouble."

"Trouble? I wouldn't call it trouble. He was following in his father's footsteps."

"I don't understand."

"Prem and I used to play jokes on each other. Tufan was trying to do the same. Let's just say I woke up to a furry companion of the four-legged kind."

"Oh." I can see her dimples again. "Tufan is a very good boy. I love him. I'll do anything to keep him with me and in my life."

"So, he's the reason you've agreed to consider this arrangement?"

Raine stares down at the floor. "Yes." I'm not sure why, but I think I'm disappointed. Or jealous? But of whom? I don't hear her question right away.

"Why did you agree?"

"I didn't."

Her eyes open wide and the swing stops.

"Let me explain. It's customary in India for marriages to be arranged by parents. Blue is the one who arranged it."

"Oh. I think I knew that. Prem and I, we were different. There was a connection between us the minute we met."

"You were blessed to have a love match."

Raine starts crying before the words complete my sentence. I jump off the rocker and move to sit next to her on the swing. She starts crying harder, so I hug her to my shoulder and hold her until her sobs slow. Her pain is still fresh. Of course she still mourns Prem.

She lifts up from where I hold her. "I'm so sorry. So sorry for wailing on you. It's just something we all do from time to time. Pooja, Tufan, and I, that is. I don't have much control over it."

I turn to face her and cover her hand with both of mine. "Listen. You don't need to be sorry. We don't have to get married. It's still too soon."

Raine is silent. I wonder what she's thinking.

"No. We need to. I need to. For Tufan. He deserves a family."

I don't disagree with her. I settle back in an easy embrace, not too close, with my arm resting on the back of the swing. Raine sinks back next to me and sips the juice. She scrunches her nose. I think Aunt Pooja got it wrong. The easy glide of the swing is relaxing. Fireflies fill the front yard. My mind wanders until Raine's question interrupts an easy silence.

"How did you know?"

"Know what?"

"This." She lifts her glass in the air before setting it down.

"Oh. Aunt Pooja. Why?"

"No reason."

· · ❧ · ·

POOJA. OF COURSE. WHY did I think the answer could be anything else? I'm upset at myself for wanting him to know me like Prem did. How could he? We only just met. But I can't help wanting to be the way I was with Prem.

Wanting him to know my favorite songs, my favorite drinks, my favorite foods. Wanting him to know my favorite flowers, my favorite candy, my favorite colors. Wanting my nightmare to go away. I can't help wanting Prem.

And Dev is not Prem. The sooner I get used to the idea, the easier it will be. I sneak a glance at the man sitting next to me. He's off in distant thoughts. I don't expect him to look at me when he does, and I jump when he speaks.

"Are you okay?"

"Yes. I'm sorry. My mind is jelly right now. What did you say?"

"It's all right if you don't feel like talking."

"No, I want to. I mean, we probably should."

Dev exhales a deep breath. "I'd like to know more about you. I know you work for a construction company. But what exactly do you do for them? Office work?"

Typical. Most men can't image a woman on a construction site. Let alone a five-foot-three woman on a construction site. "Uh, no. Not office work. I'm a project manager and supervisor. I actually work onsite to oversee the job." There it is. Incredulity. I've seen it so many times you would think I should be used to it. But I'm not. It's annoying.

"You mean you actually oversee the building? The workers?"

"You mean the 'men' workers?" I feel like teasing him a little.

"Um. Well, yes." Dev squirms in the swing to better face me. "Do you find it difficult?"

I expect him to tease me, but he doesn't. I realize I don't mind answering him. He's taking me seriously. I clear my throat. "No, it's not. I agree, it's probably not the norm, but my laborers respect me. We've worked together on projects for about four years. I know their work, and they know what I expect. Together we get the job done to specifications."

Dev bends his arm on the back of the swing to support his head. "So you're telling me you've had no bad experiences, no one giving you a hard time, no one pushing you around because you're a woman?"

"I didn't say that. Of course I've had men give me a hard time. It's part of the job. But I've learned how to deal with it."

"How?"

"I can dish out as well, you know." I really wish he would stop with the questioning, or he might find out just how much I can dish out.

"Hmm. What's the worst situation you found yourself in?"

"The worst?" I have to think. Should I tell him about the time the porta-potty delivery was late? Or when two of my laborers got into it with nail guns? No, better leave those for another time. "Probably conflicts related to union versus non-union. Tempers flare when we employ non-union laborers."

"How do you deal with it?"

"I avoid hiring non-union workers. Pick your battles. You know?"

Dev reaches his hand out. The jolt I feel from his fingers against my cheek freezes the seconds it takes for me to realize he's only sliding the hair away from my face. I can't tell if he knows how uncomfortable I am now. But I know I have to get used to his touch so I don't move. I look down because I can't look him in the eyes. I'm too nervous. It's not the same as with Prem. My Prem. Gone.

CHAPTER FOUR

The house is quiet and dark. I'm stretched out on the couch with my hands folded behind my head. "I can't do it."

My mom takes a sip of her tea and cradles the cup in her hands. "Devaj, what are you talking about?"

"It's too soon. She's still mourning Prem."

"Of course she's still mourning Prem. It doesn't change anything. It's an arrangement."

"How can you say that?" I sit up to face her. "Ma, I refuse to marry her this soon. I won't."

My mom takes another drink. "I understand what you're saying, but take some time. Get to know her. Take her out. You know? Love will come in time."

I stare at her. Her words "get to know her" echo in my head. Right now, my problem is not getting to know her. It's why I agreed to this to begin with. I look at my iPhone and check the time. Almost dawn. I stand up and go to my room to put on my running shoes. My mom's voice trails after me. "Where are you going?"

Running. I have to get out of this house. That's all I know. I walk past my mother, sitting in front of the large window overlooking the porch. I don't even look at her. I want no more conversation. I need to think. Think for myself. I check my pockets to make sure I have my phone and wallet, open the door, and leave.

. . ⚘ . .

WHITE FLASHES EXPLODE against the stencil designs on the walls of my room. I count the seconds before the loud boom that follows. Angels bowling in heaven. My mom used to say that every time it thundered. I didn't figure out the truth until fourth grade science class. Three seconds ...three miles away. I look at the clock, five thirty a.m. I check my phone to find out the weather forecast. Ninety percent chance of rain all day. I'd say more like one hundred percent. It feels like someone's throwing rocks against my skull. From the inside. I sit up on the side of my bed and ruffle through the drawer of my nightstand. My migraine pills are almost gone. I swallow a double dose because I know I'll need it and drink the last of my bottled water I keep by the bed. I call my foreman and find out the day is shot because of the rain. He'll check back before noon to see if we can get anything done this afternoon. Looks like I'm working from home today, so I get dressed slow and steady before I head downstairs.

Blue is staring out the front room window. Rain is raging and overflowing the edges of the gutters. I can see it splash when it leaves the end of the downspout. I need to fix that before it causes water damage to the foundation. Blue's navy sari is draped in perfect symmetry over one shoulder and wrapped tight around the curve of her waist. I'm surprised to see anyone up this early. I guess it's the jet lag. "Good morning." Blue turns around to look at me. Her brows are furrowed, and I can tell something is wrong. "What is it?"

"Devaj. He's not back yet."

"What? Back from where?" I walk closer to where she's standing.

"He went out running earlier before it was light."

I walk outside on the porch. Wet grass and pine scents decorate the air around me. Shades of silver and dark gray canvass the sky. Blue joins me. "Which way did he run?"

She points north. I always know where north is. Everyone in Lakewood knows since we're on the shore of Lake Erie. "I'm sure he's fine. There are plenty of places to wait out the rain."

"But at six a.m.? I don't even see anyone moving around out here."

I laugh. It's true. The world isn't that active at six a.m., but I know a few businesses are open that early. "Trust me. He'll be fine. Let's go have some breakfast. Unless... Are you tired? Maybe you would rather sleep?"

"Sleep? No. I've been up almost all night, but I don't think I can sleep right now. Not until I know Devaj is home."

I come back inside and head for the kitchen. Blue follows. I know Tufan will be up soon. I think I'll take him to school myself this morning. I cook the turkey bacon first in the cast iron skillet my grams gave me. I crack open four eggs in the center. I always think of grams when I cook in her skillet. Eggs, bacon, and soda bread. That's what I'm making today. It reminds me of her.

The front door squeaks open and snaps shut. I can hear the commotion and mixed voices in the foyer. I think Blue and Dev are arguing, but I don't really care. I want to finish making breakfast. The eggs sizzle in the oils. I lightly salt them and spoon some of the hot oil on top to get a thin white layer on top of the yolk. The touch of someone's hand on my back startles me. Oil misses its target and splatters the top of my other hand.

"Ouch!"

"Are you okay?" Dev shuts off the burner, pulls me to the sink, and runs cold water on top. I feel the instant relief, but I know it's going to sting for hours. I hate getting burned.

"It's fine." As I take my hand away from the running water, I realize the entire side of my body is damp somehow. I look down the length of my side. Wet. I look at Dev. Wet. Soaking wet and dripping where he stands in his bare feet. His white t-shirt is painted on his chest. I cover my mouth because I can feel it starting. The everything's-better-after-two-glasses-of-wine feeling. It happens sometimes when I take my migraine pills on an empty stomach. I may be in mourning, but I'm not dead.

"What happened to you?" If I can turn my thoughts serious, it might go away.

"Isn't it obvious?"

I look straight into the amber glow in his eyes, trying to focus. Droplets of water hang at points of the hair edging his face.

"Jet lag. I forgot to take my clothes off before I took a shower."

If Blue hadn't told me he went for a run, I might believe him. Almost. My face burns hot because I remember.

Yesterday he forgot to *put on* his clothes. Everything's better after two glasses of wine.

· · ❧ · ·

IT'S NEVER BEEN HARD for me to talk to women. I can't figure Raine out. I try to be funny and she's serious. I try to be serious and she laughs. I know she's grieving. That must be it. I grab a towel laying on the counter.

"Come over here. Sit." I'm still holding her hand in mine. I sit down next to her and start drying her hands. It's not too bad, but I know oil burns hurt. "We need to put something on that to help the pain." I start opening drawers.

"What are you looking for?"

"Toothpaste."

"Excuse me? Do you have a sudden urge to brush your teeth?"

"What?" I can tell she's holding back laughing, but I don't understand why. "No, you put it on burns." Now she is laughing. "What is so funny?"

"I've never heard of anyone putting toothpaste on a burn."

I stop looking for the toothpaste and sit back down next to her. "It's true. It works. I know from experience."

"Really."

"Yes. I was working on my cars with Gio and opened an overheating radiator before it had cooled. The water sprayed me in the face."

"Ow! That must have hurt."

"Hurt? I can't remember anything that hurt worse. Well, maybe I can. But anyway, Gio grabbed some toothpaste he had in his tool cabinet and pasted it all over my face."

"Did it work?"

"What do you think?" I turn my face from one side to the other. "Any scars?"

"None that I can see, although they could be hiding under the stubble." Her closed-lip smile still allows her dimples to show. I really can't tell if she likes it not. I decide to try and find out.

"You don't like my designer stubble?"

"Designer? That's what you call it?" She takes my chin in her hand and moves it from one side to the other. "I'm not sure." She stands up and leans into my chest. I'm not sure what she's doing. She reaches over my shoulder and pulls a tube from a drawer. "Here."

"What's this?"

"Neosporin. It's what we put on burns here in the States."

"Ah." I take the tube and squeeze some out onto the back of her hand and rub it lightly with my thumb until it absorbs into her skin. "Do you put a bandage on it or something?"

"No. I think I'm going to leave it like this for now. I may put one on later." She stands up to check the eggs on the stove. "Ugh. How do you like your eggs?"

I look over her shoulder. "Overcooked."

"Perfect. Go get some dry clothes on, and I'll get these plated."

"You may need a dry set yourself."

She looks down the front of her wet top. "Shit."

. . ⚘ . .

WHY CAN'T I GET IT together? What was I thinking, leaning into him like that? I pull my lavender tank top off and open the closet to find a replacement. I pull out a green one. It works. The yoga pants I'm already wearing match. I never should have taken those pills. I need to call the doctor and find out if it's okay. Oh God. Please don't let it hurt the baby. I place my hand on my stomach and head down the hall to Tufan's room. It's almost time for him to get up anyway. A few minutes early won't hurt. The door is open and the light is on. The blinds are pulled allowing some light into the room, but the gloom of the storm still darkens everything. Dev is sitting on the edge of the bed wearing dry clothes. Tufan sees me and stands up on his bed and starts jumping. "I can go. I can go. We can go."

"What? Where? Where are we going?" I look at Dev, who's holding a mailer in his hand.

Tufan falls on his bottom and snatches it from Dev's hand. "No. Not we, us. Men. It's for men only. I can go because I'm a man. See?" Tufan shows me the mailer and points to a line and reads, "You're invited to a special event. For Men Only: Stay Strong, Live Long." I look at Dev, and he shrugs his shoulders. I want to laugh, but I don't want to discourage Tufan. He's so excited about being able to read. He reads everything. Not always a good thing.

"Why not? I'll take him."

"You do realize this is just a free health screening at the Cleveland Clinic?"

"But they're going to have dinner and free raffle prizes!"

I look at them both and swallow hard. "We'll have to see, Tufan. We might have something more fun planned. Why don't you get dressed now and come down for breakfast? I need to speak with Uncle Dev for a minute."

I bite the insides of my cheeks to keep from laughing. Dev follows me to the kitchen. I shake my head because I can't believe the events of this morning. I begin to set the table. I place eggs, and turkey bacon on each plate. Forget the soda bread for today. We'll go with the store bought.

Dev sits at one of the places, holds a fork in his hand, and waits. "So, what did you want to speak about?"

I stop. I place the last fork by a plate, unlock my teeth from my cheeks, and sit. "The free health screening is going to offer information on the risks of colon cancer in men."

"Oh." Dev's fork remains dangling from his hand.

.. ❧ ..

"HOLD STILL, TUFAN." I watch Raine's patient attempt to get his raincoat on.

"I don't want to wear it. Can't I just wear my clothes? Uncle Dev went running in the rain. I want to play in the rain too."

"But Uncle Dev didn't do it on purpose, and he had clothes to change into. You'll be at school. How will you dry off? Hmm?"

Aunt Pooja walks past me, gives Tufan a big hug, and kisses the top of his head. "Be good at school, and I will be there to pick you up."

Raine hands Tufan his backpack and grabs her keys from a hook near the backdoor. I wonder about my ability to be a father for Tufan. To be a husband for Raine. To be married to one woman. I look around at this life. It's so far from what I'm used to. I pour myself a second cup of coffee and walk into the living room. I'm trying to stay awake all day so I can get myself used to the time difference.

"Dev?" Raine is calling from the kitchen. "Dev?"

"Yeah! I'm here."

"Do you think you can drive us?"

"What's wrong?"

"I don't think it's a good idea for me to drive. I'm feeling light-headed after taking some migraine medication this morning."

"Oh. Sure. I can drive. It can't be that much different, can it?" I walk out to the truck. Tufan is already in the back seat. It will definitely be different than my Spyder. I'll have to be careful of the speed. I start to open the door. Raine calls out.

"Are you sure you can drive?" She's standing right next to me.

"Of course."

"Uh, you'll need to go to the other side then."

"Right. I forgot." I walk to the other side and climb in. Raine is already in the passenger seat with her seatbelt on. I start the engine and pull out.

"Slow down! You can't go that fast here."

I slam on the brakes at the end of the driveway. Tufan falls forward between the front seats. Raine looks back. "Tufan, how many times have I told you? Seatbelt. Now." I hear a click.

"What are you waiting for?"

"Which way?"

"Oh, yes. That way. The school's on Elmwood."

"Left it is." This is the same way I ran this morning. I drive to the end of the street ending at a stop light. I remember the strange blue egg-shaped monument in front of the library on the right. This isn't difficult. "Now, which way?"

"Right." I'm sure more than one horn blows louder than the screams erupting inside the truck. Raine grabs the wheel pulling a sharp right toward her. I slam on the brakes and drift to the side.

"I thought you said you could drive?" Her voice screeches.

Who would have imagined a sound like that being possible from the wisp of a girl she is? No one grabs the wheel when I'm driving, and I'm annoyed. I look in the rearview mirror and my eyes meet Tufan's. His face is pale. I want to yell back at her, but the fear I see in him settles my anger. I grit my teeth instead. "Yes, I can drive." I feel like I do when my mom grills me about my cars. "I just need to adjust to driving on the right side of the road. It was a momentary lapse. In India, we drive on the left."

Tufan squeezes between us. "Uncle Dev really knows how to drive, Raine." Tufan flips his head back and forth from me to Raine. "Tell her, Uncle. Tell her."

"Tell me what?" Now they're both looking at me.

"I said I can drive." My teeth are still grinding.

"No, no. Of course you can drive. Uncle Dev races cars. He has any car you can imagine. Tell her Uncle. I've seen the pictures. My dad showed me."

Raine is facing forward now. Her jaw tightens, looking like she may be grinding her own teeth. "C'mon. We need to get you to school." She won't even look at me.

. . ❧ . .

ONCE TUFAN IS SAFELY at school, I reach over, turn off the engine, and take my keys. "I need to drive now." I start to get out, but Dev touches my arm to stop me.

"What? Why?"

I hesitate before opening the door. "Because I didn't realize you don't drive on the same side of the road in India. If I would have known, I never would have asked you to drive."

Dev hangs his arm over the steering wheel and turns in his seat to face me. "I didn't hide it from you and you didn't ask. It won't take long for me to adjust."

"I would prefer if you don't adjust while Tufan is riding with you." I can see the muscle in his jaw tighten and release. Maybe I shouldn't be so hard on him, but I can't help it. He scared the crap out of me. My heart is still beating wild from the experience.

"Listen. I need to acclimate myself to driving here if I'm going to live here, yes?"

I know he's right, but I'm not sure I'm ready for another potential head-on collision.

"Let me drive with you a little more this morning. Take me around town where I can get some practice. Somewhere with less traffic. What do you think?"

What I think is I want to go home, crawl back into bed, and sleep. I'm not sure practicing in the rain is the best idea, although it's not raining right now.

"There was this park I was at this morning. It can't be far from here. Let's drive there."

"There are parks all over Lakewood. Do you remember the name?"

"No, but it had a large pool. They were filling it."

Lakewood Park. No doubt. School will be out in a week, and the pool opens the first week after school's out.

"I know what park you're talking about." I lean forward to look at the sky once more. It's still gray, but it's not raining. "I guess we can."

"Great." He holds his hand out, palm up.

"What?"

"Uh. I need keys to drive."

I look at his hand. I'm still not sure I'm up for this driving experience, but I drop the keys in his palm, and we drive to the park.

"The pool is almost full."

Dev drives past it to the end of the lot and parks by the Women's Club Pavilion. "Should we get out and walk? I saw that bike path earlier, but it started to rain so I didn't get to run it."

I check the sky again for any changes. It's still the same. "I guess."

It's colder by the lake. I zip up my jacket and put my hands in my pockets. We hit the bike path and work up a brisk walk. We walk past the volleyball courts and make our way to the edge.

"Wow! I had no idea. When everyone said Lakewood was on the shores of Lake Erie, I had no idea it was an ocean!"

"Didn't you Google it?" Dev's reaction makes me laugh. Every time someone reacts like this, it makes me proud of our lake. No one really gets the concept of how big the Great Lakes are until they actually see one.

"Yes, but I guess I didn't think it would be like this."

"Didn't you see it this morning?"

"Not really. I only got to the pool and then the rain started. I waited as long as I could under the pavilion, and then I just ran back."

The closer we come to the cliffs, the more excited I get. "I love this park. It has always been my favorite." We stop at the fence bordering the edge of the cliff where a line of stand-alone gliding swings are installed. I can sit here for hours just watching the water from the top of the cliff. "Let's sit for a while."

Before I can actually move in that direction, Dev is on his way down the stairs to the break-wall and stone walkway below. I jog to catch up with him at the bottom.

"The only thing missing is the salt water. I can't believe this is all fresh water." He walks to the edge and climbs out onto the rocks of the break-wall.

I'm too nervous about slipping to follow him so I stay on the walkway. "I agree, but I'm not sure I miss the salt water."

"Really? It's good for your health. My house in Mumbai is on the shore of the Arabian Sea. I never get enough of it."

"I love the sea too. I've been to Ocean City, but I don't miss the salt or the creatures that live in salt water."

"Creatures?" Dev climbs back and joins me on the path along the bottom of the cliff. I can tell he thinks it's funny. The show of his perfect white teeth proves it. I guess it is.

He takes my hand in his. "Can I?"

My words are stuck by the surprise of his question so I allow it.

"So tell me about these creatures."

"You know. Jellyfish, sharks, scorpion fish." I can't even think clearly. All I'm aware of at this moment is my hand in his, warm and soft.

Now Dev throws his head back and laughs. "Scorpion fish? I get jellyfish and maybe sharks in certain places, but I've never heard of someone afraid of scorpion fish specifically."

"It's because of a friend I had in high school. He was scuba diving not far from the beach. He said he almost got stung by a scorpion fish. They're deadly you know." I can feel the soft caress of his thumb on the inside of my wrist.

"Whoa! Look at that!"

Dev amazes me with his excitement at small things, like a child getting his first bike without training wheels. He pulls me up the side of a low hill where the city installed an outdoor amphitheater. I agree with him. It's exceptional. Giant, concrete stairs carved into the side of the hill. I follow him up to about the center, and he drags me across to sit. The stone steps are perfect seats with a couple feet of grass behind each length of stone. Enough for a lawn mower to pass. The grass is damp, but the cement is cold and dry. Sitting there in the wide-open space, with nothing in front of you but the Great Lake Erie in all her glory, gives me chills.

Dev must have seen me shiver because he puts his arm around me and holds me close. "It's breathtaking."

"Yes, it is." I don't share that being so close to him is what's really taking my breath away at this moment. I feel so guilty sitting here with him. Prem's cousin. I feel guilty because I'm enjoying his closeness. Enjoying being with him. Enjoying his touch. Enjoying him.

"Imagine how beautiful it would be to come here at night to look at the stars."

"Naz and I did that once with a group of friends. We came here to see the Aurora Borealis."

"You can see that here?"

"Not usually. It was an odd thing. Something about a solar storm, I think. Anyway, all the weather channels were telling people there may be a chance to see them around midnight."

"What color were they?"

"There were too many lights reflecting from downtown to see them, but we did see some falling stars. Even though it's pitch black to the naked eye over the lake at night."

"I know. I have that view from my house in Mumbai."

I want to ask him more about his home, but I can't find the words. My emotions are rattling, mixed up and foggy. Dev stands up first and holds his hand out to help me up. "Let's sit on one of those gliders for a while."

The gliding of the swing always relaxes me. I look out over the gray water of the lake. I watch darker clouds in the distance rolling east toward Cleveland's skyline. Dev is sitting so close his leg is touching mine. It feels intentional, but I'm not sure. I decide to stay put and just enjoy the moment.

"What are you thinking about?" Dev's question startles me.

"I don't get the chance to come here as often as I used to. I'm just thinking about times past."

"So tell me something. About times past."

I put my hair behind my ear because it keeps blowing in front of my face. "I was just remembering when I used to come here to watch the sunsets. The only thing here was the fence. Nothing else. There was only a cliff that ended in the water. It reminded me of England or Ireland."

"Have you ever been to England or Ireland?"

I smile. "No, but they're on my list of places I want to visit. Trace my ancestry. And I love the classics. Jane Austen, Elizabeth Gaskell."

"It is a truth universally acknowledged that a single man in possession of a good fortune must be in want of a wife."

I can't believe it. "You've read Pride & Prejudice?" I feel like a school girl meeting her idol for the first time. I want to wrap my arms around him, hold tight, and scream. Prem always teased me about my choices of entertainment. Oh my God. No. I feel sick. I just compared Dev to Prem.

"What's wrong? Are you okay?"

"I'm all right."

"You don't look all right."

"That's comforting."

Dev laughs. "Seriously. What is it?"

"I feel like I'm cheating."

"Cheating?"

"It's silly, but I like that you've read Pride & Prejudice."

"Raine, entertainment is my profession. I attended the Bombay Scottish School and studied at the Royal Academy of Dramatic Art in London. My curriculum was more than theatre."

I keep forgetting he's an actor by profession. Probably because he's famous in India and not here. "Prem always teased me about it. You didn't and I like that."

"So what's the problem?"

"I feel like I'm betraying him."

Dev adds force to the glider to intensify the swing while placing his arm along the back of the bench. He's not touching me exactly, but I'm aware of his arm behind me, waiting. Waiting for something I'm afraid to give. At least now. I place my hand on my stomach to hold my baby.

"You're not, you know. Not betraying him."

"I can't help how it feels. It feels too soon."

"Try to look at it the way we do in my culture. It's a business arrangement. If we feel like we are compatible, we don't wait to be in love. Love comes with time."

As soon as he says the word *love*, I feel it in my chest as if an open wound in my soul is being scratched. "The truth is, I want to be a part of Tufan's life. He's my son. I may not be his birth mother, but he's my son. The only way Pooja will allow that to happen is if I marry you."

Dev turns to face me taking my hands in his. I can feel the tender compassion radiating from his touch. "Raine." He caresses the top of my hands. "Listen to me. We are not betraying Prem. I know it's hard, but he's gone and Tufan needs a family. He needs a mother who loves him. I want to help make that happen. Prem would want this."

I watch our tangled fingers hang between us. "How can you be so sure?"

"Because family always came first with Prem. I loved that about him."

"Were you two close?"

"As close as the ocean separating us would allow. We skyped a lot. He spent many summers with us when he was in school." Dev turns forward again and forces the glider into another swinging session. His arm is back in its position behind me.

"You must miss him too." I can feel the tears stirring behind my eyes, but I'm able to keep them back for the moment.

"I do. I'm sure it doesn't compare to your loss, but I do miss him. I miss his laugh, you know?"

I know exactly. The memory of Prem's golden smile is what begins whittling away my control. "When he laughed, I could never keep a straight face when something got him going."

"I know. And Tufan has the same laugh."

"Yes, he does." The tears waiting to fall push forward a little more coupled with my memories of Prem and Tufan together. I wipe each eye under my lashes. "I love to hear Tufan laugh. It reminds me so much of Prem."

Dev takes my hands in his again. "Hey, these are happy memories, yes?" He bends his head to look up at me.

"I know. Yes, they are. And you're right. Family always came first with Prem. It's why we live with Pooja."

"It's why my mother has a suite in my house in Mumbai. And helped arrange our marriage. And followed me here." Dev's smile is bright too.

I have to laugh a little because men living with their mothers always seemed odd to me until I knew Prem. I would never guess Dev for a man who still lived with his mother. But Prem made me feel safe, protected, loved. I look at Dev. Will this man be the same?

"Family first."

"Family first." I repeat.

"And you must admit there is some attraction between us, yes?"

My face betrays my feelings. I can feel the heat grow hotter. I nod in agreement. More tears threaten the corners of my eyes. I wipe each one with my left ring finger. Dev takes my hand back into his. I want to tell him about Prem's baby, but I'm afraid. "And you know, I am a single man with a good fortune and in want of a wife. I choose her to be you, if you will have me?"

I have so much warring emotion exploding inside. The words won't come. Dev just proposed to me quoting Jane Austen. In another life, I would be jumping all over him. All I can do now is nod my head yes.

Tears stream down my cheeks. Dev holds my face between his hands, wiping them away with his thumbs. "Why don't we go tell the Aunts we've come to an agreement?"

"The Aunts?"

Dev smiles. "It's a thing we do in India. It's shows respect to older ladies. Kids call older ladies in the family Auntie.

I feel like it fits us. Pooja is my aunt and Blue, my mom, is auntie to Tufan and can be auntie to you for now. So, the Aunts."

"Okay."

Dev leans in slow and stops an inch before touching my lips with his. I look right into his eyes. Amber eyes, the color of topaz. The wind swirls my hair around us. I can feel his breath on my skin, but he doesn't kiss me yet. I close my eyes and it's instant. Gentle and awkward, but soft lips close the gap.

CHAPTER FIVE

What was I thinking? Asking Raine to marry me this soon. Mom is happy. Aunt Pooja is happy. I guess I'm happy. And Raine. She's still grieving.

I pick up my iPhone to check the time. Where the heck is the driver? Gio texted me two hours ago to let me know it arrived. How long can it take to drive from Hopkins airport to here? Air Cargo confirmed door-to-door delivery. I need to get out of here. The ladies for Raine's painting party are starting to arrive. I can hear Naz downstairs. Tufan runs into me the minute I open my door to leave. "Uncle Dev! Uncle Dev! You need to come down fast."

"What's going on?"

"You have to see what's in the driveway!"

"Hold on." I run to the window. He's right.

Tufan grabs hold of my hand and pulls me down the stairs, past the ladies, and out the front door. There she is in all her sleek, silver splendor. The driver is standing next to the passenger side door taking notes on his electronic clipboard. "You Devaj Shukla?"

"Yes, I'm Dev." I walk all the way around her. I've missed this baby. I can't wait to sink into the front seat and hit the road.

"Can I see a Photo ID?"

"What?"

"I need your photo ID before I can release the vehicle to you."

"Tufan, run up to my room and get my passport. It's in the top drawer of the dresser."

"Can I have the keys? I want to hear the engine."

"Keys are in the ignition."

"Right." I hop in and start. I've missed that sound. I rev the engine a few times. It sounds good. Tufan returns with my passport, I sign the paperwork, and open the glove box for my Ray Ban sunglasses. I adjust the rearview mirror and see the delivery man leave in his flatbed tow truck.

"You want to go for a spin?"

Tufan's grin spreads from one side of his face to the other.

"Hop in."

He doesn't even get the door open before Raine, Naz, Aunt Pooja, my mom, and another girl I don't recognize step out onto the porch.

"Devaj! Where did this come from?" I can tell from my mom's familiar exclamation this is not going to go well.

Raine squeezes between the ladies grouped on the porch and bustles down the steps to meet me. "Dev? You can't drive this here."

"Why not?"

"For starters, the driver sits on the right. You've only just gotten used to driving on the right. Now you're adding this to the mix?"

"Raine. It's not a problem. I'll be careful."

"No. Not with Tufan."

"C'mon, Raine." Tufan runs around the front of the car to beg her to let him go. He takes her hand in his, jumping and shaking at the same time. "Please? Uncle Dev is a good driver. He's a professional driver. My dad told me. Please?"

My mom comes down the stairs and the others follow. "Devaj. I can't believe you brought this car from India."

Raine looks at my mom. "What do you think?"

My mom shrugs her shoulders. "He is a good driver. This much I know."

I'm not sitting here listening to a bunch of women discuss the safety of my driving. "Tufan, get in the car. We'll go have a boy's day out and leave the ladies to their party."

Tufan looks up at Raine. She crouches to his level and gives him a hug. "Make sure you keep your seatbelt on all the time." Raine glares at me over his shoulder.

When she stands up, she leans against my door. Her whispers are heavy and fierce in my ear. "You better be careful. I can't handle another loss in my life." Her words are like a punch to the gut, and the fire in her eyes matches the color of her hair. I'm not sure how to respond in front of all the female eyes pasted on me. All I can think to do is reach out and pull her lips to mine. So, that's exactly what I do.

• • ⚘ • •

I'M SO ANGRY, I COULD spit nails. If I had a nail gun, it would be aimed directly at his smiling, scheming face. How can I say no to Tufan now? So I aim my words like nails. Nails aimed right into the side of his head. "You better be careful. I can't handle another loss in my life..." What happens next is not what I expect. His lips claim mine. His fingers tangle with my hair, holding my head firmly in place. I want to pull away, but I can't. I don't move. I let him in, and he kisses me. Kisses me full and complete. I'm sure I'm kissing him back, but it feels like I'm standing outside of myself. All I know is that his touch calms one anxiety and builds another.

Tufan's voice echoes in the background. "Let's go, Uncle Dev. Let's go."

And then it was over.

I step back from the car and lock my eyes with Dev's. My attraction to him surprises me. I feel different with him. I want him to kiss me again. And I feel guilty that I do.

I look away when someone takes my hand. It's Dialah. On my other side, Naz wraps her arm around me. "Come on, sis. We need to finish getting ready. Celine will be here in a few minutes."

"Celine?"

"Celine Weston. My friend? The tattoo artist? She's going to do the henna painting."

"Oh, right."

Dialah and Naz walk me back in the house. The Aunts have redone the family room in the back of the house to prepare for the wedding the day after tomorrow. The entire room is decorated in flowers. Golden marigolds, multicolored daisies. Even the gerbera variety. We didn't have anything close to this many flowers when I married Prem. I told Pooja I wanted simple like before, but Blue must have insisted on more. I feel like a pawn in a chess game.

Dialah brings in a tray with glasses and a pitcher of ice tea. She pours a glass and hands it to me. "Drink."

Naz has scarlet and gold clothing draped over her arm. She hands me a long skirt. "Put it on."

I look around. "Here? In front of everyone?"

Dialah and Naz laugh. "Of course not. Go in the pantry. Put this on too."

Naz hands me a *choli* to match the skirt. The gold lace and trim of the top is spectacular. I love Indian traditional dress. I'm excited to see what I'll look like. I sip my ice tea. "Dialah! This isn't ice tea."

"Well, it is. Kind of. We decided to serve everyone Long Islands. More bang for the buck."

I head for the pantry to change. "I can use a little bang about now." I don't want them to know I don't plan on drinking it.

I can hear Naz and Dialah laughing. "That's not what I meant." It is kinda funny. I hurry up and change.

"Two more days, honey. Two more days." Dialah's words tie my stomach in knots. Dev and I haven't even talked about the wedding night. I don't know what he expects. His kiss is still fresh in my mind. Kissing is one thing, but I'm not sure if I'm ready for anything more. Someone opens the door a crack. Dialah.

"Do you need help? Celine's here."

"No. I'm good."

Dialah steps in. "You don't look good. What's wrong?"

"Nothing. Really." I know she doesn't believe me.

"Raine. How long have we been friends?"

"Too long."

"Ha! So, out with it."

There is no way I'm going to tell her. "It's nothing, really. C'mon. Let's go get tattooed." I shove her out the door.

"Wait." Dialah reaches back in and grabs my drink. "You forgot this."

I take it and pretend to take a sip. I'll have to figure out a way around the Long Islands. Maybe open a bottle of red wine. Dr. Hill said a glass of red wine occasionally won't hurt the baby. Naz introduces me to Celine. My eyes go straight to her neck. She has a tattoo collar on her neck.

"It says Romance." Celine hands me a piece of paper.

"What?" I don't realize I'm staring.

"It's the first thing everyone sees. In addition to my day job as a tattoo artist, I write romance."

"Wow! How fun is that?"

"I love it. Hence, the tattoo." Celine's beautiful smile compliments her long, black hair. I've never met a real romance author before, and I wonder if she's famous. I haven't had time to read in a long time.

"I need you to complete this before I can start."

I look down at the paper she hands me.

"It's a waiver and a questionnaire. It's required by the health department. I've revised it for henna. I have all my customers complete one. It helps me make sure you're healthy enough."

"For henna?" I didn't even consider it might be dangerous for the baby.

I see the others filling out their questionnaires so I pull Celine to the side. "I'm guessing this questionnaire is confidential?"

"Absolutely. HIPAA laws require it."

"Good. Here's the thing. I'm pregnant and no one knows. I need to keep it that way."

"Oh, congratulations! It's not a problem. I only use brown henna and none of my colors contain PPD."

"PPD?"

"Some people are allergic to it. It's the same stuff that's in some hair dyes. And only a concern if we were using black henna."

"Ah. That's good to know. And you're sure it's safe for pregnant women?"

"Yep. Some women even tattoo their baby bump."

Now that is not something I've ever seen, but at least I know it's safe.

"How about you come over here so I can start with you first. Do you know what you want?"

"Um. I'm not sure. Naz?" Pooja, Blue, Naz, and Dialah circle around where we're sitting. "Design suggestions?"

Naz answers first. "Celine, what do you think?"

"Do you want both hands and feet?"

Everyone answers.

"Yes."

"Yes."

"Of course."

"Is there any other way?"

I really don't want to be covered in henna designs even though I think they're beautiful. "Can I just have something floral and exotic on my right hand and arm to compliment my jewelry and then another one to compliment my feet?"

Blue and Pooja object in unison. "No."

They look at each other and Blue explains, "She needs both hands and feet. It's a protection."

Pooja didn't cover me in henna when I married Prem. Why now? "I really don't want that much."

"Come, child." Blue places her hand on my shoulder. "What is one more hand? Hmm? The designs she will make are beautiful. You will love them and so will Devaj. Yes?"

Why do I have such a hard time saying no to her?

. . ⦵ . .

"IT'S TIME TO GO."

"Now? Can't we stay a little longer, Uncle Dev? I don't have school tomorrow."

"I know, but it's nine o'clock, and the library is closing."

"Can we go for ice cream first?" Tufan takes my hand in his and shakes. "Please?"

"Great idea. Do you know where to go?"

"Yep. Menchies." Tufan directs me out the front door, skipping his steps beside me. "We can walk from here."

"Even better."

An hour later, we're driving back up the street. I pull all the way to the back yard and park in the garage next to Raine's truck. My Spyder is tiny compared to the size of her Sienna.

Tufan runs inside. I don't take long before I follow him in. All the ladies are in the family room. I'm not sure what to expect. I'm hopeful things have calmed down. I walk in and see Tufan with his arms wrapped tightly around Raine's neck. "Doesn't she look beautiful Uncle Dev? I never see her dress like this."

Raine stands up, her body tightly swathed in red and gold. The curve of her hips is lined by the gold edges of the sari wrapped over her shoulder, allowing me a tiny glimpse of the white skin of her tummy. I don't know what to say. She puts her wine on the counter and walks toward me. All I want to do is hold her close and mingle my fingers in never-ending curls. Curls the color of burning wood. The closer she gets, the more urgent my need. I'm surprised by her arms when they wrap around me, and the weight of her body causes me to fall back a step. I'm not sure what I did, but I'm not complaining. I can smell the floral fragrance of her shampoo. I close my arms around her waist. Her voice is kind instead of harsh. "Thank you."

"For what?"

"For taking him to the library."

"If that's all it takes to make you happy, I think I'm the luckiest man alive."

Raine steps back. Her face flushes pink. I like that I have that effect on her. "I was worried. I'm happy you only took him down the street. I want you to have American road rules down before you drive everywhere."

"I know. I'm sorry I upset you. Are you enjoying the *Mehndi* night?"

"I guess." She raises her hands and shows me the front and back. "What do you think?"

I don't want to tell her what I think. I'd rather show her. But I don't. Instead I take each of her hands in mine and kiss her fingers on the top of each. Pink rushes to her face. I can hear my mom and Pooja in the family room. "Raine? Dev?

Are you going to join us?" Any more will have to wait until the first night.

.. ∞ ..

DEV AND I EXCHANGE garlands of colorful flowers. My favorite gerbera daisies are included with the floral arrangements. There are so many marigolds of different varieties, along with daisies, lilies, and irises. I think I even recognize zinnias in the mix.

I told Blue and Pooja I didn't want to do the traditional seven steps around the fire, but Blue insisted. I'm sure it's because of some superstition. So now I find myself walking around the fire pit. Dev dabs red powder on my forehead and places a beaded necklace around my neck. My fingers touch the black beads, a symbol I belong to him. I can't help but compare it to a choker. I'm married. Again.

"My beautiful girl." Blue hugs me tight, and then I'm transferred to Pooja.

"See? I told you everything would work out. I'm so happy for you." I see the tears in the corner of Pooja's eyes.

Tufan wraps his arms around me. I bend down to give him a hug on his level. I'm so happy now that he's mine. Really mine. I've already got a meeting with my lawyer, so I can make it legal. I hold my belly, my baby.

I can feel Dev's arm around my shoulder. "I'm starving. Let's eat."

I can't help but laugh. The last thing I can think of is food. Everyone moves into the formal dining room. The bright white tablecloth is accented by a table runner of orange gerbera daisies and deep purple flowers. I'm not sure if they're violets or irises, maybe neither. The glass vases on each end have floating candles over a large daisy sunk to the bottom. I've never seen the dinnerware before. The plates are circled with deep blue, almost purple, around the outside of the plate and in the center is a floral design. I turn to Pooja. "It's exquisite. Where did we get it?"

Pooja nods to Blue. "It's our gift to you. The set includes sixteen place settings."

I can't believe it. I've never had a dinnerware set. I always thought it to be an unnecessary extravagance.

Blue motions to everyone to be seated. "We saw this pattern, and it spoke to us. We knew it should be yours." I'm speechless. Dev pulls out my chair to allow me to sit. We're at the center of one side of the rectangle table with our backs to the wall. Tufan is next to me, the priest sits next to Dev. Naz, Dialah, Pooja, and Blue are across from us on the other side of the table. Caterers begin to serve the food. It's Indian cuisine. Garlic *naan*, *pakoras*, *aloo bonda*, and different curries and chutneys are offered by servers. I choose mint chutney. I can't wait to have some *Paalak paneer* and curry chicken for main courses. Forget about not being hungry. My stomach growls. I never eat this much. I look at Pooja. "Where did you find the catering?"

"Namaste India Gardens. It's Southern Indian cuisine."

"I had no idea the restaurant catered to this type of event."

"I explained to the owner we're having a small wedding at home. There was no problem. I asked him to be prepared to create all the dishes you love. He's a very nice man. They can cater up to two hundred guests."

"This is all very lovely. Thank you both so much for arranging everything." Pooja and I share a silent acknowledgment. I know she must be thinking of when Prem and I married. How can she not? I'm also thinking about it. I still miss him. Still I feel like he's here. Still with me, only on vacation or something.

I know I shouldn't be thinking about him now that I'm married to someone else, but I know Dev must understand. *Think of it as a business arrangement.* That's what Dev said. I'm trying. It's so different from how I have always believed marriage to be. I remind myself that it's for Tufan. For my baby. For my family. For Prem.

Once the wine is poured, Dialah raises her glass for a toast. "I'm not sure if it's customary to offer a toast or not, but it is for me. So, I'd like to wish you both a long and happy life together. May you be blessed with everything your heart desires."

Blue adds to the wish. "And what my heart desires, many grandchildren!" My face flames. I'm sure it's pink.

Pooja's sly smile is directed at me when she leans forward to whisper, "We have your room all ready for the first night."

There's no doubt in my mind I've flushed red all the way to the top of my ears and beyond. I peek over at Dev sitting next to me. If he heard her comments, he isn't letting on. Everyone sips their wine. I drink mine down complete. The young Indian boy standing by the sideboard immediately refills my glass. I know I shouldn't have too much, but I'm nervous. I need to relax, and it's red wine. It's should be okay for the baby. The baby. I need to tell Dev. I'll sip the next glass. Everything's better after two glasses of wine.

BOLLYWOOD BARGAIN

· · ⚶ · ·

TUFAN SQUEEZES ME TIGHT. He doesn't want to let us go. He's got one arm around me and one arm around Raine in a three-person hug.

"Let's go, Tufan." Naz is taking him to stay with her tonight.

"I don't want to leave. Why can't I stay here? Naniji and Auntie Blue are staying. Why can't I?"

I don't like him staying away from home, but like most of the ceremony arrangements, I didn't have much to say in the matter. "It's only for a few days. You'll have fun with Auntie Naz. She's got plenty of things planned for you."

Tufan lets go so we can finally stand up. He looks back at Naz. "What kind of things are we going to do?"

"Well. How does Cedar Point sound for starters?"

"Really? Cedar Point? Can we go to the water park?"

"Yep. It's all set for tomorrow, but we have to leave and get a good night's sleep. What do you say?"

"Let's go! Bye, Uncle Dev! Bye, Raine! Have fun on your first night!"

I grab Raine's hand because I know she's nervous about what my mom and Aunt Pooja have planned. I need to reassure her that it's going to be all right.

"C'mon, you two. Off you go. Pooja and I will settle things with the caterers and get everything cleaned up."

My mom pushes us, actually pushes us up the stairs. I am so thankful right now their rooms are on the first floor. If it wasn't for Naz, they would have had me waiting like a pampered sultan while they guided her to my room.

73

I've never been nervous with a woman before, but Raine is different, and now she's my wife. I hold her hand as we go up the stairs together. I can't believe what they've done to my room. They refitted the bed with all new bed clothes and matching curtains for the windows. They even have the bed decorated with flowers, roses, and jasmine, I think. Raine looks sick.

"I've never been to a wedding where we didn't dance the *bhangra*." I have to tell her something before she faints from fear. She has her hand on her neck when she looks at me, and I can tell she's terrified.

"The bhangra?"

"I'm surprised you didn't dance it when you married Prem. It's a *punjab* folk dance. Like this." I do a few steps around the bed and around her to try and lighten things up some.

"Yes, we did. I forgot what it was called."

She smiles and laughs when I stub my toe on the love seat backing the end of the bed. I sit down to rub the pain away. I pat the spot next to me. "Please."

Raine sits. But it's as far away as the seat will allow. I reach out to her and hold her hand. "You don't have to be afraid."

She doesn't look up. "I'm not."

I don't believe her. I take her chin and turn her in my direction. "I know it's soon. We can go at our own pace. Take it slow. Okay?"

Her green eyes stare back. No dimples. Her hair is bundled behind her head, and I can't wait to loosen it, but I don't. She nods her head and frees her chin from my grasp.

"Tell me what's wrong."

"Nothing's wrong. I'm just not comfortable here. With this." She looks back at the bed covered in flowers. I look back too.

"I understand. Why don't we go away for a few days?"

"Away?"

"Yes. I know we said we wouldn't, but I think it would be good for us. We don't have to go far. Show me somewhere around here you like and we'll go."

I can tell she's thinking about it. She's twisting the newly placed ring on her finger. The small cleft in the side of her cheek promises me she'll agree. "I'd like that."

"Good." I stand up and grab the comforter off the bed and shake the flowers to the floor.

"What are you doing?"

"Getting ready for bed."

She turns around fast and sits.

"Raine. I promise nothing is going to happen tonight. Tonight, we'll just sleep."

She stands up and comes to where I'm standing, turns around, and waits. I'm not sure what she wants. The dark red waves I love are wound in loose curls all over the back of her head. I pull one between my fingers to loosen it from the others. It hangs down below her waist. I loosen another.

"What are you doing?"

I don't know why, but I lean down and kiss the side of her neck where it meets her shoulder. She cringes. "I only wanted you to unbutton the back so I can change out of it."

"I'm sorry." I move her hair to the side and hang it over her shoulder to the front before I begin to unbutton her choli. I take my time. Her skin is soft and creamy white. I want to help her some more, but as soon as I reach the last button, she moves away into the master bathroom and behind the closed door. What is wrong with me? I just told her all we're going to do is sleep. I couldn't resist. She's my wife now, and she's beautiful. I remove my clothes and hop into bed. I wonder what she's going to wear. I'm not kept wondering for long because the door opens and she walks out. She's wearing an oversized t-shirt. One of mine. "What's this?"

"You don't recognize your own clothes?"

I'm not sure if she's playing with me or if she's being sarcastic. I decide to ignore it.

"Of course I do. I'm just not sure why *you* are wearing them."

"Probably because your mom and Pooja had other things in mind for me to wear." Raine holds up a hanger with dark green, lacy lingerie. "This is all there is."

I don't say I wish she would wear it. I don't say I want to see it on her. I don't say put it on. I don't say anything. I just stare.

She throws it on the love seat and walks to the other side of the bed to slip in beside me. The king-size bed gives us plenty of space in between. She's laying on her back with the sheet pulled to her neck. I hit the switch on the wall above my head to turn off the lights, then roll on my back. I place one arm behind my head and the other across the flesh of my stomach right above the sheet covering my hips. I can hear her breathing and turn to look. She's staring at me, eyes wide. I want to talk to her, but I can't. I don't know what to say. A few more minutes pass in the dark. And finally she asks me. "What are *you* wearing?"

"The same thing I was wearing the first time you came in my room."

CHAPTER SIX

I t's raining when we pass over the bridge to Catawba Island. I'm glad because I wasn't looking forward to untangling my hair after driving in Dev's Spyder. It's the first time I've seen it with the top closed. It's so tiny, I feel like we're in a match car race on the highway. I'd much rather be in my truck, but Dev insisted we take the Maserati. He won't tell me where we're staying. All I said was a bed & breakfast might be nice, and he was gone. It's all arranged. I'm not sure I like the idea. He's never even been here. When we pull up to a dark brown house sitting on the edge of the lake, I don't know what to expect. The sign says, "Our Sunset Place Bed & Breakfast."

"I've never been to a bed & breakfast before."

"I had my agent find it and book it."

"Your agent?"

"Sure. Tony also functions as my personal assistant, has been with my family for years." Dev runs around the side to open my door. He reaches down to take my hand and bows. "M'lady."

I laugh. I can't help it. When he does things like that, it makes me uncomfortable but pleased. I'm not used to it. I look around. There are no other cars in the driveway except ours. I wonder if we're too early. I can see Lake Erie behind the house and hear the faint sound of the waves crashing against the shore.

"How can you trust Tony to find a decent place?"

Dev walks me to the door and rings the bell. "Trust me. Tony knows."

I don't know how Tony knows, but I have no choice now. A woman my height with short blonde hair and a smile that reminds me of my mom answers the door. "Hi! Mr. and Mrs. Shukla, I'm guessing?" She opens her arm wide directing us to enter.

Dev responds first. "Yes. Sandy?"

"That's me. Come on in and welcome. I have the Vineyard Room all set up. I'm so happy you've decided to stay with us, Mr. Shukla. I've spoken with Tony this morning, and everything you requested is being arranged."

Everything he requested?

"Thank you, Sandy."

"If you'd like to give me your keys, I'll ask Bart to bring in your luggage while you and Mrs. Shukla enjoy a nice glass of wine on the deck."

"You can call me Raine."

"Raine? What a beautiful name. I hope you enjoy your stay."

Dev gives Sandy his key, and she closes the door behind her. The view is phenomenal. I wish it wasn't raining. I look around the room. A bottle of chilled red wine and two glasses sit on the table in front of the picture window. Lake Erie is gray and menacing. I love watching the waves roll in when there's a storm coming in. The king-size bed has four posts shaped in odd sized cylinders from the bed to the ceiling. Zig-zag nausea erupts in my stomach. I run to the only other door in the room, praying it's the bathroom. I make it just in time.

•• ᦓᦓ ••

I KNOCK ON THE DOOR. "Raine?" I can hear she's sick, and I don't want to intrude on her privacy. "Do you need anything?"

"No."

"Can I come in?"

"No."

I don't know what else to do. I've done everything I can think of to help her feel comfortable. I leave the room to look for Sandy. She's in the kitchen.

"How is everything? Can I get you anything?"

"I'm not sure. What can I give to someone with an upset stomach?"

"Hmm. Upset stomach?"

"Yes."

"I had planned on preparing chicken paprikash for dinner, but that can easily be changed. How about a chicken soup?"

"Can we have both?"

"Absolutely. Whatever you would like, Mr. Shukla."

"It's Dev. Call me Dev."

"Okay, Dev. Dinner will be at five o'clock. A walk outside in the fresh air might help."

"Good idea." I walk back into our room. Raine is lying on the bed with her eyes closed. I'm not sure if she's asleep.

I see one eye open. "How do you feel?"

"Not sure. I'm so sorry."

"Sandy's making chicken soup."

Raine inhales a deep breath. "I'm not hungry."

"How about a walk outside? The fresh air might help."

She doesn't move. I walk to the picture window where a stone patio frames a full view of Lake Erie. I can see a sun lounge not far from there. I walk to where she lays on the bed and sit down beside her. My insides tighten. I don't like to see her like this. I swipe her thick waves back from her pale face. I'm not sure what makes me do this, but I decide I'm not giving her a choice. I stand up and lift her into my arms.

"What are you doing?"

"What does it look like?" She's light in my arms. She wiggles, and I can't help but enjoy the playfulness of it. "Trust me. You'll feel better."

I walk her straight out of the room where Sandy sees us and opens the door to the patio. I carry Raine directly to the sun lounge and plop her down in the two-seat pillowed lounge shaped like a heart. I take the seat next to her and wrap my arm around her shoulders.

"I can't believe you just carried me all the way here."

She's forced to lean against my chest. Our legs are stretched out in front of us. I lean my head back.

"Why? You're not that heavy."

Raine raises up, pressing her hand on my chest. It feels good there, so I put my hand on top of it to hold it in place. "Not *that* heavy? That's comforting to know."

I can't help laughing. I look down at her. "You can't be more than, what? Five feet?"

"Five feet, three inches to be exact."

"Pfft. Told you. Light as a feather."

Sandy shows up with a tray, two wine glasses, and a bottle of wine. She places both glasses on the small side table next to me. She pours one glass and hands it to me. I pass it to Raine.

"No. I can't drink that."

I take a sip myself.

Sandy pulls a can out of her apron pocket. "Ginger ale for you, dear." Sandy pops open the can, pours it in the second wine glass, and hands it to Raine.

Raine takes a sip and sneezes. "Vernors. I swear I can never take my first sip without sneezing. Every time it gets me. Even when I try to not breathe in."

"Are you sure it's not from being sick?"

"I doubt it. Can you put my glass on the table? I'm not going to drink anymore right now."

Raine settles back close against me. Her hand is back in its place, and I cover it with mine.

. . ⚓ . .

I LIKE HOW DEV'S HAND covering mine makes me feel. Protected. Owned. His. My stomach does a somersault. I remembered Prem's hand on mine the first night we met. Now, I'm here. With Dev. And Prem's baby. I close my eyes and relax against him. The sound of the waves below is soothing. I don't want to move. Everything is warm and calm and then I hear nothing.

Dev moves next to me. I can feel his fingers slide along the side of my cheek.

His voice whispers, "Raine."

I like the sound of my name in his voice. I feel his breath on my cheek.

"Raine, it's time to wake up."

I open my eyes. The sun is setting in the west. It's cloudy, but the yellow glow is still visible. "What time is it?"

"I'm not sure, but Sandy wants us to come for dinner."

"Dinner? I thought this was a bed & breakfast. They don't normally serve dinner."

"Tony arranged something a little different for us."

"What?"

"Tony rented the entire house for us for the next few days."

"The entire house? That must have cost a fortune. We don't need the entire house."

"Tony knows what I like. Even arranged with Sandy to provide the meals."

"So, we have room service too?"

"In a manner of speaking. We don't have to have all our meals in our room. Unless you want to."

Dev's smile throws me into a minor panic. "What? No! That's not what I meant."

I stand up and push my hair back behind my right shoulder. I pull out a scrunchie I slipped in my pocket and decide to pull it up in a loose bun. I really need to get used to being with him in the same way I was with Prem. He's my husband now. That thought pushes me closer to all-out panic. What will he expect of me tonight? Here. In this house. This house we have all to ourselves. I lose my balance and fall back slightly. I catch myself on the edge of the lounge. Dev catches me also. Before I have a chance to move forward, he sweeps me into his arms again. "What are you doing?"

"What does it look like?"

"I know what you're doing, what I mean is why?"

"Would you believe me if I told you I like it?" Dev walks me back to the stone patio and waits at the door.

"How can you like carrying someone?"

Sandy opens the door, and Dev carries me into the dining room and sets me down in front of the table. He pulls out a chair for me to sit.

"I feel like I need to dress for dinner."

"If you think you're not dressed, I would love to see what you consider to be undressed."

My face flames. I look at Sandy, hoping she's not paying attention. She's not. I think.

Sandy brings the Dutch oven to the table and ladles chicken soup for both of us. I taste a spoonful. The full-flavored broth soothes my insides. I take another chicken-loaded bite. Sandy rolls a cart with two covered plates to the edge of the table and opens one to show Dev. The steam rises, wafting up to the ceiling. The aroma reaches me, and the nausea returns in full force. I can barely hold it back.

"I'm so sorry." I cover my mouth and look at Sandy and then Dev. "The smell. I don't ..."

I push my chair back and run for the bathroom. As soon as I get there, I splash cold water on my face. It helps ease the nausea, and my stomach settles again. I'm so embarrassed. How am I going to go back out there? I dry my face, smooth my hair, and head back just in time.

Sandy's words freeze me where I stand. "I had the same sensitivities when I was pregnant."

•• ⧫ ••

WHAT THE HELL? I LOOK at Raine standing in the hall. Her face is pale again. I walk over and help her to sit down. She shakes my arm away. I'm not sure why she's mad at me. I'm quite sure I'm the one being set up here, and I'm not sure how I feel about it. Sandy comes over and ladles some more chicken soup in Raine's bowl. "It's okay, dear. I understand." Sandy pats Raine's shoulder before leaving us alone.

"Why aren't you eating?" Raine's question snaps me back to the present.

"I am." I take a bite of my chicken paprikash. "Does this bother you?"

"No. Not anymore. It must have been the intensity of it built up under the cover."

"Yeah. That must be it." I don't care how I sound. I'm mad. "Raine."

"Yes?"

"Are you?"

"Am I what?" Really? She's going to play it this way? I'm not backing down.

"Are you pregnant?"

She stops eating and places her spoon to the side of the plate and takes a sip of water. She dries her mouth with her napkin and places her hands in her lap. She looks at me. Her eyes are sad and glossy. I start to feel a pang of regret, but I need to know.

"Yes."

I toss my fork to the side of my dish, down a full glass of wine, and then refill it to drink some more.

"Please, Dev. Don't be angry. Please let me explain."

"I'm not sure there's any need to explain. It's all very clear. You didn't want to be a single mom. Does my mother know? Does Aunt Pooja?"

"No. I haven't told anyone yet." The whimper of her voice melts a little of the anger I'm feeling but not enough. "So, what exactly was your plan? Pass the baby off as mine?"

Her eyes are full with tears now, and I don't care. I can't believe I've been tricked into this. I can't believe I didn't see it.

"No. I'm not sure how I thought it might be explained, but I had no intention of tricking you. I was going to tell you. I couldn't find the right time. And I was ..."

"Was what?"

"I was afraid, okay?"

"Afraid of what?"

"Afraid. Pooja. She... I couldn't bear to lose Tufan. And I couldn't bear for Prem's child to grow up without family."

I don't know what to say. Not what I expected. "What do you mean? You wouldn't lose Tufan."

"Pooja told me she would not allow Tufan to live with me. I wanted to move out and go somewhere else. Everything about the house reminds me of Prem, but I wanted Tufan with me." Her voice cracks. Guilt splits me in two. "Pooja wouldn't let me."

"I still don't understand why you haven't told anyone."

"I don't know. I felt like it was something between me and Prem. A promise from him to me. His gift. It felt special somehow. Meant for me alone."

"And Tufan? Don't you think he might enjoy some good news? Something left to look forward to from his father? A brother or a sister?"

"Stop. Please. I know. I didn't know when or how to tell everyone. I enjoyed holding this to myself, Dev...."

Raine reaches out to touch my arm, but I'm not ready to give her that. I pull away. She looks down and wipes her tears with her napkin. "I didn't mean to hurt you or lie to you. I promise I was going to tell you."

I feel my anger slow inside. I know I have no right to be mad at her. I don't know why exactly, but part of me hoped she married me for more than just Tufan. And now this.

"Pooja told me the only way she would allow Tufan to be with me is if I married you. I wanted my baby to be with family. To be with Tufan. To be with me. And have Pooja close."

I'm not sure where I fit in all this, and I know I need to have a conversation with Blue as soon as we get back.

• • ～ • •

IT'S DONE. NOT HOW I wanted Dev to learn about Prem's baby, but it's done. I feel relieved and sad at the same time. I know it's unreasonable, but I want him to be happy. I want him to understand. I want him to support me. I don't even know what he's thinking right now. I leave him sitting at the table. I take a quick shower and put on my pajamas.

I want to cry. They're tight. Tighter than I like them. Dev joins me.

"What's wrong?"

"Nothing." I hold my hand on my stomach. I refuse to tell him my clothes are tight. I refuse to talk to him any more tonight about my baby.

He walks over and sits on the edge of the bed. "Look, Raine. I'm not happy you kept this from me. You should have told me before we were married, but I understand why you did it."

"Are you still mad?"

"I'm not as mad as I was."

"So you are still mad."

He turns his entire body to face me. "What did you expect? Tell me."

I don't know what I expected, and I don't know what to say, so I stay silent.

"Look, is there anything else I need to know?"

"I'm not sure what you mean."

"Exactly what I said. Is there anything else you need to tell me?"

"Of course not. What else could there be?"

"I don't know, that's why I'm asking."

I'm so frustrated with Dev right now, I want to slap him. Instead, I pick up a pillow and throw it at him.

"What the hell was that for?"

"I don't like the way you're talking to me."

"Well, don't worry because you won't have to put up with it for much longer."

"What's that supposed to mean?"

"I wasn't going to tell you this until we got back, but I've decided to take an acting job in Shimla."

"India, Shimla?"

"Yes. Shimla is in India."

"So just like that you're leaving. What will people say?"

"Does it matter? I need time and so do you. Tony told me about it earlier this week, and I wasn't sure, but now it's what I need."

"What you need? What about what I need? What your family needs?"

"Look, Raine. This is what I do. This is my job. You'll need to get used to it. So let's just enjoy the few days we have here while we have it."

Right. Not a chance.

· · ⁓ · ·

I CAN TELL RAINE DOESN'T like riding on Route 6 with the top down. I don't care. I'm struggling with the news of her pregnancy. How could she do this? Does my mom know?

"Dev, please. It's too much." Raine holds her hair in place while it roils around the top of her head.

"Can't you put it up like you did before? In that band thing?"

"I lost it." I reach into the glove box while we're stopped at a red light. I know I have a band. I used it to put my hair up.

"Here. Use this." She takes the band and swirls her hair. In seconds, it's tied back. I want to hold her hand. Twist her stray hair between my fingertips. Kiss her at red lights. But

I don't. I can't shake how upset I am at the idea of Raine keeping her pregnancy a secret. I need to get over it, but I'm not ready. Not yet.

"Do you really have to leave as soon as we get back?"

"I think it's best. I need time to prepare for the part. I can't do that here."

"Why not?"

"Too many distractions."

"But what about Tufan? He's going to miss you. And Blue. Will she leave with you?"

"I'll miss Tufan too, but we can always Skype or use Messenger as much as we want. I'm not sure what Blue will decide."

"Dev. I know you're still upset with me about keeping the baby from you. But do we have to tell Pooja and Blue yet?"

"And how long do you think you can keep this a secret?"

"I just...just for a little while longer. Please?"

I don't know why, but I can't seem to deny her anything. Despite everything, I want to protect her and make her happy. "I tell you what. I'll leave it to you. You tell them when you're ready. You'll have to tell them soon, anyway."

I see her watching the houses as they pass by while she's holding her hand on her midsection. All of a sudden it hits me. I know why I'm so mad. I wanted the baby to be mine. Something I know I can never have.

CHAPTER SEVEN

Tufan waits with me while we watch Dev straighten his carryon.

"Why can't you stay, Uncle Dev?" Tufan's tiny voice breaks my heart. I can tell he's trying to be brave. I wish things could be different, but Dev is determined this is what he has to do.

Dev stoops in front of Tufan. "Here. This is for you." Dev pulls out a phone from his pocket and hands it to Tufan.

Tufan takes it. "You're giving me your phone?"

Dev smiles and shuffles his hair. "No, kiddo. It's yours. It's just like mine, see?" I'm not sure I like the idea of a five-year-old having his own phone.

"Look, Raine! It's an iPhone!"

"I see, Tufan. We'll have to set some ground rules on its use though, right, Uncle Dev?" I stare at him so he knows what I mean. I start to feel the frustration building inside me again. Giving a five-year-old an iPhone. Unbelievable.

Dev looks at me, and I'm not sure if he's going to agree, but he does. "It's so you can Messenger me anytime you want, okay? But Raine is right. You have to be responsible. No calling anyone without permission, and Raine sets the rules. But here, this is how you Messenger me."

Dev shows Tufan how it works and then stands up to look at me. He tightens his lips and streams out a long exhale. I know he wants to say something but doesn't. He looks down at Tufan playing with his new phone. Dev motions me to follow him into the hall. "Listen. I know you're not happy with me leaving, but I need to do this."

"All I've been hearing about is what you need. What happened to family first? How about what I need? What Tufan needs? What this baby needs?"

"What the baby needs? You mean the one I just found out about? The one that belongs to another man?"

"Don't make it sound like I cheated. I was married. To *your* cousin. And it's not like we're in love or anything. Your mother and aunt got us into this...this business arrangement."

"I'd keep my voice down if you want to keep your secret."

It irks me that Dev is able to keep his voice at one steady, disdainful monotone. I stop speaking and grit my teeth. I want to slap him.

Instead, I punch his chest, and he grabs my wrist. I flatten my hand while he holds it in place. He takes my other hand hanging at my side and holds it. His fingers intertwine with mine. I'm so angry with him for leaving me. I bend my forehead into his chest just below his chin and push forward. Dev holds me in place. I hate myself for not wanting him to leave. For feeling like I need him. I look up. He doesn't say anything with words, but he's telling me so much. Telling me so much with his hand now resting on the small of my back and holding me tight against him. Telling me so much with the soft caress of his thumb on the back of my hand pressing his chest. Telling me so much with the closeness of his lips to mine.

His whispered words breathe against my lips just before he touches his lips to mine. "We'll be fine."

. . ᘛᐤᘚ . .

KISSING RAINE ALMOST makes me change my mind about leaving. I tell myself if she asks me one more time to stay, I will.

"Devaj!" My ride to the airport must be here. My mom's voice breaks the magic of our kiss. The kiss currently sending me to the vast ends of the universe and back. The kiss I don't want to end. Raine's kiss. I look down. Her eyes are still closed when I pull away. Her words "family first" echo in my ears. I know she's right. But I still need some space, some time.

Tufan follows me down the stairs, dragging my duffel with two hands and holding his new phone with his chin. "Be careful. We don't need you falling down the stairs. And give me the phone."

"If I fall, will you stay?"

"Don't play games, Tufan. Be careful." Raine's voice is close behind me on the descent down the stairs. She doesn't ask me.

I give Tufan his phone back when we reach the bottom of the stairs. My mom and Aunt Pooja are waiting by the door. I kiss them each on the cheek, give one more hug to Tufan, and walk out the door. Raine follows me to the cab sitting in the driveway.

She waits while my luggage is loaded. "I wish you wouldn't go."

I place a lingering kiss one last time on her cheek before getting into the cab to leave. I watch her stand at the edge of the driveway while we pull out. I lied. I have to go to India, no matter what she or I want.

· · ❧ · ·

HE'S GONE. AS QUICKLY as he came, gone. I hold my stomach. It hurts. Not from the baby, from heartache. I know this feeling. It's loss. I feel Dev's loss. I don't know if he will ever come back, really. Blue stayed so I guess that's a good sign. I hope it's a good sign.

I walk back inside. Tufan, Blue, and Pooja are sitting in the front room. Blue is working on Indian lace. Tufan is playing on his new phone, and Pooja rocks in the rocking chair with her hands crossed in her lap staring at nothing. Everyone misses him. I decide to call Naz.

"Can you come over?"

She doesn't live far, so it doesn't take her long to get here. We run up to my room. Our room now, I guess. I sit on the bed and cradle a pillow in my lap. Naz sits across from me on the edge. "Dev left."

"What? How come nobody told me?"

"It wasn't planned. He got a call from Tony. Something about filming in Shimla."

"Yeah. I'm not a huge fan of Toni. I met her once and decided I didn't need a second time."

"Well, I've only heard of... Wait. "*Her*?" Now my stomach drops all the way to my feet. And not because I feel loss. "Tony is a *her*?"

"Uh-oh. You didn't know?"

"Obviously. I just assumed Tony was a guy."

"Nope. Toni with an 'i' not a 'y.'"

"I think I want to be sick. Did he ever date her?"

"I'm not sure. I know they were raised together. Her parents were in the business with Dev's parents or something like that. Their families have been friends for years."

I lean back and knock my head on the wall. "Ouch."

"I'm calling Dialah. We need a girls' night."

I don't disagree. I really need my friends right now. We walk downstairs to sit on the porch. Pooja and Blue are still sitting quietly in the front room when we pass by. Tufan has gravitated away from his new phone and now plays with Honey on the floor. "Watch she doesn't get behind something. You know how she likes to chew the wires."

"I know, Raine. I promise. I'm keeping her occupied." I know he will, but I feel like I have to remind him anyway.

It's a perfect summer day in my opinion. I love it when it's seventy-six degrees. Not too hot and not too cold. Naz and I sit on the porch swing just as Dialah pulls into the drive. She doesn't even reach the porch before asking, "What happened?"

"Dev left." I'm so tired I can't say more than two words at a time. Tired like I've been carrying weights around my ankles and arms for days. Tired like I can't breathe. And tired like I want to sleep a hibernation sleep.

"I know that. Naz told me. I want to know why." Dialah joins us in the rocker next to the swing.

I don't want to speak. I don't want to tell them, but I know I have to start telling people about the baby. I inhale a long, deep breath, preparing myself.

Naz runs her hand along my arm. "Honey, I know it's hard, but just talk to us. It will help, I promise."

Tears well in the corners of my eyes. I know she's right. "It's just hard." I wipe a tear that falls.

Dialah pulls her chair to face me and pulls my hand in hers. "Take your time. We're here for you."

I don't know where to start so I just blurt it out. "I'm pregnant."

Dialah gasps, pulls her hand back while falling back in her seat. Naz places her hand on my arm. "Honey, a baby is a good thing. A happy occasion, no?"

I can tell Dialah gets it immediately, but she doesn't say anything. Naz looks at Dialah. "Tell her, Dialah."

"Naz, think."

"Think about what?"

I watch my two best friends stare each other down. I settle it. "It's Prem's, Naz."

Naz turns to look at me. I swear she should be the blonde one sometimes.

"Oh my God! Raine! Does Dev know?"

"Really, Naz?" Dialah's voice is raised. I probably would be laughing at the entire conversation if it wasn't me at the brunt of it.

I decide I need to settle it. "Naz, listen." I turn to face her sideways in the swing. "I didn't tell anyone. Dev found out at Catawba. He thinks I hid it from him so I could pass the baby off as his."

"You would never do that. Why does he think that?"

"I tried to explain, but I don't know that I wouldn't feel the same if I were him. I really didn't intend for it to end up like this. Now he's gone."

"Is he divorcing you?"

"What? No! I don't think so. He said he needed time, and he decided doing this film in Shimla would allow him to come to terms with it, I guess."

"He's an ass." Strong words coming from Naz.

Dialah's eyes widen. "Don't you think you're being a little harsh, Naz?"

"Me? What about you? You should be more supportive of our friend."

Dialah turns to me and squeezes her lips tight. "You're right. I should be more supportive of you, Raine, but you should've told him before you were married."

"Don't you think I know that?"

"Well, why didn't you?"

"I don't know. I couldn't. It was personal to me. Precious. A part of Prem still with me. I want him to just be with me. I wasn't ready to share this part of him with anyone else."

Naz wraps her arm around me and pulls me close to her. Dialah moves to my other side and holds my hand. Naz wipes a tear from her eye. "We'll figure this out. It's all about family. No matter what, you're family and that baby is family. Dev knows it. Give him his time. He'll come back."

I hope she's right.

. . ⌒ . .

THE WEEKS DEV'S BEEN gone feel like years. He only speaks with me for a few minutes whenever he speaks with Tufan. Today it feels like everything that can go wrong, does. I'm trying to wrap up the second phase of a construction project so we can move forward next week after the fourth of July. Everyone is pushing to finish so we can enjoy a long weekend. My foreman Jimmy sits across from my desk.

"Raine, what do you think?"

My brain fazes, again. I didn't even hear his question.

Jimmy puts his iPad on the desk. "Why don't we call it quits for this week and pick up again on Tuesday?"

"What? No. Do you want to finish this week or not?"

"Of course. But I can tell your head's not in it, and I don't want to waste any more time."

"Waste time?"

Jimmy stands up and walks to the door. "It's clear something's going on with you. You've not been one hundred percent for weeks now. At this point, a couple more days won't make a difference."

"What are you talking about? Of course a couple days will make a difference! It makes a whole lot of difference, and you know it."

Jimmy rests his hand on the doorknob.

"Look, Raine. I was told not to say anything, but Wally's coming out later this afternoon to have a talk."

"A talk? Wally the boss? That Wally?"

"Yes. And you didn't hear it from me."

"And why is he coming to visit?"

Jimmy sighs deep. "Apparently, Ken had some issues with the last few sub-lots of Phase II and went to Wally about it. I'm sorry."

Jimmy opens the door and leaves. Everyone knows Wally only visits when someone's being let go.

• • ⤮ • •

A LEAVE OF ABSENCE. It could have been worse. He could have fired me outright. I leave the trailer carrying my box of personal items, and Jimmy runs over to me to help. Does everyone know I'm pregnant?

"Thanks Jimmy, but I got it."

"No. Give it to me. You need to be careful."

"Excuse me? Careful? Really?"

Jimmy's face turns red. I know he means well. "It's just... I mean..."

I decide to be kind. "I appreciate it. How long have you known?"

"Not long."

"Do all the men know?"

Jimmy doesn't answer. He opens the backdoor to my truck and plops the box in the back seat. "Most of them."

He holds his hand out to me and I shake it. "Thank you. I'll see you in a few months."

I hop in and drive away. I'm not as angry as I thought I might be. I knew I would have to stop working at some point, but I wasn't expecting it to be so soon. Too much of a risk. I can still hear Wally's voice when he told me. Pregnant women don't belong on a construction site. Probably not in those words, but that's what I heard. I can still do some things from home. At least I think he meant that. I guess I get it, but part of me wants to call an employment lawyer. Although if I did that, I may never be able to work construction again. People talk in this industry. It's the way it is. Even now.

I pull in the backyard next to Dev's Maserati. I shut off the engine of my truck and sit for a few minutes remembering our trip to Catawba. Will we ever do that again?

I grab the box from the back seat and head in. Blue and Pooja are preparing dinner. "You're home early."

"Well, it looks like I'll be home early every day, for a while anyway."

Blue stops mid taste. "What's that?"

"I've been given a leave of absence." I don't want to explain so I take my things upstairs and close my door before any more questions can be asked. I throw my box on the ground and lie across my bed. I grab my iPhone from my pocket and plug my earbuds in. I need my escape. I close my eyes and listen to my absolute favorite song.

"... if you like midnight driving with the windows down ... if you like to do whatever you been dreaming about ... Baby, I'm perfect ..."

Prem. Dev. My baby. No one is perfect.

• • ⌘ • •

LOUD KNOCKING. THAT'S what it is...loud knocking, shaking me out of a deep sleep.

"Raine? Dinner is ready." Blue's voice is soft compared to the banging my door is enduring.

"I'm coming." I stay where I am, lying on my back and staring at the ceiling. I'm not hungry right now. I just want to sleep.

Blue doesn't leave. Instead, she opens the door and stands there. "I said I'm coming."

"I want to be sure." I can feel her eyes boring into me. She's not leaving until I sit up.

I'm not ready to sit up, so I continue to lie there, stretched out on the bed. "I'll be down in a minute." I pull my top down because I suddenly realize my belly is exposed.

I can tell she's still standing at the door waiting. I sit up. Blue's eyes are glossy. She doesn't say a word. "Come down stairs and eat. Everyone is waiting for you."

"Fine. Let me change first." Blue waits. "Are you going to stand there while I change?"

Still, she doesn't say a word, but only turns and leaves. I put on my yoga pants. I can't believe it. Even my yoga pants feel tight around my waist. Whatever. I pull my hair back and head downstairs.

Tufan, Blue, and Pooja are already seated. Pooja opens the top of the pot in the center of the table. Chicken vindaloo. I do everything I can to stop it, but I can't. I run straight for the bathroom, heaving the entire time.

I open the door of the bathroom to return and run smack into Blue and Pooja. Blue's eyes shine as bright as her smile, wide across her dark face. Pooja is no different. They both hug me tight.

"The smell of cooked chicken made me sick too." Blue's expressions of joy invade my personal space. Pooja is hanging at my side, helping me back to the table.

"Stop." I stand completely still, shake them from my side, and raise my hands in the air. "Just stop. What is wrong with you?"

"You need to be careful. For the baby." Pooja smiles.

Tufan yells from the dining room. "Baby? You're having a baby?"

Tufan runs to my side and holds my hands. "Is it true? Am I going to be a big brother?"

His excitement radiates across his face. I look at Pooja. I look at Blue. I end with Tufan. "Yes. It's true."

Now how do I tell them it's Prem's.

CHAPTER EIGHT

What are they watching? I stand next to Pooja, Blue, and Tufan in the family room. They're all huddled around the family computer set up in the corner of the room.

"Look, Raine. Indian movies. They're on Netflix. I also found some on Amazon video. Here. Sit with me." Tufan moves over so I can pull a chair next to him. This particular one is in English. I'm surprised Blue and Pooja are interested.

"What is this?"

"It's called Bride & Prejudice."

"What? Are you sure it's 'bride' and prejudice?"

"Yes, I'm sure. Look." Tufan stops the movie to show me what it's about.

It's an Indian version of Pride & Prejudice set in modern times. "Wow! How come I never saw this?"

"I don't know, but you can watch with us now."

I laugh. "My question was kind of rhetorical."

"Huh?"

"Rhetorical. It means a question not meant to be answered." Tufan's confused expression makes me remember he's only five. "Never mind."

Tufan shrugs his shoulders and returns his attention to the computer monitor. This is not going to work. "I have a better idea. Give me a minute and I'll show you how we can watch this on the flat screen."

"Really?" Tufan jumps up and starts moving the chairs back in place. He shuffles Pooja and Blue up so he can move theirs too. I open the Amazon video app on the flat screen and search for Bride & Prejudice. Perfect. We all settle back down on the couches. Tufan snuggles close to me. Something's missing.

"Raine? Can we have some popcorn?"

"Why didn't I think of that?" That's not what's missing, but I go to the kitchen and make a large pan of popcorn over the stove. I'm not a fan of microwave. Plus, you can pop so much more in a pan on the stove and make it however you want. I just add a little salt and bring the pan and bowls out for everyone. Tufan snuggles back against my side. His wide eyes are glued to the flat screen, keeping a continuous flow of popcorn from the bowl to his mouth.

I hand bowls to Pooja and Blue. "Have you seen this movie?"

Pooja shakes her head.

Blue plops a kernel into her mouth. "I've heard of it. I know the director. I've not seen it though."

I've always loved the colors and the singing in Indian movies when they realize they're in love. The wedding processions are the best. The funniest thing pops in my head. Does Dev sing and dance like that?

Pooja and Blue wander out midway through the movie, so I decide to ask Tufan. "Do you know any movies your Uncle Dev played in?"

"Of course! Do you want to watch one?"

I want to say yes, but I feel a little strange watching it. I feel like I should already have seen them. I give in and nod my head.

Tufan grabs the control and searches like a pro. "There! Let's watch this one. He plays a superhero!"

"A superhero? I don't know... Let me think." I playfully tap my finger on my chin.

"Come on, Raine! Please! Please!"

I'm not sure I want to see Dev as a superhero right now, but I finally give in. How can I not?

. . ᴄᴧᴎ . .

TUFAN'S FINALLY IN bed, so I can return to the family room to relax. I enjoyed watching Dev on TV. I search his name to see what other movies he's done.

"You should watch that one." Blue joins me.

"Oh? What's it about?"

"It's full of action, adventure, spies, love. It's my favorite. It won an award, this one. It should have won more."

"Okay. Let's watch it."

"Would you mind if we watched the news first?"

"The news?"

"Indian News. May I?" Blue holds her hand out for me to give her the remote. She switches and scrolls until she reaches what she's looking for.

As soon as the music starts for what looks like an Indian version of E!, Pooja joins us. "Has it started?"

"Just now. Here, sit next to me." Blue moves over and pats the seat beside her for Pooja to sit.

I smile at the two of them in their colorful saris like two excited fan girls. I watch as the show begins. I can't understand anything except a stray English word here and there. I pull the lever on the side of my chair so I can prop my feet up in the recliner.

"Look! There he is." Blue points to the screen and squeals, grabbing Pooja. "I never get tired of seeing my son on TV."

I close the recliner to pay more attention. Dev looks good. Very good. His hair is trimmed, and he's wearing his designer beard again. I have to admit I like the look on him. I can't understand what they're saying. I want to ask Blue to translate, but she's so interested in watching I don't want to interrupt her. I start to feel excited and proud knowing this man is my husband. Then all of a sudden, the only thing I feel is the floor falling away from under me. A beautiful Indian Princess folds herself to him, and he responds by wrapping his arm around her and kisses the top of her head. I can't help the tears beginning to erupt in the corners of my eyes.

Blue speaks first. "It's not what it looks like."

She moves to the seat next to me and tries to take my hand in hers. I pull it away. I don't know what to do. I want to be swallowed by something and never come out.

"It's all for show, dear. I promise. I've been in the business all my life. There is nothing there. She's his co-star and the advertisers want them to be seen together."

It bothers me a little to see him in films with another woman, but this is not a movie. It's different. "It doesn't look like show to me."

"Raine, he's an actor. It's what he does."

I look at Pooja. She doesn't say anything.

"I don't care."

I leave them both and head straight to my room. I'm going to be swallowed up.

. . ❧ . .

MY LIFE WAS MUCH EASIER without Indian TV invading it. Prem didn't care one way or the other, and Pooja never pushed for it. She probably didn't even know it was possible. Now, constant escapades of Dev and his life are splashed across the screen every time I walk in the family room.

"Look, Raine. They're showing the trailer for Uncle Dev's new movie. Wanna see? Wanna see?"

No. Not really. But of course I would never want to hurt Tufan. So, now I constantly see him with this other woman and just swallow the swell that develops in my throat each time.

"I can't wait to see him. When is he coming back?"

"I don't know. Why don't you ask him the next time you Messenger him?"

"I would, but I haven't been able to reach him for a few weeks. He must be really busy with his new movie.

I bet. He sure looks really busy. I can't keep up. I need to get control over things. "Are you looking forward to seeing the fireworks tonight?"

"Oh, yeah! I almost forgot about those. When will they start?"

"I'll look it up. It's usually after sunset. Whenever that is."

"I love sitting outside on the lawn to watch them."

"Me too, hon." I'm so glad we can see enough of them from our house. It's so much more enjoyable to watch from your own home. I remember my mom telling me about the time there was an accident, and the fireworks ended up going off on top of the crowd. She said there was such a panic, that it was amazing they even got out of there. One of her friends was on a blanket right at the edge. The men covered the women and children to try and shield them. Since then, she watched from home to see what she could see. The finale is what everyone waits for anyway, and it's visible from a lot of places in Lakewood.

"I'll call Naz and Dialah and see if they want to join us. What do you think?"

"If you want." Tufan could care less. And why should he? He's too busy watching Dev. I tousle his hair as I grab my phone sitting on the table. I glance at the TV. Dev is awesome, but I want to scratch his co-star's eyes out. I never imagined it would be this difficult to watch. I remember when he left. The touch of his lips on mine. His hand tangled in my hair. I can't watch this.

I call Naz first. Then Dialah. "They're on their way."

Tufan is playing with Honey in the middle of the floor. Attention span of a five-year-old boy. I wish I was five.

· · ⚬ · ·

IT'S EIGHT O'CLOCK, and I can't find anything in my closet I feel comfortable in. All my yoga pants are tight around the waist. I sit on the love seat at the foot of the bed and stare at the giant pile of discarded clothes. I hear Dialah and Naz downstairs talking to Tufan, then their footsteps on the way up the stairs a few minutes later.

"Raine, what's wrong?" Naz sits next to me.

"Nothing fits."

"It's time for shopping." Dialah comes and pulls me to my feet. "Let's go."

"No, not tonight. I promised Tufan we would watch the fireworks together on the front lawn."

"Fine. We'll go tomorrow. I'm sure there are sales everywhere for the holiday weekend."

She's right. There are. "That doesn't help me now." I can't believe I want to cry over something as silly as this.

Naz pops up. "I have an idea! I'll be right back."

Dialah and I look at each other, and in two minutes, Naz is back with arms full of fabric. Lengths of it. "What is this?"

"Um, you are living in a house with two Indian women, are you not?"

"Saris! Of course." Dialah takes some of the fabric from Naz's arms. "Look, Raine. Which color do you like? I'll wear one too."

Naz throws the rest on the bed. "We'll all wear one."

I flip through the colors. Some are full, bold colors and some are lighter, pastels. I like the bolder ones. I pull on a dark, emerald green fabric. The edges are gold. "How about this one?"

Naz pulls it out of the bunch and holds it out so we can see the length of it. "I like it. Come here. I'll wrap it for you."

"Don't I need an underskirt or something?"

"No, it's just us hanging out here at home. I don't care. I think you'll be more comfortable anyway, unless you want a skirt?"

"Just wrap me."

Naz completes the task in no time and moves on to Dialah. Dialah chooses a deep, rich blue.

"I love the way it brings out the color of your eyes."

"Really?" Dialah spins around and the bottom of the sari flairs out like a spindle. I do the same. I feel like we're in high school, dressing for prom.

Naz wraps herself in a coral fabric. It also has gold trim. I notice all the saris have a gold trim of some kind.

"Naz, that color is amazing for your skin tone."

"You think?"

"Absolutely!" Dialah and I answer in unison.

Our schoolgirl giggles must have been heard throughout the house because Blue comes from one direction, Pooja from the opposite, and they converge at the door.

"Naz, where did you get these?" Pooja walks in and starts sifting through the fabrics.

"They were hanging in one of the guest rooms."

"That would be mine." Blue walks over and sits on the bed next to the saris.

"Auntie, I'm so sorry. I didn't know. I thought maybe they were my mom's that she put away or something."

"No, they're mine, but don't worry. I don't mind. You all look lovely in them. The colors you chose suit you."

Naz continues to apologize and make excuses. I can tell she's still worried she overstepped. "I only thought of dressing in them because Raine is officially in need of maternity clothing. We needed something comfortable for her to wear until we go shopping tomorrow."

"Don't worry, dear. I completely understand." Blue's smile lights up her face every time a reference is made to the baby. I swallow hard and try not to think about what might happen when she learns the baby isn't Dev's.

Tufan joins us next holding Honey. "It's almost time! C'mon. We need to get set up. Hurry." Tufan tugs at my hand first then reaches for Pooja and pulls us both downstairs together.

"Slow down. We have plenty of time. It's only a little after nine."

"I know, but they start at nine forty-five o'clock."

Dialah and Naz laugh and I repeat it to him. "Nine forty-five o'clock. Hmm. Are you sure?"

"Yes, I'm sure. I read it on the flyer I found on the table. It talks about all the things they're having at Lakewood Park. C'mon, I'll show you."

"Okay. Okay. I believe you." We all flow in a line downstairs.

"I set up all the lawn chairs already, see?"

I look outside and sure enough. All the lawn chairs are set up. All ten of them. "Tufan did you count how many we are?"

"No."

"We're six. So how many chairs do you think you should put back?"

"Really, you're making me do math, now?"

"It's not math." I look at Dialah and Naz as they duck in the kitchen.

"It kinda is," Dialah yells out. "Just sayin."

"Fine." I bend down to Tufan and kiss his cheek. "You did a great job with all those chairs. How about we put four back in the garage? I'll help you."

Tufan shrugs. "Okay. I can do it myself though." He skips out the screen door and begins dragging one chair at a time to the back yard.

I watch Naz pass in front of me carrying a tray outside with a pitcher and glasses. "Long Island Iced Tea."

"Umm, I..."

Dialah follows with another tray. "I know. I got yours. Juice. Minus the Schnapps."

Pooja exits next with her palm leaf fan, then Blue links her arm with mine and walks me out.

The fireworks don't disappoint. My absolute favorite part is the finale. It's always louder than I anticipate. The sound slams through the air. The crackling stars and colors fill the sky in brilliant designs of silvery purples, pinks, reds, blues, and yellows.

I can't help feeling someone is missing. And that I'm missing him.

• • ⚜ • •

SHOPPING FOR MATERNITY clothes was not as fun as I thought it would be. I couldn't find much that I liked. The Paisley Monkey had the best choices of all of them. I've always loved the clothes they display in their window. It's right next to TJ's so I always see what they have when I go to the butcher. I've concluded I'm not ready to be fat. Naz and Dialah tell me I'm not that big, but I've never been overweight before, and I can't get used to seeing myself with this baby bump. The clothes I found from the maternity shop are still laying across the love seat in my room. I hold the one I like best up against me to see myself in the mirror. The lacey black fabric stretches across my midsection. Whatever. It'll have to do. I certainly can't keep wearing Blue's saris for my entire pregnancy, although they are very comfortable.

I can hear Pooja and Blue arguing downstairs. Their voices are louder than usual. Maybe Tufan did something, and they're disagreeing on how to handle it. I hurry and slip on pants with an elastic front. Ugh. I can't believe I have to wear these. I grab the first over-sized shirt I can find in the closet, pull it over my head, and make my way downstairs.

Both ladies are sitting on the couch in front of the flat screen.

"We should have told him."

Pooja starts to answer Blue, but sees me first. "Good morning, dear. Did you sleep well?"

I can tell she's straining to sound normal. "I slept okay. What's going on?" I come around the corner so I can see the screen.

Blue fumbles with the remote without success. "Nothing. We're just watching the weather."

"The weather?"

I doubt it. I sit down next to them and take the remote from Blue. It's definitely not the weather. I turn up the volume so I can hear. The interview is in English. It's Dev. And *Her*. She has her hand on his knee. I want to throw up. The reporter is asking about their off-set romance. Dev smiles, *she* gushes. I really am going to be sick.

Blue links my arm with hers. Again. I wonder if this is going to be her new thing with me. "It's only acting."

I look over at Pooja. Her arms are crossed in front of her. She's not saying anything. Blue pulls my arm tight against her side. "I promise you, it's only acting. Look, he only smiles. He knows he's on film, if he shows any negative feelings toward her, it won't be good publicity for the movie."

I don't care. It hurts to see him with her. It hurts like blades shooting through my heart. I'm upset that it bothers me. Prem would never do this to me. I miss my Prem. I have to get out of here. I need space. So I go to the only place I can think of...Lakewood Park.

CHAPTER NINE

Cleveland Hopkins Airport. I wasn't sure how long I'd be gone when I left in June. Now it's the end of August. I look out the window. Everything looks the same. I don't know why it would look any different since it's only been almost three months. I haven't told anyone I'm arriving today. I didn't want to interrupt their day when I can just get a cab.

I recognize some of the photographs lining the airport corridors this time around. I like not having photographers in my face everywhere I go. I grab my luggage and head up the escalator to get a cab.

"What's the address?"

"Do you know Arthur Avenue in Lakewood?"

"Yeah, I know Lakewood."

"Good. I'll show you the house once we get there."

In twenty minutes, we're turning onto the street. My heart starts pounding because I'm not sure how Raine will react when she sees me. We barely spoke while I was gone. Only a few words when Tufan and I talked on Messenger. At least I know my mom and Aunt Pooja will be glad to see me. I can't wait to see Tufan. I'm surprised I missed him so much. I didn't get to talk to him enough while I was gone. Raine, well, I'll have to see. Tufan chattered on excitedly about the baby, so I know it's no longer a secret. After I pay the cab, I walk in the open front door and call out.

Nothing. I walk into the kitchen. No one. I walk through the back of the house to the family room. No one. I look at my watch and count the time difference. It's only six thirty p.m. here.

"Anybody home?"

Why would they leave the door open when no one is home? I walk out to the garage and Raine's truck is there, still parked next to my Spyder. I can't wait to take it out again. I drag my suitcase upstairs to my room. Everything looks the same. Maybe they just went out for a walk and forgot to close the door. I decide the best thing I can do right now is take a quick shower to get all the dirt off from the trip. It's as hot here as India was when I left. Maybe they'll be back by the time I'm finished.

· · ✧ · ·

THE HEAT IS SO STIFLING that I'm regretting the walk to Grant Elementary School. Tufan is so excited about starting first grade. I couldn't say no when he begged us to walk to orientation. The doctor said exercise is good, so I agreed. I wish I hadn't. At least Pooja and Blue are walking slow with me. Tufan keeps skipping ahead of us. It makes me nervous because I'm afraid he might decide to jump out in the street. Naz and Dialah always laugh at me, saying I'm overprotective, but I can't help it. Maybe they'll understand when they have kids.

We finally reach the house, and Tufan runs straight in.

"Great. Which of us was the last one out?" I look at Pooja and Blue, who offer no response. "We have to stop forgetting to lock the door when we leave."

My overprotective instincts kick in again. What if someone broke into the house while we were gone?! I pick up my pace, hurry up the front steps, and follow him in faster than I'm used to. My heart beats strong in my chest, and I feel like I can't catch my breath. "Tufan? Where are you, buddy?"

"I'm here. Watching TV."

"Really? Already? You just got home. Don't you want to play outside or something?"

"No. It's too hot."

"I can't say I disagree." I sit in the recliner and put my feet up. I need to have air conditioning installed. I wonder if the subcontractor we used on my last job at work will give me a deal. I can hear Pooja and Blue fumbling in the kitchen to get dinner going. I'm almost asleep when I hear something drop on the floor upstairs. I open my eyes and Tufan is still in front of the TV. I'm sure I heard it.

I get up and check to see if Pooja and Blue are still in the kitchen. They are. I eye the stairs. I don't hear anything now, but I'm sure I did before. I know I won't relax until I make sure no one is up there. I creep up the first step. Then another. And another. I decide I'm being stupid and walk the rest of the way up. I check all the rooms, ending with mine. I peek in the door, seeing everything the way I left it. Well, not everything.

Dev walks out of the master bath wearing nothing but a towel wrapped around his waist. I scream out loud and might have even peed myself a little. "Where did you come from?"

"Uh...the bathroom." His words are muffled by the toothbrush wedged in his cheek. He takes it out and rinses.

"You know what I mean. We didn't even know you were coming home. Did you tell anyone?"

I can hear footsteps scrambling up the stairs. Tufan shoves me aside. "Uncle Dev! You're home! You're home!" He launches at Dev and lands in his arms, almost ripping the towel from its secured place. I turn around quickly to avoid another embarrassing peepshow.

Blue reaches the top of the stairs followed by Pooja. "What's this?"

"Uh, the prodigal son returns." I don't know what else to say, so I say something stupid. Blue's mystified eyes linger on mine as she leans into the room.

"Devaj! Why didn't you tell us you were coming?" Pooja pushes past me into the room where Blue hugs Dev, who's still awkwardly holding Tufan with one hand while his other is holding the towel in a tight grip.

"I wanted to surprise you."

"Well, you did." Pooja kisses his cheek. "Come on now, we need to let him get dressed." Pooja pulls Tufan away and shoos him out. "You go on downstairs now. Let your uncle get dressed and visit with Raine." Blue takes Pooja's hint and follows them out. "We'll see you when you come down for dinner. Lock the door." She winks at her son before closing the door behind her.

"It's good to see you, Raine. You look great."

"Great? I don't feel great. You try walking around carrying sack of potatoes permanently sitting on your bladder."

Watching him stand there and stare at me, wearing only a towel, releases weeks of bottled-up emotion. It's not fair. He gets to have perfect chiseled abs. I get to pee every half hour.

I'm so confused right now between the perfect baby growing inside me and wishing I could have my perfect flat stomach back. It doesn't help that my husband's perfect body is staring right at me, and I can't even touch it. Perfect. Just perfect.

· · ⌘ · ·

RAINE LOOKS MORE THAN great. She's beautiful. Mussed up hair, baby, and all. I take a deep breath. I want to tell her more, but I'm not sure what she's thinking right now. Two things I've learned recently. One. Never tell a woman something you don't mean. And Two. Harmless flirtation is never harmless.

"Can you please put some clothes on now?"

"What?" I look down. "Oh." I grab a pair of shorts and a t-shirt from my suitcase and turn around to put them on.

When I turn back, she's lying on her back in our king-size bed holding her stomach. Crying.

"What is it?" I lay down on my side next to her, and she turns her back to me. "Raine, what's wrong?"

"Nothing."

"I'm sure it's not nothing." I don't know whether to touch her or leave her alone. My hand hovers a minute before I decide to place it on her shoulder. She doesn't cringe. That's a good sign. She does, however, start crying harder. So I take my hand away. "I can't help you if you won't tell me what's going on."

"What's going on? Really? I'll tell you what's going on." She turns halfway in my direction. I know I'm going to regret asking the minute she starts. Her voice has an interrupt-and-you're-dead tone to it. And then she starts.

"You leave, not even two days after we're married. I get you're upset with me about not telling you about the baby. But that's not how you solve problems. Especially in a marriage. Then, our conversations over the phone are no more than the niceties. And to top it all off..." Here it comes. "I have to watch you and your girlfriend splashed all over the flat screen while your mother tells me it's only acting. How's that for what's going on?"

She rolls over so her back is to me again.

"Raine, listen ..."

She shoots one last sentence in my direction over her shoulder. "Oh, and what's with coming home without letting anyone know? I almost peed myself. No. In fact, I did pee myself. You might as well get used to it. That's what happens when you're seven months pregnant." I can hear her sniff on her side of the bed. "And, yes, I'm still wearing the same peed-in underwear because I'm too tired, sick, and hormonal to do anything about it."

Now I'm speechless. Completely. Nothing to say. At all. What is there to say? I decide to do the only thing a man in my situation can do. I get up, open a drawer, and hand her a clean pair of underwear before lying back down on my side of the bed.

"Thank you." I think I hear one more sniff before I fall asleep, but I'm not sure. It might have been more.

• • ∽✦∾ • •

I CAN'T BELIEVE I JUST told Dev I peed myself. And to make things worse, I told him I was too tired to change my own underwear. I look at the pair he gave me. I start crying again. He doesn't know I can't even wear these anymore. I have to wear granny panties. My tears keep rolling while I scroll myself up to a sitting position. I can hear his rhythmic breathing. He's already asleep. I stand up and put my wanna-have-sex panties away and snatch a pair of the til-death-do-you-part variety. I feel a twinge at my conscience for telling him I all-out peed myself. I really didn't, but he has no idea what it's like to have no control over your bladder. I can't sneeze without leaking.

I go downstairs. Tufan is sitting with Honey, watching TV.

"It's eight o'clock, Tufan. We need to get you ready for bed."

"Can't I finish watching this? It's almost done."

"What is it?"

"It's another Indian movie. This man, he marries this girl even though her face is scarred from a fire when they are engaged because she rescued her cousin from a house fire, and everybody thinks he's not going to marry her now, and they're in the hospital, and ..."

"Okay, okay, okay. How much longer?"

"Twenty minutes."

"I'm surprised you like that kind of story."

"It's okay. I like watching it because it shows India, and I want to go there and visit."

"Right." I hadn't thought about that until now. Tufan should visit. I've no doubt Blue and Pooja wouldn't mind taking him, and we can surely stay at Dev's house in Mumbai.

Burning rises from my stomach all the way up to my throat. Heartburn. Time to OD on Tums again. The thought of flying over the Atlantic Ocean, or any ocean, scares the crap out of me. I hate flying. I can't stop the realization I'm going to have to face it eventually. A trip to India. Gah!

"Tufan, as soon as that movie finishes, I want you upstairs to brush your teeth, change into pajamas, and bed. Okay?"

"Yes. And put Honey back."

"What? Oh, right. I see you're learning."

I walk through the house out to the porch and find Pooja and Blue rocking in peace in the high back rockers. I pass them to head for the swing.

"Are you hungry?" Blue's hands are working nonstop on her Indian lace piece.

"No."

"You have to eat, you know. I don't think you eat enough." Blue doesn't even look up when she speaks.

"I eat plenty. Trust me."

"I would like to see you eat more."

I want to tell Blue straight where she can put all her unsolicited advice, but I chomp on my handful of Tums instead.

"Is Devaj coming down?"

"I don't know. He was sleeping when I left him."

"He'll probably wake up early morning. I'll leave some food out in case he's hungry."

"I'm sure he's more than capable of fixing himself something to eat."

"Raine, what's wrong with you?" Pooja's censuring is not helping my mood. Nothing helps my moods.

"Nothing is wrong with me. Why does everyone think something is wrong with me? I'm pregnant, the size of my truck, and my husband has a girlfriend, not that I care. It's not like we married for love or anything. It's business. It's acting. It's always something." I don't even wait for them to respond. I stomp through the house and up the stairs to my room. Heedless of Dev sleeping, I slam the door, pull off the knit dress stretched too tight on top of my body, and sink into my side of the bed. I don't bother with pajamas anymore. I'm still wearing my bra and panties. It's enough. I can no longer stand the restraints of clothing twisting on my body at night. Tears stream down my face, but I'm trying to be silent in my grief.

I lay my hands on my bosu-ball belly and wait to feel him move. I enjoy the movements and knowing he's alive. I still don't know if it's a boy or girl. The last ultrasound didn't allow me to see, but I like to think of him as a boy, for Prem. I massage my stomach. My large stomach. I'm crying hard now. I can't believe I'm so unhappy. This is Prem's baby, my baby. What happened to the joy I'm supposed to feel?

Dev moves in the bed next to me. His arm reaches across the pillows and rests when it touches my hair. I turn on my side, and my cheek falls on the palm of his hand. I can feel the caress of his thumb on my temple. I still can't tell if he's awake or not. He scoots closer to me and cradles me in his arms. I can feel the skin of his rock-hard abs against my belly. He's definitely awake. He must have removed his clothes after I left. I don't care because it feels good lying here so close to him. His lips find mine in the dark of the night. His kisses are soothing to me. I allow myself to explore him a little. More than I ever thought I might. I can't help it. The feelings inside me are raging. It's been so long. I'm done fighting it.

. . ❧ . .

I FORGOT HOW MUCH I missed her. Missed the wildness of her hair. Missed her kisses. It feels different somehow. I like it. I'm not going to stop until she does. The way she's kissing me back I don't know if I can stop even if I want to. I pull back and kiss the top of her nose. Her tears have stopped, but her cheeks are still wet. I wipe them with the pads of my thumbs and kiss each cheek when I'm finished. Her round belly presses into mine, warm and inviting. I smooth my hand around her side and across her middle. Something moves under my touch and it startles me.

"Did you feel it?" Raine whispers low and presses my hand flat to her stomach, holding it in place. "Just wait."

It happens again. "I feel it." Even in the dark I can tell she's smiling.

"He's going to be a soccer player, I'm sure of it."

"You found out what you're having?"

"No, not exactly. I like to think of him as a boy. For Prem."

I take my hand away and place it behind my head. I can feel an instant surge of angst in the center of my chest. I swallow hard to make it go away. It doesn't. Am I ever going to get over this? Jealousy of a man who's no longer alive? My own cousin. A cousin I cared about. Someone who's given me the gift of his most precious possessions.

Raine clasps her arm tight across my chest and snuggles close, tangling her legs with mine. "Do you love her?"

"Who?"

"Her. Pria."

"*Pria*? Of course not!" I can't believe she's asking me this.

"That's not what it looks like."

I don't want to talk about this, but I don't want Raine to be upset again. I like having her close against me. "Listen." I can't help twisting a curl around my forefinger while I talk. "I know what it looks like. I know what they're saying. It's not true. None of it."

Raine bends her head up to look at me. "Dev, I saw you on TV with her. She was all over you. I know I shouldn't care, but technically we're married."

Raine tries to pull away, but I hold her in place. "Technically? Raine, we are married. And despite what you may think, I want to be married to you. I never would have married you if I didn't."

"So, why did you let her put her hands on you? Why didn't you move away or avoid her?"

"It's complicated." I'm not sure how I'm going to explain it. She wasn't raised in the entertainment world. "She and I are co-stars in a movie. We need to have good reviews. And her family has influence. I have to be careful…"

Raine turns her back to me now. The spot she leaves feels hollow, and I don't want to let her go, so I crawl up against her and hold her. "Which is why I have lawyers to handle things for me. Naz, too. Whatever happens next, they'll deal with it."

"I don't understand what she hopes to accomplish. Does she just want to sleep with you? Marry you? Destroy your career? I don't get it."

"Honestly, Raine. I don't get it either. I think she wants the publicity because believe me, India is soaring with it. Which is one of the reasons why"—I kiss the top of her head—"this little town on the edge of Lake Erie is fast becoming my absolute favorite place on earth."

I don't tell her the other reason.

CHAPTER TEN

"I'm telling you she's having twins." I can hear Blue's voice all the way upstairs. Pooja's voice is muffled so I can't make out what she's saying. I don't care anyway. The two of them are constantly bickering about something, more so than usual. I woke up this morning with a pain shooting down the back of my leg that feels like a dentist drill when it hits a nerve. I have to place each step carefully or the pain zaps me in all directions. I wish Dev was here to help me down the stairs. I woke up and the room was empty. Empty of him, anyway.

Pooja and Blue are shelling peas in the kitchen. Sometimes I feel like that's all they do. Shell peas, string beans, and clean okra.

"I'm not having twins."

Pooja jumps up from her seat to help me into the room. "I know, dear. Let Blue think what she wants, yes? Are you all right?"

"I'm fine. I think it's just the weight of the baby. He's getting bigger is all."

Pooja clasps her hands to her mouth. "Are you sure? It's a boy?"

"No. No. I still don't know. I like to refer to him as a boy." I circle my hand on my belly as I talk. "I don't like calling my baby an 'it.' I'm hoping for a boy, but I'll be happy with a girl too."

Blue stands up and opens the refrigerator. "What can I make you to eat? Anything you want. We cooked for Devaj and Tufan before Devaj took him to school so that you could rest. Now it's your turn. I'll cook whatever you want to eat."

If these two don't stop telling me to eat, I'm going to slap someone, but it's early so I'm able to keep my tongue checked behind my teeth. "How about a little coffee?"

"No, no, no. Caffeine is no good for the baby." Pooja shakes her head in a coordinated effort.

"Dr. Hill says I can have one cup a day." They're making me feel like a child begging for candy.

Pooja places the peas on the table and folds her arms across her chest. "Hmpf. I don't like it. You need to eat things nutritious. Keep your strength up. You're going to need it. Trust me."

What can I do? Once again, I succumb to the whims of these ladies of the house. I allow Blue to make me eggs in my gram's skillet.

I take one bite and realize how hungry I am. I can't get enough. Of course there's a comment from the ladies. "Protein. Your body is craving protein."

I nod and agree, while I munch on the last, savory, delicious bite. I hear Dev roar up the driveway under the kitchen window. He took Tufan to school in his Maserati. My stomach squirms because I remember the first time he drove here in the U.S. I close my eyes and take a deep breath. I can't control everything. Tufan's at school and Dev's home safe.

My stomach squirms again except this time it's more like a cramp. A tight, hard, charlie horse cramp. Right across the top and lower abdomen. I can't breathe. Pooja's on one side and Blue's on the other, both are rubbing my back. I can't speak. It hurts.

"Devaj!" Pooja yells first.

"Devaj!" Blue yells next.

I exhale fast and take another deep breath. I'm not sure, but I think I might be going into labor. It's too soon.

"Devaj!" They yell in unison.

Blue runs out the backdoor to get him to come faster. Seconds go by.

"What is it?"

"It's Raine. She needs to go to the hospital."

"Okay. I'll take her. Let's go." The cramp in my stomach eases a little, and I start to stand up. Dev has other plans. He whips me up in his arms and swings me out of the kitchen, down the hall, and out the backdoor.

"I can walk, you know."

"I'm not taking any chances." He doesn't even open the door to his Maserati. All he does is set me down in it. The space is much smaller than I remember. Although, I wasn't carrying around my watermelon belly either. He races around to his side, fires the engine, and squeals out. I can feel another cramp coming on. What if I am in labor? It's too soon. Way too soon.

We stop at the light at the top of my street. Dev looks at me. "I'm not sure where to go."

I'm holding my breath trying to get my stomach to relax, and the last thing I want to do is give directions to St. John

Medical Center. "Just get on I-90 and go west. Can you do that?"

"That I can do."

Twenty minutes later, Dev's carrying me into the waiting room. The nurses immediately direct him to put me in a wheelchair. "Are you the father?"

Dev doesn't answer and looks at me. I'm not sure what I should say. I say the only true thing I can. "He's my husband."

·· ∽ ··

I DON'T KNOW WHAT TO say when the nurse asks me if I'm the father. I'm not. I look at Raine because I have no words. My gut wrenches deep inside. Raine's quick response saves the dead air hanging between us. "He's my husband."

"Follow me down the hall. I'll show you where you can wait near the patient rooms." We pass desks and rooms and stop at two double doors you can only pass with a code or key. Maternity is plastered above the doors.

"What's happening? My stomach is tight. I feel like I can't breathe." Raine's voice is breathy and scared.

I want to be next to her and hold her hand through it all. I know it's too early. Is she losing the baby? I start to feel the tingling beginnings of fear.

Two nurses walk with us, the older one pushing the wheelchair. "Don't worry, hon. We'll get you hooked up to the monitor and get everything checked out. Is this your first?"

"Yes."

I can tell Raine is scared. I'm scared. What if she is in labor?

We reach the room, and the second nurse directs me to the waiting room across the hall. I walk over to a room filled with large couches and lounge chairs. Not your typical waiting room. I walk to the window and look out. There's so much open space all around the hospital. They even have a soccer field with goals on each end. A bike path trails the boundary. I'm guessing it goes all around the hospital. I'm not sure how long I'm standing there staring, but I hear my name being called and I turn around.

The same nurse directs me to follow her. "She's all set up."

I walk in the room to see Raine dressed in a hospital gown and an electronic belt fastened around her stomach. Another large couch is along the back wall. The whoosh, whoosh on the monitor sounds in the background.

"How are you doing?"

"I haven't seen the doctor yet, but she'll be here in a minute I'm sure."

"Are you still having pain?"

"Not as intense now. Maybe it stopped."

I pull a chair to the side of the bed so I can sit next to her. I take her hand in mine. "Raine..."

She covers my hand with her own. "It's okay. Let's not talk about this now. We'll talk later when I know everything's fine."

Dr. Hill walks in and introduces herself to me. "It's good to meet you. I'll need you to step over there while I take a look."

I take a seat on the couch and wait. All I can focus on is the whoosh, whoosh of the monitor. It soothes me and scares me at the same time. Dr. Hill circles the bed, poking and prodding and then does *that*. Raine squirms on the table. I immediately look out the window. I wasn't expecting Dr. Hill to place her fingers there.

I listen while Dr. Hill briefs Raine on what's happening. "You're only dilated one centimeter. It looks like Braxton Hicks contractions."

Like I know what those are. I'm embarrassed to ask what she means, and fortunately I don't have to because she goes on to explain it in more detail.

"Your body is getting ready to have this baby. We'll have to monitor you closely. Have you had your Lamaze classes?"

Raine shakes her head.

"I highly recommend them. Can I ask why not?"

Raine doesn't answer immediately. "I don't have a partner selected."

Dr. Hill looks at me. "I don't understand."

"I travel. For work."

"I see. Is there a friend or someone you feel comfortable with who could take you?"

Raine's tears fall down her cheek. I can't tell if she's having another contraction or not. It doesn't matter. Right now all that matters is Raine. And the baby. "I'll do it."

Raine looks up from twisting the sheet in her hand. "What?"

"I'll be your partner for the Mazze."

Raine smiles enough for me to see the dimples that frame her lips. "Are you sure?"

"Yep. Whatever you need."

Dr. Hill looks at one and then the other. "Okay, then. I'll give the nurse my instructions and she'll help you get scheduled for the classes. I want you to stay a little longer for observation and then you can go home."

"You don't have to do it, you know. I can get Dialah or Naz."

"Why didn't you?"

"Honestly, I didn't think it was time yet. I'm coming up on seven months in September, but if you really want to..."

I take my seat by her bed and envelop her hand in mine. "I'm sure."

Whatever the Mazze is, there's no doubt in my mind I can handle it. How hard can it be?

· · ⚭ · ·

DEV AND I WALK DOWN the hall of the medical offices attached to the hospital. Almost a week has passed since my emergency room visit. I'm nervous when I walk in. The room is full with about ten couples. Everyone is smiling, but I'm not. I don't like thinking about the day I go into labor. I'm excited about my baby, but I'm not looking forward to the pain. Why am I even here? I want the drugs.

"Welcome! Have a seat." The instructor, Helen, tells us to sit in two open spaces on the floor in front of her. Great. I hate sitting on the floor. It's too hard to get back up. Helen begins by telling us she's had eleven children, all without drugs and all using the techniques she's going to teach us. "Let's begin."

Sparks fly as soon as I lean back against Dev. He wraps his arms around me and massages my stomach. It's relaxing and intoxicating at the same time. I'm not sure he knows exactly what he's doing to me, but then again, after his first night back from India, maybe he does. I try not to think about it and focus on the breathing. Which is apparently important. Whatever. I'm still taking the drugs.

Helen also teaches us, or rather teaches Dev the importance of foot massages.

"I haven't had any swelling in my feet. I don't think it's necessary."

Helen looks in my direction. "You will. Maybe not yet, but almost all women get some swelling in their feet, maybe even grow a shoe size."

"What?" Dev helps me up from the floor and over to a seat next to a table lining the wall. "I really don't think it's necessary."

Helen winks at me. "You'll thank me later."

Dev kneels in front of me and removes my shoe. I feel like my face is burning hot. Dev concentrates on each area of my foot. His slow, methodical movements relax me.

"How does that feel?" He's using just enough pressure so it doesn't tickle.

"Nice." I don't want to tell him how nice. It excites me.

One of his hands begins to massage up the back of my calf, almost to the back of my knee. "Okay. That's enough." I pull my foot back and start putting my shoe back on.

"What about your other foot?"

"It's fine. I think we understand the concept."

"I think I'd like more practice." Dev removes the shoe I just put back on and continues his efforts. I watch his hands touching my skin as he continues slowly up and down my calf. I can feel my heart begin to race. I swallow hard to stifle the storm beginning to rise. Goosebumps appear on my leg.

"Are you cold?"

"No." I try to pull my leg back, but Dev doesn't let me.

"Are you sure?" He strokes my leg with both of his hands to warm it before propping it firmly on his thigh. His inner thigh.

"Yes, I'm sure." I start to remove my foot, still Dev doesn't let me.

"Uh-uh." He reaches for my other leg, removes the shoe, and begins at my toes. I can barely sit still. I try to focus my thoughts anywhere else, but I keep returning to the delicious way his hands and fingers massage my entire foot before making their way up. I can't take it anymore. I decide to sit back, close my eyes, and let myself enjoy.

Dev continues his training until Helen announces the end of today's class. I open my eyes and Dev is looking right at me. His dark, golden eyes meet mine. He doesn't say anything. I stand up and he helps me slip each shoe on. He stands up too, but he lets his hand linger close to the side of my leg as he does. All the way up the side of my leg. Past my knee. I feel the fabric of my dress drop when he lets go.

"Are we good?" His words are close to my lips when he speaks.

So close I want to answer him with mine but not with words. I can hear the shuffle of people leaving around us, but I don't care. Dev's arms are holding mine at the elbows, and I hold him at his waist.

"Raine?"

"Yes?"

"How are you feeling?"

I can't stand being this close any longer. Before I talk myself out of it, I kiss him. He kisses me back. I can't think. He pulls me flush against his chest, and I circle my arms tight around him, kissing him more. He cups my face with his hands. I feel his soft caresses when he pulls back slightly.

"What was that for?"

I don't know what to say. "Thank you?" I can feel my face begin to tingle, probably pink. I'm embarrassed and I don't know why. He is my husband. I pull away and turn my back to him while I put my coat on.

"I see more foot massages in your future."

No doubt my face is flaming now. As soon as I've buttoned my coat, Dev takes my hand and we walk out to the car. I can barely speak.

Dev won't stop looking at me, and I can't stop sneaking glances at him. The entire drive home consists of one-word conversation. My body is telling me I'm ready for more, my head is telling me no, and I'm not sure what to tell Dev.

• • ⤙⤚ • •

"RAINE, RAINE, RAINE!" Tufan runs into my room and jumps on the bed. "Come on, get up!"

I can't move. I'm so tired. "What is it?"

"Uncle Dev is taking us for a drive."

"No. I'm not going anywhere."

"But you have to."

I sit up in my bed. Dev is gone. He's been sleeping in one of the guest rooms. I'm not sure why. It might have to do with my current need to take the entire king-size bed for myself. I'm sure it's not because I'm snoring. I don't snore.

"Tufan. Stop, honey. I can't go anywhere. Do you see this?" I point to the massive protrusion across my midsection.

"I know, but you can still walk. Uncle Dev will carry you if you want. I know it. Please, please, please?"

I can't stand it when he begs, and Tufan knows it. "I'm sorry, Tufan. I just can't. This baby is due in three weeks. I am not in the mood for a drive."

"Fine." Tufan lands on his bottom and bounces off the bed. "I'll tell Uncle Dev."

After a wake up like that, no way I'm falling back to sleep now. I crawl out of bed, get dressed, and head downstairs. No one is around. "Tufan?" Nothing.

I walk into the kitchen. No one.

I walk into the family room. No one.

I hear engines revving outside. Dev is outside with his Maserati, wiping the dashboard and panels with a cloth.

"I thought you had a mechanic for that?"

"I do. Giovanni is in India taking care of my other cars."

I sit down on the top step of the stairs, holding the railing as I go.

"Where is everyone?"

"Drug Mart, I think."

"Did they walk?"

"Probably. I'm not sure where they went. They said they had some shopping to do."

"Oh." I watch Dev wipe the windshield and then walk over to where I'm sitting. "So, how many cars do you have?"

I shield my eyes from the sun. In this light, he looks like a Greek statue. His t-shirt is pulled tight across his chest, and I can see the faint outline of his muscles.

"Do you really want to know?"

"If you want to tell me."

"Last count, twelve."

"Twelve? Do you own a dealership? What do you do with them all?"

"I collect them. I'm a collector of luxury cars." His smile is a mile wide. He wipes his hands with the towel and tries to sit next to me. "Scoot over."

I'm as close to the edge of the step as I can get. "Do you have to sit here? There's plenty of chairs in the garage."

"Yes." He nudges in and snuggles in close to me. "See? We fit."

I'm glad we fit, but I don't want to let on how glad.

Tufan bounces a basketball and takes shots at the hoop attached to the front of the garage. The ball keeps hitting the backboard, and he runs to chase it down.

"Why don't you shoot some hoops with him? Show him how it's done."

"Me? Nope. Not my game." He gets up and opens the trunk of his car. "Now this..." He drops a soccer ball on the inside part of his foot and begins to dribble it between his foot and knee, alternating between two feet and two knees. "...I can do."

Tufan runs over. "Whoa! How do you do that so fast?"

Dev moves them over to the backyard, dribbling the ball as he goes. "Come over here and I'll show you."

I watch them as they play together, kicking the ball back and forth. Dev helps Tufan learn to kick the ball with his knee. More than once he misses. I wish I could join them, but I'm sure that's not a good idea.

Dev yells over to me. "Watch this." He bobs the ball back and forth.

"Tufan, I'm going to kick the ball to you, and I want you to kick it back to me up in the air. Can you do that? I'm gonna bounce it off my head."

"Really?"

This, I have to see. Tufan readies himself, flings one foot forward to kick, and misses.

"How about this instead?" Dev walks over and places the ball in front of him. "When I say go, just kick it up in the air in my direction."

Dev runs backward a few yards away. Tufan kicks and Dev runs forward to slam his head into it as it makes its downward cycle. I'm not sure what just happened. All I hear are happy wails from Tufan and one wail from Dev, not so happy. I get up and waddle as fast as I can to where Dev is weaving and holding his head.

"Ugh." He won't move his hand away.

"You have to let go if you want me to see what I can do."

"No, it's fine." He turns away so I can't see his face.

Tufan runs to slip under Dev's arms and look up. "Are you okay? You're bleeding."

"I'm not taking no for an answer. Let me see." He is bleeding.

"Uncle Dev, I'm sorry, I'm sorry." I can hear the panic begin in Tufan's voice.

Dev must hear it too because he immediately starts telling him not to worry. "It's not your fault, it's mine, buddy."

"Why don't you go inside and play with Honey while I get your Uncle Dev all fixed up, okay?"

"Are you sure?"

"Yep! Go on now. I'll get him good as new. I promise."

I turn to Dev. "Let's go, David Beckham."

Dev is still holding his head back while I direct him into the half bath off the back porch. "Sit." I close the lid on the toilet seat and shove him down. "Put your head back and pinch your nose together with these."

I hand him a wad of tissues, grab a washcloth from the drawer, run it under cold water, and begin to pat his face down to get the blood off. "Take off your shirt." He takes it off. Too fast, I think.

His nose stops bleeding. I wipe his face with the cold cloth. "I hope you don't have any photo shoots or filming anytime soon."

"Why?"

I give him the hand mirror sitting on the shelf above him. "Shit."

"Yep." I step between his legs, so I can get a better look at the swelling going on between his eyes, and he pulls me down on his knee. Now he's grinning mischief from one ear to the other. "What are you, fourteen?"

"Yep." And then he kisses me.

. . ⚜ . .

"TAKE OFF YOUR SHIRT." Raine's demand sends charges zinging through my body. She's standing so close that I can't help tugging her into my lap.

Yep. Fourteen is about how old I feel right now. I decide to act it and kiss her. I can tell she wasn't expecting it, but I don't care. I keep kissing her. She doesn't pull away at first, and when she does, her eyes are closed.

"You really need to stop kissing me so much."

"Why is that?"

"Haven't you learned anything from Lamaze class?"

"Do you want to practice your breathing? Do you need a foot massage?"

"No. And no."

"I'm not sure what you mean."

"Remember when Helen talked about the hormones raging inside pregnant wives?"

I know exactly what she means, but I'm not sure she's ready. I'm not sure I'm ready. Although when she refers to herself as my wife, I can't help feeling an odd satisfaction somewhere near my heart.

I decide to try something different. "I know what we can do for that." Maybe I need to rephrase. She squirms in my lap. Part of me wants to give in and take her upstairs, but I don't. "How about we go racing? I know you'll love it."

"Racing? Are you serious?" Obviously not what she's expecting.

"Come on. It always helps me when I need a boost."

"Ugh! That's what you want to do?" She stands up and throws the used washcloth in the hamper by the door.

"Racing. You want to take a pregnant woman with raging hormones racing?"

It takes me a second to realize I need to clarify. "I'm talking about going to the track to *watch* live racing. Amateur racing. It's the best."

"Hmm. Tufan told me something about it earlier."

"I'm telling you. You'll love it. Let's go. Just you and me."

"And Tufan? He wanted to go too."

"He has school tomorrow, and I'm sure we can keep it between us. What do you say?" I watch her roll the decision around in her head. She's going.

· · ᦕᦓ · ·

"RACING. WHAT THE HELL was I thinking?" At least we're driving in my truck. I need space. The seatbelt even pinches.

"Just leave it off."

"What?"

"Don't wear it."

"I can't. It's the law. What if we get pulled over or pass a cop? They can stop you if you're not wearing one. Haven't you seen the signs? Click it or ticket?"

"Lame. I'll pay it."

"Aren't you even worried about my safety?"

"Of course I am, but I'm also concerned for your comfort, and I think it can go either way. So if you don't want to wear it, don't."

"I'm wearing it." I pull it on and try the best I can to adjust it. Visions of the Pillsbury Dough Boy, the Michelin Man, and the Goodyear Blimp invade my mind like a slide show gone rogue. Why did I agree to go racing? I haven't been to a race track in years. In fact, the last time was with my dad. I did enjoy it, but it's not what my pregnant hormones need, and I'm sure Dev knows it.

An hour later, we pull into the empty parking lot of Lake County Speedway. "Where is everyone?"

Dev drives to the gate to check the sign. No events are scheduled for tonight. "I don't get it. I checked the time online before we left."

"Well, something's off." I pull out my iPhone to check the times myself. The website is the first on the list. I scroll down.

"I'm telling you. I checked it."

"Yep. You're exactly right."

"See?"

"Exactly right if we were here last year. They obviously haven't updated the site."

"What the... No." Dev snatches my iPhone form my hand.

He hands it back and slouches in the seat. "Now what do your pregnant hormones crave?"

I'm sure he doesn't want to know, so I suggest the next best thing. "We could head out to Geneva-on-the-Lake."

"Geneva it is."

"No, it's Geneva-on-the-Lake."

"That's what I said."

"No, you're not getting what I'm trying to tell you. It's Geneva 'dash' on 'dash' the 'dash' Lake. That's the complete name, not Geneva by itself."

Dev stares at me like I have horns on my head, but puts the truck in drive and pulls forward. "What's fun to do at *Geneva-on-the-Lake*?"

"Only my absolute favorite thing in the world! Well, maybe not absolute." I'm so excited. I love singing Karaoke. I'm looking forward to seeing the surprise on his face when we walk into the Swiss Chalet.

• • ∞ • •

IT REALLY DOES LOOK like a Swiss Chalet. How did this ever get built on the shores of Lake Erie? The building belongs in the Swiss Alps. We walk in and Raine goes straight to the man sitting at the table behind sound boards and monitors. Karaoke?

"What do you think?" Raine spins around. "I love this place. It's so much fun. We should come here on a Friday or Saturday sometime."

I'm not sure I agree. "If this is what it takes to make you happy, we'll do it."

We sit in a booth to order. I order a beer, and Raine gets a hot herbal tea. We haven't even gotten our orders in before it's her turn to sing.

"I'm going to sing my absolute favorite song. Pay attention." She walks up to the mic and the music begins. I'm guessing it's going to be One Direction. It's not. I can tell she's nervous, but she has a beautiful voice. As soon as she's done, she slides back into the booth and sips the tea the waiter brought while she was gone.

"So? How'd I do?"

"Sugar? By Maroon 5? I thought for sure you would sing something by One Direction."

"I will."

"So, Sugar *isn't* your absolute favorite song."

"No, it is."

I hold my beer to my mouth for a minute before I drink. "You are so confusing sometimes."

"I try. And you haven't told me how I did."

"You did good. Only off a few times, and I could tell you struggled a little on the high notes."

"Well excuse me, Simon Cowell. It's your turn next. We'll see how good you do. And you have to sing an English song."

"Not fair."

"And you have to dance like you do in your movies."

"What? Whose rule is that?"

"Mine. There's plenty of room on the stage."

"Only if you come up there with me. I'll need a co-star." That silenced her. I'm not sure why I said it, but it's true. Performing is much easier for me when I have someone with me to work off of.

"I'll come. As long as it's something I know."

"Done." I walk over to the DJ and tell him what to play. She probably doesn't know I can sing. Or maybe she does. I'll have to remember to ask Tufan what movies they've watched.

She grabs a mic, and as soon as the song starts, her eyes widen in the dim light of the chalet. I walk her over to a stool on stage next to me and help her up just in time for me to start the first line. "You're insecure... Don't know what for... You're turning heads when you walk through the door... Don't need make up...to cover up... Being the way that you are is enough ..."

I start to do my dance around her stool and continue singing. "Everyone else in the room can see it... Everyone else but you..."

Raine joins me in the chorus. "Baby you light up my world like nobody else... The way that you flip your hair gets me overwhelmed, but when you smile at the ground, it ain't hard to tell, you don't know... You don't know you're beautiful."

I decide to tease her and pretend I'm the one who doesn't know I'm beautiful. A few of the restaurant patrons laugh, and we continue singing together and performing in the same way. I sing and dance my way around her until the end of the song. We step down off the stage and go back to our booth. My beer is waiting, and I drink it almost to the bottom.

"Can I have sip?"

"Are you allowed?"

"It's just a sip. I'm sure it's not going to hurt anything at this stage."

I pass my glass to her.

"Did you mean what you said?"

"About what?"

"You know, about what we were singing about."

"Raine, I'm a professional. It's what I do." As soon as I say it, regret grabs me by the throat.

"Oh." She takes her napkin and starts to fold it before placing it in her lap.

"Raine, I didn't mean..."

"It's okay. I understand."

"No. It's not okay and you need to listen to me. I only meant that when I'm on stage, I'm performing. It's what I do." I take her hands in mine. She won't even look at me. "I'm just not accustomed to my performances paralleling my own life so well." I bend down to try and catch her attention, but she still won't look me in the eye.

She removes her hands from mine, adds hot water to her cup, and dips her tea bag. "Look. I know our marriage is not like most. We have an understanding. I just thought there might be more, that's all. You don't have to make excuses."

"I'm not making excuses." I'm really not, but I don't know how to explain it to her. Everything I think to say might come out wrong.

"It's just..." I can tell she's struggling with what to say and I wait. "You keep kissing me."

"Uh, it's not just me. You kiss back."

"I need you to tell me what you're feeling."

Why do women always need men to tell them what we're feeling? Isn't it obvious? "I thought it was clear how I feel about you."

"It's not. We get married, and a few days later you leave to shoot a film in India. We haven't even had time to really get to know each other."

"You're forgetting the fact that you were pregnant and didn't tell me."

"But I explained that to you."

"And I told you I needed time."

"So, have you had enough time?"

"These things can't be rushed." I never respond well when I'm pushed, and she's pushing.

"Can't be rushed? Dev, I'm going to have this baby in the next month. Hopefully. How much more time are you going to need?"

"I'm here with you and Tufan now, aren't I? I'm taking Lamaze with you, aren't I? Isn't it clear?" I hate arguing with her.

"No, it isn't."

I don't know what else to tell her, so I sit back and say nothing. It's true. I have kissed her. A lot. But I thought she wanted it too. I need more than a beer right now, but I know I have to drive. "Are you ready to leave?"

"Yes."

I help her up and we start to walk to the door. She stops. The fish-eyed look on her face scares me. "What is it?"

She looks down at the floor. I do too. Clear liquid is pooled at her feet.

CHAPTER ELEVEN

"I need to talk to you." It's only been an hour, and my mom pulls me into a private room near the waiting room.

"I have to get back to Raine. What is it?"

"Is it true?"

"Is what true?"

"The baby. It's a month early."

"Yes, but Dr. Hill assures me everything should be fine. They have the equipment they need to take care of any problems resulting from a premature birth. The lungs are the main concern, and even though a month early, they should be fully developed." Saying the words makes me feel like throwing up, but I don't.

"That's not what I mean."

Typical. She can never just say what she means. "Then you need to be more specific."

"I mean are you still mad?"

"About what?"

"The baby. It's Prem's."

I close the door so we can talk more privately. The last thing I need right now is for us to be overheard. Raine and I still need to come to terms with it, and I don't need anyone else butting in with their opinions. "You know?"

"Yes, I know."

"And Aunt Pooja?"

I'm not sure what I see in my mom's expression. She sits down in a chair across from me. "Yes." Her eyes tear up. "We both knew."

"Why the hell didn't you tell me?" My chest tightens and the familiar hollow returns to my stomach. The same one I get every time I think about the idea of children of my own.

"Because this baby is still a Shukla."

She's not wrong, but I can't help the anger I have right now. I can't even look at her. "You should have told me."

"I know. I'm sorry we caused you to leave."

I'm not going to tell her I left because I believed Raine wanted to pass the baby off as mine. I'm not going to tell her I left because I wanted the baby to be mine. I'm not going to tell her I left because I was jealous.

"I needed to shoot the film in Shimla. It's my job. Raine understands." I know she doesn't, but I'm not going to explain my reasons to my mom or anyone. Especially since I haven't had a real conversation with Raine yet.

My mom cups my face between her hands. "Devaj. I only want you to be happy. Promise me you will be happy."

A knock on the door saves me from answering. "It's time."

· · ⚘ · ·

"SHH. SHH. SHH. WHERE the hell is the doctor with my epidural? I can't stand it anymore!" I grab onto Dev's hand and squeeze hard. The pain is excruciating. Why doesn't anyone listen to me?

"It won't be long now."

"How freakin' long do they need? It's a hospital! Oh my God, oh my God. I can't stand it. Please make it stop." I'm trying so hard to keep it together.

"Focus, Raine. Focus on your breathing."

I glare at Dev. "Shut up. Just shut up. Leave me alone. I'm not doing this shit. I want the epidural. I want the drugs. I want it all. Wake me up when it's all over."

I can't even stand the sight of the man. "Get away from me." Dev steps back.

Pooja takes his place. She whispers something in Dev's ear and he leaves. She doesn't touch me. She takes my cup of ice from the table and offers me pieces from a plastic spoon. "Here, have some. It might help."

It doesn't. I want out of this bed, out of this hospital. Hell, I want out of this universe. It's not fair. I can't believe everyone tells me "it's worth it." It's not.

Dev comes back in. "Better?"

"Better? If you like having strangers jam their fingers between your legs and up your private parts every twenty minutes without your permission, maybe." The words freely flowing from my mouth surprise me. I never talk like this and the awful thing is, I Just. Don't. Care.

Dr. Hill comes in and fingers me up the wazoo. Again. The slap of her rubber glove when it comes off sends my nerves on a joy ride. I want to scratch her eyes out when the lid of the contaminated items basket claps closed. She sits on a stool with wheels and rolls herself across the floor next to me. "Raine, I know we talked about giving you an epidural, but here's the thing. You're dilated too much. I'm also concerned about the baby being three weeks early. I want to be sure we have a healthy birth and are in a position to provide neonatal assistance, if necessary."

I can't even think straight. All I hear is "neonatal," and then my insides rip from my chest to my belly button and farther down. It takes me a minute to formulate my question. "Dilated too much? What does that mean?"

"It means you went from three centimeters to eight fast, and we need you to try and continue through to ten centimeters so you can start pushing."

"Start pushing? What the hell have I been doing all this time?"

Dr. Hill smiles and looks at Pooja and Dev. "It might help if you help her get on all fours on the bed and massage her lower back."

"Like hell!"

"Come on, Raine. Let me help you."

"We both will." Pooja's voice is soft, but I still want to choke someone.

"Fine." I'm mortified. The hospital gown is split in the back for easy access, and of course, I'm not wearing underwear. There is no way on God's green earth this is going to relax me. Even though both Pooja and Dev are facing forward as if that's going to make it any less awkward. I only last through one contraction in this position before I make them help me back down on my back.

"No, I am not going to walk down the hall." Who the hell walks when you're trying to have a baby? I'm in so much pain all I want to do is scream. More finger poking does not add to my present comfort.

"It's time." Dr. Hill stands to the side and waits while the nurses prepare me for delivery. I see one of them look at Dr. Hill. "The bed's not ready."

I look from one to the other. "What the hell does that mean?" What is with my potty mouth? I feel like every word that wants to come out needs peppered with hell, shit, and damn. "I'm sorry. It just hurts so damn much."

"It's okay, honey. It's part of the process." Dr. Hill gives her nurse instructions to position me on my back.

My legs are bent, and I lean against Dev who's sitting on the bed behind me. This is not like the movie from Lamaze class. Where's the opening at the end of the bed? Why isn't someone standing at the bottom ready to catch my baby? Why don't they... My train of thought gets interrupted by the sharpest, hardest, ripping spasm I've experienced so far.

"Push."

I can't believe Dr. Hill wants me to push. I feel like screaming, "You push, bitch!" But I don't. I do the only thing I can do. Push.

Four times. Four times in a row. That's how many times it takes to have the most sensitive part of my body stretched like a rubber band top to bottom.

The only thing Dr. Hill does is stand on the side, arms crossed in front, commanding the troops like a rowing captain. I'm bent so tight that if my legs were crossed, I swear I'd be a pretzel.

Dr. Hill steps in after the fourth push then sudden, instant relief. I relax against Dev who's whispering something in my ear. I don't even know what he's saying. I can't think. I'm so tired.

"It's a boy."

I start to cry. "Where is he? Can I see him?"

Dev's voice cracks when he speaks. "The nurses have him."

I don't hear anything. The nurses are cleaning things up for me down there, but all I can think of is why isn't he crying. Tears stream down my face and then, finally, the most amazing sound. Crying. Loud and angry.

My joy expands even further when he's placed in my arms. I have no words for this feeling. I only know it's immense, immovable, and overwhelming.

"You did it. The newest member of the Shukla clan. He looks like you."

The last thing I care about right now is the Shukla clan. I don't see me. I see Prem. I can't help falling in love. For the first time in my life, I know what true love is. Sweet child of mine.

• • ⚜ • •

POOJA SITS WITH LITTLE Prem bundled tight in her arms. It's been three days since coming home from the hospital. Pooja's eyes are glued to the little bean as she glides back and forth in the rocker. "Why did you never tell me?"

I'm not sure what she means. "Tell you what?"

"That you were carrying my grandchild. Instead, I had to pretend I didn't know until the opportunity presented itself." Her voice is calm and not angry.

"You knew?" I move over to sit on the cloth-covered lid of the toy box, already filled to the brim with toys.

"Prem told me. How else do you think he convinced me to help you two get married so fast?"

I watch Prem sleep in her arms. I feel a little guilty for not trusting her enough to tell her months ago. I want to be mad at her, but I'm not. Instead, I enjoy the expressions my little one makes. I wonder what he dreams about. Watching him cuddled in her arms causes my milk to drop, and I can feel the warm leakage. I'm not too concerned because nursing pads keep it under control. I don't want to wake him up yet anyway. It hasn't been two hours. The pediatrician said to let him sleep until he wakes up to nurse.

"I wanted to tell you."

Pooja looks up at me while continuing to glide back and forth. "Why didn't you?"

"I don't know." I'm lying, but I can't tell her I kept the secret on purpose. "It was hard for me after Prem died. So many things happened at once. So many decisions I needed to make. This was one thing I controlled in my life. One thing entirely mine. One last gift from the love of my life."

Pooja stops rocking and takes my little one to his bassinet, carefully propping him on his side. The nurse at St. John's showed us this little trick. Wrapping him so tight makes him look like a Russian nesting doll, but it helps him feel secure. The small bassinet also helps. Something to do with a how a smaller space feels more familiar to him.

Pooja comes over and sits next to me. She puts her arm around me. I can tell she's holding back tears too. "Daughter, I couldn't understand why you wanted to leave us. Why you wanted to take Tufan away from me. I couldn't let you take the last thing I'll ever have from Prem. My little one."

I turned to look at her. I'm shocked. "Pooja. I thought you would want to go back to India, or to family or something. I didn't know. I would never keep Tufan from you. I wanted to keep my baby with family. Prem's baby with family. Give Tufan a family."

"And you don't consider me family anymore?"

"No. No. That is not what I mean at all." I know I'm screwing this conversation up royally. I take her hands in mine. "Believe me. It's not that. You are Tufan's family, this baby's family, and my family. It's why I agreed to marry Dev. I needed to deal with my grief, I guess. I was struggling. I'm still struggling."

"Are you unhappy?"

"Unhappy? No." And I'm not. I know I still love Prem. I don't think I will ever stop. But I'm also very aware of my feelings for Dev.

"Do you regret marrying Devaj?"

The truth of that question is not one I'm ready to face. "It has been difficult, but I don't think I regret it."

"I'm sorry for pushing you." Pooja looks down at her lap and our entangled hands. "I didn't want to lose you either, you know. I love you like a daughter."

My heart opens to her words in a way I never thought possible. I hug her close. "I love you too."

• • ❦ • •

I HEAR PREM'S TINY cry, but I can't open my eyes. The thought I might regret sleeping in the same room with Raine and the baby crosses my mind. I push it away. I don't want to be that kind of father. Or that kind of husband. Raine's been through enough heartache in her life. I only wish she would let me in. I wish she would come to me with open arms like she did before. Before Prem was born.

I watch her pick him up and begin to nurse him in the glider positioned in the corner of our room. She is so good with him. "Do you need anything?"

"A glass of water would be nice."

I hit the button on the wall above my head to switch on the light. Tufan bumps into me on my way downstairs. "Hey buddy, what are you doing up? It's late."

He rubs his eyes. "I don't know. I just woke up. I had a dream about Daddy."

I pick him up and hug him. "I miss him too. Do you want something to drink?"

"Can I have some milk?"

"You bet."

I carry him downstairs with me. I pour his milk, fill a glass with ice water for Raine, and we climb back up the stairs together. Tufan snuggles into the loveseat at the foot of our bed, drinking his milk. Raine looks up and smiles at him. "Nice milkstache, kiddo."

"Huh?" Tufan looks at me, confused.

It takes me a minute to figure out what she means. I point to my upper lip.

"Oh!" Tufan wipes his mouth with the sleeve of his pajamas. "Can I hold him?"

"Not right now, hon. He's still eating."

"Oh." Tufan finishes his milk and curls up on the loveseat. I put a blanket over him and kiss his cheek. I lift his legs across my lap so I can sit with him. I know he's missing his dad, and I want him to know I'm here for him. I watch Raine. She doesn't know I'm watching her. This feels right. This family I've acquired. I want to photograph her right here, right now, in this light. I'm afraid it may be the last time we might be like this. Exactly like this. Tufan is fast asleep now. I'm not sure why I feel this way, but I do.

I'm lost. I see Raine's hair of twists and turns shooting in all directions. Her beautiful face and perfectly shaped nose.

"What?" Her question catches me off guard. "You're staring at me."

"Does it make you uncomfortable?"

"A little." She adjusts Prem in her arms. He's finished. "Do you want to burp him?"

It doesn't take me a second. I take him from her arms and put him on my shoulder. Raine tucks a cloth under him.

"You might need this."

The weight of his sleep is relaxing. I rub his back with my hand until I hear his soft burp. I know I can put him back down now, but I don't. I want to continue to hold him right here. Over my heart.

Raine kisses Tufan and walks him back to his room. I sing my promise softly in Prem's ear before I slowly put him back in his bed. "Just know you're not alone, I'm gonna make this place your home."

• • ✺ • •

EXHAUSTION. THERE IS no other word for it. The recliner in the family room is now labeled mine and has molded to my posterior. Poor Tufan wants to do fun things like we used to do, and I don't have the energy for it. Dev comes in the room with my latest craving. Popcorn.

"Hey, Tufan. Can I have the remote, buddy?"

"What are you going to put on?"

"I don't know. Let's see what Raine wants to watch."

They both look at me, waiting for my answer. I don't know what I want to watch. It's like I'm stuck in hibernation mode or something. Tufan rescues me and asks to watch an Indian movie on Netflix. Works for me.

Dev takes Prem from my arms. I just finished feeding him. It's Dev's turn to do his thing. Prem will sleep for at least a couple hours on a full stomach. This has become our pattern. I nurse, and Dev burps. As soon as Prem is free from my arms, Tufan scrambles over to cuddle up with me in the recliner. I know he's probably feeling a little left out and jealous. I've heard this is normal for older siblings going from being the only child to second-in-line. I still love cuddling with him. It's the least I can do since I don't have the energy for much of anything else. Dev settles on the couch next to us.

"Throw me some of that popcorn."

Dev does just what I asked. Kernels of corn fly through the air, hitting Tufan in the back of the head.

"Hey!" Tufan leaps off my lap and tosses a handful at him.

Dev puts his hand over his face. "Whoa! Not so many at a time, buddy."

"We have to eat those, you know. Hurry up! Five second rule." I shove the recliner closed and pretend to race and pick them up. I let Tufan beat me. He settles back in his place after eating the last of the handful of popcorn. Dev gives us each our own bowl while Prem hangs comfortably on his left shoulder.

The movie doesn't disappoint. It has all the parts I've come to love about Indian movies. The singing, the dancing, the action, an underlying moral, and the colors. Bold, exotic colors.

"Do you know them?"

"Who?"

"The actors?"

Tufan sits up half-asleep. "Of course he does. Uncle Dev knows everyone in the movies." He plops back down on my shoulder.

I giggle at his half-awake, half-asleep declarations.

"It's true I know a lot of people in the industry. If I don't know them personally, I probably know of them."

"So, do you know them?" I point to the flat screen.

"As a matter of fact, I do."

"Hmm. Have you ever played in a movie with a wedding procession like that?"

"Of course. Especially, if the movie is a love story." I think about Dev and me. Our love story. Do we even have a love story? "It's quite extravagant. Do people still do wedding processions like that? With elephants?"

"Some do."

"I can't imagine what that might be like. The only thing I've seen done is brides and grooms arriving or departing in a horse and carriage."

"Same thing."

"How is that the same thing? A horse is not the same as an elephant."

"Well, the ride is the same."

"It can't possibly be the same. An elephant is so much higher than a horse."

"You're still riding an animal in a saddle."

I stare at him hard. Then I get it. "You've never even ridden a horse, have you?"

"Of course I have." He doesn't keep eye contact. He's lying.

"Which side of the horse do you mount?"

I can tell he's calculating his answer and trying to buy time. "Whatever side the horse lets you."

"I knew it."

"What?"

I decide to prod him. "You have no problem driving a hundred miles an hour in a car, but you've never ridden a horse?"

"I think Prem's waking up."

"Forget that. It's not going to work. We both know he's out for at least another hour. Seriously, how is it you've never ridden a horse? I know you must have had to for your movies."

"Ever heard of stuntmen?"

The idea of Dev and his action-packed life of fast cars and fast lifestyle being afraid to ride a horse creates a slap-happy giggle I can't control. "I can't believe you're afraid of horses." I half snort, trying to be serious.

"I'm not afraid of horses."

"Then why don't you ride them yourself?"

163

"It's just easier."

"Really?" I still don't believe him. "C'mon. Tell me the truth."

Dev takes Prem from his shoulder and puts him in a football hold in his lap. "It is the truth. That, and the fact I like to have control over what I'm driving. When you're riding an animal, you never have complete control."

"I get that, I guess. But driving can have the same issue because you don't have control over the other drivers."

"I know. But still. I know I have complete control over what I do and what I want my car to do. You know?"

"Maybe. I just don't see the point of driving so fast."

"Have you ever driven fast in your life?"

The truth is I haven't. After the teasing I just gave him, I'm not about to admit to it. "I've driven fast."

"How fast?"

"Fast."

"C'mon now."

"Fine. Probably about eighty miles an hour."

"Only eighty? Try a hundred and ten, a hundred and fifteen."

I'm not ready to succumb to defeat. "I'm not racing the Indy 500, so I don't see the point."

"Ah. The Indy 500. That's my race."

"No. No way. Don't tell me you're also a professional race car driver."

"I don't have to be. Anyone from India can race in it."

I have no idea what he means. "Dev, you do know you have to qualify."

"But I do qualify."

I know he's teasing me because he's about to laugh. I just don't get where the joke is.

"What do you call them... Native Americans? They qualify too."

I'm ready to strangle him. "It stands for Indianapolis, you nitwit, not India. Not Indian. The *Indianapolis* 500."

Now he's laughing and so am I. Prem wiggles in his arms. I look at the clock. It's about that time but not yet. "Seriously. I do want to race the Indy 500 one day."

It's a little bit funny, this feeling inside. A little fear. A little excitement. A little dread. I don't think I could bear to lose him too.

CHAPTER TWELVE

"I'm not going, I can't." Toni can plead as much as she wants. It isn't going to work this time. "I told you why. Raine just had the baby. I can't leave now."

"The baby isn't even yours."

"How the hell do you know that?"

Toni doesn't answer, but I already know. Toni's persistence is not going to make a dent in my resolve to stay stateside. "Never mind. I don't care."

"Dev, you need to come. It'll be good for you."

"Good for me? How?"

"Don't tell me family life suits you. I know you. You'll never settle. Why not just do what you know you want to and come home?" Home. For the first time in a long time I feel like I am home.

"Tell them I'm taking a leave of absence, I'm on paternity leave or whatever you want. This is home now." It's strange to me how good it feels saying that out loud.

"Dev, we need to do more promo for the movie. I don't think you understand how important this is."

"No, it's you who doesn't understand what's important. I fulfilled my contractual obligations on this one already." For the first time in my life, my priorities feel straight.

"But don't you miss your life? The ocean? Racing your cars along the coast?"

If Toni only knew how much those things don't draw like they did before. "I just told you I am home, and I can race here."

"Race there?" I can hear the scoop of disbelief in her voice. "Like that's even a thing there."

"Um, Indy 500 ring any bells?"

"Do you really think you'll qualify?"

Why does everyone keep asking me that? I haven't considered it yet, but I'm not about to tell Toni. I decide to change the subject back to the real reason she called. "I'm not coming. Do what you need to do."

"Are you sure?"

I can hear the silence. I know Toni too well. The truth is I'm not sure. We don't always agree on publicity methods. I decide I don't care this time. "Yes, I'm sure."

"Great. Now don't forget to send me pictures of the babe."

"No. I don't want them leaked." More silence. "Toni, do you hear me?"

"Yes, Dev. I hear you and I don't agree."

"I don't need you to agree. You work for me, remember?"

"Actually, I don't. I work for the production company." I hate when she gives me her stuck-up-urban-professional tone.

I give her a version of my own. "You may work for them, but I'll have my lawyers on you faster than you can push your submit button if you go against me on this."

"Alright, alright. Don't get so worked up. Just consider this. Your fans love to hear about your life, and this is something you can control. What's more positive than a baby? Even Prince William allows pictures of their babies."

"I'm not the future King of England."

"Regardless, you need to keep your social stats up. Keep your ratings up. I want you to reconsider. I'll wait before I post anything. You know it has to come out eventually. Better for it to be under your control. Am I right?"

"You heard what I said." I know she's not going to listen.

. . ⚭ . .

TONI'S PHONE CALL LAST week makes me think more about my life in India. My house. My cars. My job. My life. The last few days of spending time with Prem, Tufan, and Raine have been blessed. That's the only way I can describe it. If I had a wish, it would be for things to be this way always. It makes me happy. Truly happy. I don't think I've ever felt this close to anyone, not even my parents. I know it's time to get up, but the warmth of Raine's body lying next to mine keeps me where I am. I heard my mom getting Tufan ready for school a while ago, and now the house is completely silent. Even Prem is quiet.

In this moment, I realize it. My life is brilliant. My love for Raine is pure. I don't know what to do. I watch her sleeping. She's beautiful. I can't help feeling I'll never be with her—truly be with her—until I'm able to get my head around the secret she kept from me.

"Good morning." Raine stretches. "Wow! How many hours did we sleep?"

"I'm not sure. Three? Four?"

"I can't believe it! It feels good to sleep. How are you this morning?"

"I slept. I guess."

"What do you mean, you guess? Don't you know if you slept?"

"It was one of those nights. I have too much on my mind apparently."

"I don't know what could be so awful for you. Are we really that intense?"

"No. Of course not." I decide I'm going to tell her about Toni's call. I can't be angry with her for keeping secrets if I keep them too. At least this is one secret I'm willing to tell her. "Toni called a few days ago."

"Oh? And what did Miss Toni have to say that made you not sure if you slept?"

"Huh?"

"You weren't sure if you slept, so I assume it has something to do with Toni?"

"Not exactly. Well, a little." Raine turns on her side facing me and propping her head with her hand. She doesn't say anything. When I see her face, there's not a thing that I would change. When she smiles, it's like the whole world stops and stares for a while. She's amazing just the way she is. I want to tell her every day, but I don't. And I haven't. Her lips. I could kiss them. But I don't.

"So are you going to tell me?"

I forgot for a second we were having a conversation. Her dimples wink at me again. I don't know how I've been able to keep control of my wits this far. I clear my throat to give me a few seconds to get my head back where it belongs before

I answer her. "Yes. Toni called. She wants a picture of Prem for the press. She thinks it will be good promo for the movie. Good for my image."

"No."

"You didn't even think about it. Don't you think the request deserves consideration?" I'm not sure why I'm even arguing with her because my reaction to it was basically the same.

"No, I don't. He's not a publicity tool. I want Prem and Tufan kept away from that part of your life."

"It's not like there's going to be any paparazzi here for me. It's in India. Thousands of miles away. Even Prince William shared his children's baby photos." I can't believe I just said that either.

Raine isn't saying anything. Only staring at me. "Okay. I don't know. I'll think about it. That's all."

"Good enough." I climb over her and check in the bassinet on the way to the bathroom to get dressed. Prem is starting to squirm. Either he heard us talking or it's time for him to get up too. Probably ready to eat. "What are we doing today?"

"I'm not doing anything."

"We have to do more than just hang around the house every day. What do other mothers do?"

"Do you really want to take him to the park in a stroller? Sit by a sandbox and watch other kids run around and play?"

"Uh, no." Not what I had in mind. "There has to be something we can do."

"Dev, he's not even a month old. I'm not sure I want to take him out yet."

"Why not? We can dress him warm. I'm going crazy staying in the house. There has to be somewhere we can go. Drive somewhere? Fly somewhere? We can fly somewhere for a day. I'll call Toni and have her charter a plane for us."

"What? No! I am not getting on a plane. Not even for a day."

That gets her out of bed. She's dressed and picking up Prem to feed him before I have a chance to convince her otherwise.

I decide to try an ultimatum. "Well, I'm going. With or without you." Nothing. She looks up at me while she situates Prem to feed him. "Raine, I can't stand sitting around doing nothing. There has to be something. Tell me what you want to do."

She takes a deep breath. "It's probably not an awful idea to go for a drive somewhere. Do you have autumn in India?"

"Of course we do."

"No, I mean autumn like here in the States. With all the colors of the leaves when they turn?"

"In the northern parts of India. But not like I've seen here so far."

"Good. I know where we can go."

"Should I call Toni?"

"No! I told you I'm not flying anywhere. We can drive to the place I know."

"It's close?"

"Yep."

* * ⚜ * *

172

I DON'T TELL DEV THAT Punderson State Park is an hour away. I know he was born to run. Driving is his thing, and I'm beginning to get used to him always taking the wheel. I get Prem ready in his car seat.

"Do you think we should plan for another day? When we can take Tufan?" I can feel guilt weasel its way into my thoughts. I know he would love hiking on some of those trails too.

Dev pulls on his coat and zips it up. He puts his hands in his pockets. "Why? He's having fun at school. It's not like we can't go back on another day, right?"

"I guess." Blue joins us at the backdoor and hands me a small cooler. "What's this?"

"Lunch." She picks up Prem's car seat with him in it.

"Blue, what are you doing?" Blue carries the car seat back toward the kitchen.

"You two need a break. You've stocked up plenty of milk with that pump thing you use. Go. Take lunch. Take your pump. Enjoy your day."

I'm not sure what to say, what to do. I look at Dev. He's not saying anything. "We can't leave without Prem."

Dev shrugs. "I've learned a long time ago when my mom makes up her mind about something, it seldom changes."

I take my coat off. "I can't. I can't do it. It feels wrong."

"I understand. But it's not, you know."

Dev is still standing at the door with his coat on. Waiting. I inhale a deep sigh. "Alright." I run upstairs and grab my pump. I know I'll need to be using this in a couple hours. We walk outside. Dev walks to his Maserati. I walk to my truck. "I think the truck is the best option for today."

I can tell Dev wants to disagree, but he doesn't. Instead he puts his keys back in his pocket, and I toss him mine. No words. No complaints. We just get in and drive.

Moreland Hills. One of my dream places to live. The houses are not built on top of each other. Plenty of space. We pass a "For Sale" sign that reads, "Eight acres, equestrians welcome."

"Look at the colors. The trees are like an artist's painting, don't you think? The blending of red, orange, yellow, and sometimes pink, it's just breathtaking."

Dev isn't as impressed as I am. He just nods his agreement.

"What about those? Have you ever seen such massive evergreens?" They're lining both sides of the road and they're huge.

He looks over at me. Still not impressed. It must be a guy thing. I sit back in my seat and put my feet on the dashboard. That gets his attention. "Do you mind?"

"Mind what?"

"Your shoes. They're dirty. You're going to get it all over the dashboard."

I know he's right, but hearing him tell me what I can't do in my own truck wrangles my nerves. "So?"

He doesn't push and instead turns the radio on. It's already set to my station, and he changes it trying to find something else. I really want him to leave it alone, but I decide I'm just going to sit back and relax. At least try to. We pass by the Metroparks Polo Field. "Do you want to see what it's like?"

"What?"

"The Polo Field."

"If you want."

"Maybe we'll see some horses. What do you think?"

Dev doesn't even try to turn around. What is wrong with him?

Punderson isn't much farther, and I stop trying to point things out as we go. I tell him in plenty of time so we don't pass the entrance like we did the Polo Field. I take him all the way to the lodge. It sits on an embankment by the lake, and all the surrounding trees are in full autumn bloom. I don't even bother to mention it anymore. I guess he'll let me know if he's impressed. We get out. "Should we leave the cooler in the truck?"

"Are we gonna stay parked here?"

"We can if you want. But there is a picnic area we passed on the way up here."

"Leave it, then."

"Yes, sir!" I salute him and close the truck door. He's the one that wanted to get away somewhere today, and now he acts like he doesn't even want to be here. There's a wooden boardwalk along the side of the lake, so I head in that direction. I'm surprised when he takes my hand in his, and we walk silently together to the trail. I stop to admire the view.

"Are people allowed to fish here?" He speaks.

I don't want to fight so I keep my irritation to myself. "I'm sure they are. You have to have a license though."

"Do you like to fish?"

"I used to. I haven't fished in years. A lot of years."

"We did in India when I was young. It's been a while for me too."

I want to know what is wrong, but I know if I ask he'll probably just say nothing. One thing I've learned about Dev. He doesn't always tell me exactly what's going on with him. I'll have to dig a little to get him to open up. I'm just not sure how.

· · ❧ · ·

I KNOW WHAT RAINE IS trying to do. If she knew the mess in my head right now, she wouldn't be pushing so hard to find out. I hate being manipulated. My mom is the queen of manipulation. I can feel the familiar rage build inside me. It's been percolating since we left. My mind is racing in directions I know are not healthy, but I go there anyway. I'm fighting to keep it to myself.

"If you want to leave, we can."

"Why do you think I want to leave?"

"You've barely said two words. You're the one who wanted to go somewhere. Well, we're here, and all you've managed to do is complain about my feet on the dashboard of MY truck."

I stare at her longer than I should because her face hardens against me. I don't care. I'm mad. She lets go of my hand and walks away toward the lodge parking lot. I think about following her. I wait too long because I lose sight of her when she reaches the top of the bank. I jog to catch up, but she's already locked herself in the backseat of her truck. I knock on the window. She doesn't answer. I can't see in because of the tinted windows, so I lean my forehead against the glass and enclose my eyes with my hands to try and see. I quickly pull back. She removed her shirt and unclipped her bra in the front. Not what I expect. I know she's pumping milk, but I can't help how the sight of her naked breast makes me feel. I knock again and yell through the glass. "I'll be at the lodge. Find me there when you're finished."

She cracks the window. "There's a bar just to the right after you enter. I'll meet you there."

Perfect. Exactly what I need and it's exactly where she said it is. I order a scotch whiskey, neat. "Leave the bottle, please."

The bartender is dressed in a suit and tie, so I doubt he's actually the bartender. Manager, maybe? I'm sure he's Indian, but I'm not interested in making conversation so I ignore it.

"What room?"

"I'm paying cash."

He nods compliance and leaves the bottle. Jameson. Not bad. The way I feel I don't care what it is as long as it can take away the edge. I drink one glass down and fill it again.

She doesn't even know what she's doing to me. I swirl the golden liquid before I take another swig. Sitting there with her legs propped on the dashboard talking about horses like she's got a chance in hell of getting me on one. If she wants a ride so bad, I can think of one I'm willing to give her. I drink the entire second glass. I need to quell the urges starting again. I pour another glass. I want her. I want her bad.

I stare at the TV in the corner, but I can't concentrate. I purposely sip what's in my glass now. It doesn't help my mood when the bartender returns with a piece of paper, a pen, and a cell phone. Confirmed. He's Indian. Two months in the States without autographs or selfie requests has spoiled me. I take a selfie with him even though I'd rather not. Raine walks in as soon as we're finished.

"What's this?"

"Something for my kids. Mr. Shukla is one their favorite Bollywood actors. If I didn't have a photograph, they would never believe me."

Raine smiles and looks at me while she takes a seat on the stool next to me. "Ah."

I help her scoot in even though it's clear she doesn't need my help.

"I'll have a fuzzy navel, please."

"Should you be drinking with the... You know?" I'm suddenly uncomfortable. I make a motion across my chest, hoping she gets what I'm trying to say.

"Nursing?" She takes a sip of the drink placed in front of her. "The pediatrician said I can have a drink now and then as long as it's right after I nurse, or pump in this case."

She doesn't even flinch when she says it. It's not like I haven't seen her nurse Prem. I have. This time it was different. I hate myself for getting excited from it. It must be because there was no baby attached to it. They were suddenly just there. I shake my head as if that will help clear my brain of the image, finish what's left in my glass, and pour another.

"I guess I'm driving back?"

"What? Oh. Yeah. We'll see."

"I know I'm not getting in the truck with you behind the wheel if you plan on finishing that bottle."

I don't know what I plan to do so I just smile and take another sip. Raine sips hers and we both stare at the TV bolted in the corner above the bar. What the hell am I doing?

. . ✺ . .

DEV IS STILL ACTING strange, so I decide to leave him alone. If he wants to tell me, he will. I sip my fuzzy navel. It's so good. I've missed having one on occasion. I ask for another. Dev looks at me. I know he wants to say something, but he drinks his own instead. We sit together drinking and not talking for at least an hour.

The bartender comes over and places a keycard in front of Dev. "My compliments. It's the Saxon guest room. One of our best. Up the spiral staircase to your left. You can't miss it. It has the name in black letters on the door."

Neither one of us says anything to each other. Dev doesn't even look at me. He takes the key and clasps it in the palm of his hand. The bartender leaves us. I wait for Dev to say something and he doesn't.

I'm buzzed and I can't resist being a little playful. "Do you like causing trouble up in hotel rooms?"

His eyes light up and I know he does. I take the key from his hand, stand up, and hope he follows me. The narrow staircase coils up, and I feel like I'm going to lose my balance. I confirm Dev is behind me when he puts his hand on my waist while we climb the stairs. As soon as we reach the top, I see the names on the doors in black letters. Just like the bartender said. The Saxon room is not far down the hall. I put the key in the knob and jiggle, but it won't open.

Dev puts his hand over mine to help. "Let me." He is so close I can feel the warmth of his breath on my neck. The warmth of his body too.

The room is like a small apartment. It has a table and four chairs in the middle, a small refrigerator, and a microwave. The windows are clear, stained glass, diamonds. The four-poster king-size bed takes up most of the room. I purposely avoid looking there, afraid he'll notice and think that's all I want. It is, but I don't want to be the one to make the first move. It took a little buzz to even get me here. It's been so long. My face burns hot. He does know exactly what I want, because he turns me around and kisses me.

"Say you do… " I'm connected only to the touch of his lips to mine. I'm not even sure of all the words he whispers. I hear, "for tonight… " Then he kisses me more along my neck and near my ears. "Even if you don't…say you do. I love you."

CHAPTER THIRTEEN

Words. It's only words. That's what I've always told myself when I had to say them while shooting a film.

The first time I've ever said them, truly said them, and mean it, is now. I'm a little drunk. No, a lot drunk, but I mean it. I envelop Raine close against my chest.

I don't know how she does what she does. I'm so in love with her. I want to spend the rest of my life with her by my side. Right now, it feels like the first time. We've made out before, but all those times I knew. I knew that was all it could be. At least for the time being. I'm not sure when, exactly, I began to have more intense feelings for her. I just know I do.

Raine runs her fingers through my hair. She pulls back and looks up at me. "I do. I do love you."

That's all I need to hear. I unbutton and strip my shirt off. I don't stop kissing her. I try to keep my lips locked with hers. She laughs against my mouth. My kisses are soft and kind at first.

I open my eyes for a split second. I can't get enough of her. Raine pulls away from me only a little, smiles, touches my lips with her fingertips, and falls against me, forcing me to sit on the side of the king-size bed. I'm ready to devour her.

She straddles me and kisses me hard on the mouth. Her hands slide down the front of my chest, sending zings of heat throughout my entire body. When she moves them around my waist to the back and up, any control lurking at the edge is gone. I swing her around on her back. Her eyes are dark and challenging. My blood is boiling. I can't wait. I pull her top up over her head and throw it across the room. I'm sure I hear something rip in the process, but neither of us care. I unclasp the front of her bra.

All I think about is my mouth on hers, my tongue touching hers, and parts I can't wait to discover.

"Wait."

I hear her low whisper, but I hope I'm imagining it. I'm so focused on the heat between us, I'm confused.

She says it again. "Wait."

I lift my head up, but I still can't stop kissing her. "What do you mean?"

She presses both of her hands against my chest to hold me back. She's smiling. That's a good sign. But Raine shaking her head? Not a good sign.

"I'm sorry, Dev. We can't."

"Why not? We're married." What did she think we were coming up here to do? I'm propped on two elbows, hovering above her and struggling to hold myself back.

"I know. It's not that." Making circles on my chest with her fingers is not helping me recover any sense of control.

"Then, what?" I can't help playing with some part of her, so I tangle my hands in the curls mussed around her head.

"We have to wait six weeks."

"What are you talking about?" I can't help it. I kiss her cheek as close to her lips as I can, right next to the dimple that pops every time she smiles. I know she wants me as much as I want her right now.

"Dr. Hill said to wait six weeks to make sure everything is healed right." Her breath tickles my ear when she speaks.

Shit. That. My head is still in a fog from her kisses. I roll on my side, but I keep my arm across her now flat belly. I watch the profile of her face. She turns to face me, and I look straight in her eyes. I can tell she's as into it as I am.

"It's okay." I trace the outline of her jaw with my finger. "I don't have to have sex with you to love you."

• • ᖇ • •

TWO THINGS HAPPEN WHEN I walk in the door with Dev. Tufan runs down the hall and slams into us both. "I missed you so much. Naniji wouldn't let me call you."

I take my place in front of him to hug him tight. "It's okay. We're here now."

Dev fluffs the top of his head, and Tufan switches from me to him. Pooja follows holding Prem. "Just in time, if you want."

"If I want? Of course." I reach out and fold Prem tight in my arms. I thought my heart full before this moment. Prem's eyes greet mine and my heart overflows.

Dev's hand on my shoulder strokes the back of my hair then reaches over my shoulder to tickle Prem. "Did you miss us, little guy?"

I don't wait one second. I take him straight to my place in the family room and nurse him. I relax back in the recliner while Prem latches on in comfortable baby bliss. Blue comes in and plants herself next to us. "How did he do?"

"He was perfect."

"Really? No issues with bottle feeding?"

Blue shakes her head. "Nope. Nothing."

I don't believe her for a second. She probably wouldn't tell me if she did have difficulty. It doesn't matter. I look down at this sweet child of mine safe and bundled in my arms. If I stare too long, I know I'll probably break down and cry. I missed him so much. I lean my head back. I know Blue is interested in conversation, but me? Not so much right now. All I want to do is hold my baby and let the previous night's events sink deeper into my heart.

"You look different." Blue wants details I'm not prepared to give her. I can hear Tufan and Dev playing basketball in the back.

"Did Dev play basketball in India?" I already know the answer, but I want to change the subject.

"No. He plays soccer."

"Right."

"Raine..."

I know I'm about to get more unsolicited advice. It always starts with my first name and then a pause. I try to avoid it by closing my eyes. It doesn't work.

"Please be patient with him. My son is a good man. He will be a good husband and father. Don't give up on him."

I'm not entirely sure why she's telling me this. We've already been through the drama of the tabloids, and I don't know what story could be worse than him cheating on me with his co-star. I've learned it's best to let her say what she wants to say. "I know. I can see he's a good man. He's very good with Tufan. And Prem."

"Anytime you need time away, just the two of you. You only have to ask." I feel like asking her which of us asked her to watch Prem last night, but I don't. I already know the answer. And I'm not mad. Then it hits me. There is a story worse than Dev cheating on me. Me cheating on him. I look at my baby now sleeping in my arms. My baby whose father is not Dev. I'm scared to the pit of my deepest, darkest, inside parts.

I never thought I would love another man after Prem. I was afraid I might not learn to love Dev. Even now I wonder, how long will I love him? I know the answer and that's what scares me. As long as stars are above him. And longer if I may.

.. ⁕ ..

THE BACKDOOR SLAMS. It's Naz. "I have to speak with Dev immediately. Where is he?"

I don't wait for anyone to answer. "I'm in the kitchen."

Naz removes her coat but leaves her boots on. I look down at the snow still lingering on the black suede.

"Really?" I look up to see Naz's dark black eyes shooting bolts in my direction. "You're telling me you remove your shoes every time you come in the house?"

"I do now." I hand her a cup of coffee from the pot I just made and take a sip of my own. "What's wrong?"

Naz opens the fridge and adds half and half. "Got any whisky? We might need to make these a toddy."

I watch her stir her coffee without a drop slipping over the edge. After the weekend I just had, Jameson is now a regular member of our household. I pull out a bottle and set it on the counter along with honey and echinacea tea.

"Seriously?"

"What? You said we may need a toddy."

Naz takes a deep breath and pours a shot of Jameson in her coffee. "It's just as good with coffee."

She tries to add it to mine, and I pull my cup away. "I'm good." I take another sip and wait. Naz is always too excited when it comes to business. I watch her blow on the edge and drink down a few gulps. "Well?"

"Can you at least sit down?"

I sit at the table across from her. "Okay. I'm sitting."

"Here's the deal. I just got off the phone with Toni."

News from my lawyer after she's talked with Toni is not a good sign. If it was good news, Toni would have told me herself. I grab the bottle of Jameson and pour it in my coffee and wait.

"They're pulling out." Naz takes another gulp.

"Who's pulling out?"

"The production company."

"They can't do that. Aren't they under contract?"

"Yes, they are. You're not getting what I'm trying to tell you." Silence splits the air while I wait for Naz to continue. "They're pulling out of India completely. Closing all accounts, all offices, shutting down all productions, cancelling all contracts."

Now I get it. I drink all the rest of my coffee and fill my cup with straight Jameson. "Are you sure?"

"Pfft. Of course I'm sure. I've been on the phone with their lawyers all morning."

"I don't understand. I thought things were going well."

"Apparently, not as well as they want. The movie you filmed earlier this year in Shimla didn't make as much as they anticipated at the box office."

"Damn. I have to talk with Toni to see what she has lined up next."

Naz reaches out to me. "Uh... Why don't you hold up on that for the time being, huh? You just got married, had a baby. Why not hang tight a bit?"

"I can't, Naz. You know how it is in this business. I need to get out on top of this."

"Don't you think you've been out on top of it long enough? Why not give it some time? Let the gossip die down."

I can't believe I hear these words from Naz. She's always been one to push to stay ahead. I don't answer her right away. The truth is we are financially stable right now. "Wait. What gossip are you talking about?"

"What gossip are *you* talking about?"

Now I know something's wrong. "Spill. What else happened?"

Naz adds to her toddy. "Someone leaked a photo of the baby."

"Toni. Where did she get it?"

"I'm not sure. You know Toni. Maybe from your mom? Maybe she paid someone to hack your laptop? Your guess is as good as mine."

Naz glares at the ceiling while she finishes her coffee. Great.

"Out with it. What else?"

"What?"

I hate when she stalls. "I know there's something else. Just tell me."

"Rumors are circling the Prem's not yours."

"Shit."

• • ❧ • •

"YOU PROMISED."

I can tell Raine is trying to hold back her tears. She cries so easy. I hate being the cause. I try to be as kind as I can. "Raine, I didn't promise. You said you'd think about it."

I'm so mad at Toni right now the words "you're fired" ring in my head. Raine and I have been doing well together since Punderson. Our marriage is growing, blossoming. I love her. She loves me. Now this. "Here's what I'm promising now. I'm going to do everything I can to stop the lies."

"Dev, they're accusing me of cheating. They're saying we're getting divorced."

"I know. I'm sorry. One good thing is people here in the States don't care."

She wipes her nose and sniffs. I can tell she agrees. "I just hate the lies. How do you deal with it?"

Good question. If I didn't have my family to think about now, I'd do what I've always done. Ignore it. Let my lawyers deal with it. Naz can handle it. Things are different now. It's hurting people I love. "It's been a part of my entire life, I guess. I've grown up with it."

"Dev, it wouldn't bother me if it was only against me. But this includes Prem. I don't want him affected by it."

"Raine. I don't think the Indian tabloids is going to have any effect on him here."

"But how do you know?"

"The truth is, I don't. So that's why I'm going to do all I can to redirect attention elsewhere, find out the source, and squash it." I slam my fist in the palm of my hand so hard Raine jumps. "Sorry."

She stops crying, but I can tell she's still worried. Her brow creases when something important is bothering her. I want to help her think of something else so I ask her the only thing that comes to mind. "Now that Prem is sleeping through the night, maybe you can have time for a hobby or something?"

"A hobby? How about going back to work? I've already talked with Wally. He said they're getting ready to start a new project out in Solon. He's going to set up a conference call sometime next week to get with me on the details."

"What? No. Raine, you don't have to work."

"I know. But your contracts just got canceled."

It's a stupid idea, and I'm laughing while I talk. "No. No. No. Raine, I have plenty. You don't have to work, even if my contracts are canceled. They'll be other ones."

"But you don't know that."

"Um. Yes, I do. Contracts are always canceled, and new ones are just around the corner. Trust me, I know."

"But you said they didn't like bad publicity."

"True. But other companies don't mind the publicity. Even expect it or create it." As soon as the words come out of my mouth, I know. Fired.

CHAPTER FOURTEEN

"**Y**ou can't fire me. My family and your family have worked together our entire lives. And do I need to remind you again? I don't work for you." Toni stands up from the computer monitor so that her head is cut off from my view.

Video conferencing has its perks. This is not one of them. I'm trying to impress upon her the importance of my message, and she gets up and walks across the room mid-sentence. This would never happen if I were in her office face to face.

"It's *because* our families have known each other for so long. I can't believe you did what you did. And I'm done."

Toni comes back to her desk with a handful of files and sits down. "Dev, listen. You told me to handle it and I did. I don't understand why you're so upset about it. It's not like we haven't done it before." I hate when she multi-tasks with me on the line. I can hear the paper shuffling, and it gets on my nerves.

"What the hell does that mean?"

"You know we make up stories all the time for the press." More shuffling and now she moves her glasses from the top of her head and rests them on her nose where they should be. "You've never had a problem with it."

"Never had a problem with it? Really? So, all the lies about me and Pria? You did that?"

She stops, takes off her glass, and nibbles the tip of the earpiece. "Actually, no. That wasn't me. Pria had her own agenda on that one." Toni places the glasses back on her head and starts shuffling again.

"Own agenda? Toni, this is my life. How can you think I'd be okay with this?"

"I just told you. There's never been an issue before."

"That's because my lawyers usually deal with it, and I don't care how they clean it up."

She stops shuffling. "You mean Naz."

"Yes, Naz." It's nice to have Toni's complete attention for a change. "Her firm specializes in people like me. What are they called? Aliens of certain abilities? Something like that."

"Aliens of Extraordinary Ability. I know." Toni folds her hands on her desk in front of her. "Naz and I have talked about it. A lot. Because I need to make sure your extraordinary abilities are clear to the world."

I stare at her and wait for her to continue because I'm not used to having her pay such close attention to me. She must have something more to say. She doesn't. I say the only comeback I can think of. "Whatever."

"You don't agree on your extraordinary abilities?"

"That's not even the point. Why do you always do that?"

"What?" Toni is back to moving things around on her desk, lifting papers and folders, patting the top of each section as she goes.

"They're on top of your head."

Toni looks up at me. "What is?"

"Your glasses. That *is* what you're looking for?"

She taps her head with her hand. "Oh, right. Thank you." She rests them back on her nose, and the shuffling begins again.

"Toni. You should've talked to me first on this one. It's different now. My life is different. Raine didn't grow up in this life. I'm not sure I want Tufan and Prem growing up with it."

It looks like she's done with the shuffling because her desk is clear again, and her undivided attention is on me. Again. "It doesn't matter what you want. Fame will be a part of their lives regardless. You're not their father. You might not be a big deal over there, but here, in India? People always want to know what you're up to."

Am I talking in circles? "I am their father. And I'm telling you to keep my family out of the papers, off the Internet, out. Do you understand me?"

"Aside from the fact, and I repeat once again, I don't work for you so you can't fire me, I get it. Keep the babes clear of the press. I'll do what I can."

"Fine. And since you don't work for me, let me be as clear as I possibly can. If you don't clean this mess up, I'll sue you, the company you do work for, and anyone else I find who contributes to the lies. Got it?"

"Like I said, I'll do what I can."

I know more is coming because now she's got a pen and a pad of paper in front of her, ready to take notes. "Tell me, Dev. How do you want me to handle Pria?"

"Do whatever you want."

"Uh, uh. I'm not falling for that again." She points the end of her pen at me through the screen. "You tell me exactly what I can and can't do. I'm writing it down. See?" She toasts me with her pen before putting tip to pad.

"Where Pria's concerned? Smear her all the way across the continent for all I care. I'm having Naz throw a lawsuit at her anyway."

"I'm not sure I should write that down. Could be discoverable in a lawsuit for all I know. We don't need my written notes indicating you instructed me to smear her name."

I chuckle just a little because I know Toni and her sarcasm and I'm over it. I also know she'd probably just shred her notes if it came down to it. No matter how mad I am at her right now, I know protecting her client always comes first. "Talk to Naz. Coordinate with her on what to release. Does that work?"

"Works for me."

"And keep my kids out of it, or you're fired." I can't help sending one last barb her way.

"Right. Like I said..."

"Talk to Naz, Toni. Gotta go." I click the **x** to close the screen. Done. One of the perks of video conferencing I do enjoy.

· · ⤲ · ·

IT'S TOO COLD TO SIT on the porch, but I like being outside. I only have about an hour before it's time for Prem to wake up from his afternoon nap. Not long after that, Tufan will be home from school. I want to make the most of my free time. I take the file Wally dropped off this morning around to the backyard.

There's plenty of wood stacked by the fire pit, and I have it blazing in minutes. Campfires in the fall are the best. The smell of the wood in the cool air, the crackle when it burns, and the color of the flames mesmerizes me every time.

"Perfect." Dev sneaks up behind me, hands me one of two mugs overflowing with whip cream, and drags a chair next to mine.

"What's this?" I bring the hot mug close to my mouth. I can smell the chocolate.

"My specialty."

"Oh? I thought your specialty was something else." I had to say it. It's my turn to tease him.

Dev smiles and wraps his fingers around his mug and sips. "I'm a man of many specialties."

"Of course. I can't wait to try it." It doesn't disappoint. "Wow! It is good." I take a larger taste.

"Once you have mine, you'll never go back."

I choke on my third gulp of hot chocolate, and my face burns hot. And not from the fire. Dev leans back in his chair and stares at the flames. I'm thankful he doesn't catch on to what he just said. My embarrass-o-meter is in overdrive at the moment.

"You okay?"

"Yeah, just went down the wrong way. What do you put in it?"

"Chocolate." He smiles and sips his own.

"I know that, Mr. Obvious. Tell me what else you put in it."

"Can't."

"Why not?"

"Secret."

I want to ask him what's up with the one-word answers, but I don't. Instead, I lean back in my chair and put my feet up on a log in front of me. "I am your wife, you know. If you can't tell me, who can you tell?"

I sip again. And wait. Nothing. I look over at him. His eyes are closed now. I can't tell if he's actually smiling or just content. I know he can't possibly be asleep that fast. I look around for something to throw at him, and the only thing I find is a handful of leaves.

Dev opens his eyes, looks down at his cup, plucks one stray leaf from the side, leans back, and closes his eyes again. I turn my attention back to the work on my lap. I look over at him again and he's not moving, so I open my file to start reading the notes in the front pocket. Leaves sprinkle the pages in my lap and in my hair. I decide to play his game. I swipe them from my lap.

He leans over and whispers in my ear, "You gonna kiss me or not?"

My stomach flips. He doesn't have to ask twice. My eyes lock with his. No doubt he knows the answer. I lean close to kiss him.

He pulls back. "You're about to miss your shot."

I'm gonna kill him. I throw more leaves.

"See? You can't resist, can you?" Dev shakes his head. "I told you. You'll never go back."

My face burns all the way up to my ears, and I'm sure if you could see my scalp it'd be red too. Now, I'm really gonna kill him. I clear the items from my lap, throw myself in his lap, and give him a taste of my specialty.

. . ~~~ . .

RAINE IS SNUG AND STILL on my lap in front of the fire pit, her head resting on my shoulder. I adjust my body so we're almost in a reclining position. I look up at the sky and watch the clouds mold into puffed up shapes and designs. The fire is starting to die down. I should stoke it, but I don't want to move from this moment. I could lie like this forever, until the sky falls down on me.

I feel the vibration of Raine's voice against my chest when she speaks. "I should go see if Prem is awake. Tufan will be home soon."

"Stay. Pooja or my mom will let you know when Prem wakes up." I kiss the top of her head. "And Tufan can join us back here if he wants, but I bet my mom will get him on his homework as soon as he walks in the door with Pooja.

"You're probably right." Raine tightens her grip around my waist and cuddles close.

I don't know why I'm finding it difficult to tell her about the surprise I planned for us. I know she's already started work. I'm not happy about it, but I'm also not ready to discuss it. I enjoy how easy things have been. Naz tells me she and Toni are on top of the scandal in the tabloids. We haven't seen anything on Indian TV lately, and I learned a long time ago not to google my name.

I take a deep breath and start. "If you could go anywhere you wanted, where would it be?"

She lifts her head up so she can look at me. "Why? Are you planning on sending me away?"

"Maybe."

Now she sits up straight. I have to reposition my leg because it pinches from the weight adjustment. "What's this about?"

"The Hamptons?"

"The Hamptons in New York? Those Hamptons?"

"I think it's New York. Let me check." I try to reach my back pocket while Raine is on my lap, but it doesn't work, so she stands up so I can pull out the paper. I unfold it and try to read my notes. "I think that's what Toni meant when she said the Hamptons."

"Toni? You're still working with Toni? After what she did?"

I can tell I need to be careful how I say it. "It's complicated." The crease between her eyebrows lets me know immediately I did not choose wisely.

Raine grabs the fire poker and starts shoving the burnt logs to the side. "You told me you fired her."

"No, I said I was going to fire her."

Raine adds another log. She squeezes lighter fluid on top. Flames billow and furl. "Then why didn't you?"

"Our families have worked together my entire life. She's like family."

Another log and more lighter fluid follow. "Family doesn't tell lies about each other."

I want to tell her some families do, but I don't. Instead, I try to keep it to the facts. "The truth is, Toni technically doesn't work for me. She works for the production company."

"The one that's moving out of India?"

"Yes." Raine continues to jab the logs with the fire poker.

"Naz and Toni are working together. Naz won't let her do anything I've explicitly told her not to."

More lighter fluid becomes fire on the wood. "That's what I'm afraid of. How do you know she won't find some way around your instructions?"

"It's why I have Naz on her now. She knows I mean it. Naz will sue her and whatever production company she might be working for."

Less fire poking and less lighter fluid. Both good signs. I think. "So what do you think?"

"About what?"

"The Hamptons." She's taking too long to answer. Not a good sign.

"Why the Hamptons?"

"I don't know. I've never been there."

"How about somewhere else instead?"

Not exactly the answer I'm expecting. "Where do you want to go?"

"Ocean City."

CHAPTER FIFTEEN

I take a deep breath. The smell of salt in the air. I've been looking forward to it the entire drive. The Atlantic Ocean reminds me of Lake Erie except for the salt water and the fresh weight of the air. I don't know how Dev found this house on the beach. All the years I've been trying to come here, I've never found a house. Only condos, motels, or hotels. He tells me it's Toni and her connections. I'm still not thrilled he hasn't cut ties with her. I don't trust her. I'd rather believe it's all the new construction going up for tourism.

"What do you think?" Dev joins me on the back patio facing the ocean.

"Amazing!" I survey the area around where we are. "Where are the boys?"

"With the Aunts."

"I can't wait to walk the beach with Tufan. He's never seen the ocean before."

"Let's go get him."

We don't have to go far because Tufan is already on his way out the backdoor of this house on the beach. Dev zips up his jacket and waits while I throw on mine. It's chilly on the beach this time of year. I ruffle through the suitcase to grab one for Tufan. Pooja and Blue are happy to stay at the house with Prem. He's being fussy, tired from the trip. Even though we had plenty of room in the minivan we rented, it's still a long drive.

"Tufan, wait! I don't want you out there by yourself. You need a jacket. Wait."

Dev and I run to catch up to him. Tufan stops dead where he stands. Doesn't say a word. Dev and I come up behind him. "What is it?"

Tufan points to the ground in front of him. I don't see it at first.

Dev steps in front of us. "Don't make any sudden moves." I'm still not sure what it is. Then I see it. Long, black, slithery, and not what I want to see on the only path from the house to the beach. I don't move.

"All right. I think we're good."

"I had no idea. Do you think we should try to find it and kill it?"

Dev doesn't answer right away. "I'm not sure. Probably not. I'll check with the rental office and see what they recommend when we get back."

"I want to go home." Tufan is plastered to my side.

I bend down next to him. I can't say I'm not as uneasy about it as he is, but I know it's important for him to feel safe, so I try my best to help him settle. "It's okay, honey. That snake is gone. She's not interested in us. She didn't even stop to blink when she crossed our path."

Tufan wipes his eye with one hand and starts to giggle just a little. "Raine, snakes don't blink."

I tickle his belly just a little. "And how do you know they don't blink? I'm pretty sure I saw her long lashes when she crept by, maybe even a wink."

Tufan looks up at Dev. "Uncle Dev, have you ever seen a snake blink?"

Dev looks at me and then Tufan. "I don't know buddy. The only thing I've ever seen a snake do is stick its tongue out at me. But if Raine says she saw that snake blink...or wink..." Dev shrugs and shakes his head.

Tufan looks at Dev and then me. I can tell he doesn't know what to believe, so I help him put on his jacket, take his hand, and begin to walk him to the beach. "How about we take our beach walk and let slithery Sara go on her way?"

Dev takes his hand on his other side so Tufan is between us. Dev mouths "Slithery Sara" at me above Tufan's head. I shrug. I couldn't think of anything else to say. My effort is rewarded anyway because Tufan is swinging our hands front to back. Dev and I count off to three, lift, and swing in unison. Slithery Sara is soon forgotten.

The beach is practically empty. I know it's because we're here on the off season. It feels strange looking out over the water and not seeing a sunset because we're facing east. The colors in the sky are still brilliant shades mixed with clouds. We can see the sunset behind us still has its own beauty. I'm also not used to walking the beach wearing tennis shoes. I love walking on the sand barefoot and letting the water massage my feet as I do, but it's just too cold. Tufan runs along the edge of the water playing tag with the waves. I watch him just miss the water when it crawls up the beach with each wave. Dev puts his arm around my shoulder. I return his embrace with my arm around his waist. We can see the boardwalk in the distance. The ferris wheel is lit up in pink, yellow, and blue.

"I can't wait to take you on that." He nods in the direction of the park in the distance.

"Um, no."

"Um, yes."

"Nope. I can't."

"Why not?"

My heart starts beating hard in my chest. I'm not sure when it happened, exactly. Fear. Fear of heights. Fear of flying. Just. Plain. Fear. The terror rises from my stomach and moves up to my heart. "I just can't."

"C'mon. I'll be right there next to you."

I don't say another word because there is no way I'm going to get on the ferris wheel. No way. No how.

. . ᦕ . .

"HOLD ON."

I can't speak. I swallow hard. My legs are shaking, and my mouth is frozen shut. I'm afraid of the words that want to spill from my mouth. I'm mad at Dev for talking me into my current position in the circular car of the ferris wheel. I only agreed because it was round and enclosed. Not like the two seaters. I realize right away that it doesn't matter. I'm still terrified frozen. The only thing I can think of right now is that moment I know we'll be sitting at the absolute top waiting for more passengers to enter. Dev sits down next to me.

"No. No. You have to sit on the other side. It'll be too much weight on one side. We might tip. I can't handle it when it wobbles."

"Raine. Look at the people in front of us." He points to the car in front and slightly above of us. Only two people, together, on one side of the car. Dev turns around and points behind us. "The couple behind us are sitting on one side together too."

I take his word for it. I don't want the car to rock when I turn. I stare straight ahead. And prepare. "Will you please sit still? I can't take it."

He puts his arm around me. I refuse to move. The attendant tells us to buckle the seat belt. I'm afraid. I can feel the adrenaline juices in my stomach release. Dev reaches over me to grab my end of the seat belt. "Raine, hon. It's going to be fine."

I don't believe him. He buckles us in and pulls me close. We start to rise. The higher we get, the more nervous I feel. I look at the inside of the car we're in. That's a mistake. My eyes find one, tiny hole on the floor of the car. It's there for some important purpose I know, but the only thing I focus on is the fact I can see right through it as we go higher. And higher. I close my eyes. Dev's one arm around the back of the car scrunches me closer to him. He holds one of my hands with his free hand. I still can't open my eyes.

"You're missing the best view of Ocean City at night." No amount of coaxing is going to get me to open my eyes. I know if I keep them closed, I can control the rising panic. My insides are shaking even if my outsides aren't.

"Babe, relax."

That gets my attention. Dev's never called me babe before. I like it. He takes my face and turns it to face him. Still not opening my eyes. "I'm trying. Just let me be like this until it ends. I'll be okay because when I have my eyes closed, I can't tell what's happening."

"But you're not enjoying the ride."

"It doesn't matter. I told you before you got me on this stupid ride that I wouldn't enjoy it anyway."

"I'm about to fix that."

I have no idea how he plans to fix it. I'm afraid to ask. I don't wait two seconds before his plan is clear. He kisses me. Nice, sweet, and gentle. As soon as he does, I'm not sure what's messing with my stomach now. The ride or Dev's kisses. The ferris wheel is rapidly becoming my absolute favorite ride. Why does it have to be so short?

. . ❧ . .

TWO THINGS I DISCOVER in the course of my morning run. First, salt water taffy is not made with salt water or seawater. Second, it's addicting. I can't decide which flavor I like best. I purchased two buckets of the assorted flavors, and I've almost eaten half of one before I get home. I'm going to have to add another mile to my run tomorrow. I put both buckets on the table when I walk into the kitchen where my mom is cooking potato fritters at the stove. Raine and Tufan are doing something together at the buffet counter. Prem is on his belly across her lap, enjoying the swing of her legs back and forth.

"Look, Uncle Dev!" Tufan hops down from his stool and shows me a piece of paper with stick people and colors drawn all over it. "I'm journaling our vacation."

I'm not sure what he means, but I don't let him know. "That looks great, buddy." All I recognize are three stick figures holding hands.

"I even included Slithery Sara. See?" It takes me a minute before I remember what he's talking about. "And, Uncle Dev, I spelled Sara with no "h" because "h's" are Ew!"

I'm completely sure I have no idea what Tufan is talking about, but I do know Raine is responsible because she bursts out laughing and it startles Prem. Prem starts crying. Pooja comes to help, and Tufan tries to console his little brother in the middle of all the confusion.

"Let me take him for a while." Raine doesn't hesitate and hands Prem off to his naniji. Pooja props the little guy on her shoulder and walks to the living room shushing and rubbing his back. I watch Tufan follow them and helping her calm Prem down by telling him all about Slithery Sara.

I look back at Raine. "What was that about?"

"I was just being silly." She's still giggling. I don't think it was that funny. "It's a skit Jimmy Fallon does."

"Jimmy Fallon?"

"You know, The Tonight Show? With Jimmy Fallon?"

"Oh, that Jimmy Fallon." I know the show airs in India, but I haven't watched it. I can tell Raine is fan, though, because she keeps telling me things he's done.

"He dresses up and acts like a fourteen-year-old. It just makes me laugh. Especially when he gets celebrities to do it with him. We should watch some clips on Hulu."

I don't care either way, but I don't tell Raine.

Blue puts eggs and potato fritters in front of each of us. "Have some breakfast, you two." After all the sugar I just ate, protein is exactly what I need.

I take one bite. "You let Tufan watch it? Don't you think it's a little old for him?"

"Of course I don't let him watch it. At least not all the time. It's on too late."

"Not all the time? So you do let him watch it."

"I mean I've let him watch parts of it when people he likes are on. Superman, Thor, or Captain America." She takes a bite of her eggs. "Captain Kirk." It takes me a minute to realize she's teasing me. "You're jealous!"

"What? No! Why would I be jealous?"

"Maybe because you haven't been asked on the show?"

"First, no. I'm not jealous. Second, I haven't been asked on the show because I haven't filmed anything in Hollywood. Yet." I don't tell her I've been on plenty of similar shows in Bollywood. I like the idea she doesn't know that about me.

Raine slops up the rest of her egg yolk with a piece of bread and hops down from the stool. "I have something for you." She leaves and comes back with a pair of leather boots. "I have plans for us today."

"Can I finish breakfast?"

"Nope. You've eaten enough." She sits down and eats the last fritter off my plate. "I'll help you."

Blue places a full plate of turkey bacon between us. Raine takes three pieces from that plate. "Do you want some coffee, Raine? You look tired. Didn't you sleep well?"

"Yes, I slept well." Another piece of bacon follows.

I wink at Raine because I know just how much we did not sleep. Her face flashes pink. Her blushes have become one of my absolute favorite things about her. I will never get tired of it. I smile when I realize "absolute" just became a part of my vocabulary.

"What plans do you have for today?"

I start to sip my coffee.

Raine answers. "Horseback riding."

My coffee goes down the wrong side of my throat.

"Are you okay, Devaj?"

"Perfect." Raine flashes me a paybacks-a-bitch smile. I ignore it because there is no way in hell I'm getting on the back of a horse.

· · ∞ · ·

"C'MON. WE'LL LOOK BACK someday at this moment that we're in."

"I am not getting on."

"If I can go on the ferris wheel, you can ride a horse." I look at everyone mounting the horses brought to them by the stable hands. One man needs a stepping block to mount.

"No."

"Dev, it's not hard, I promise. You'll love it."

"No." I can tell Raine isn't happy with me right now. "I'm fine where I am."

Raine mounts a dark brown horse and starts circling the ring. I watch her bob up and down in the saddle. She clearly knows what she's doing. I'm not about to get on this animal and make a fool of myself.

Shirley, the trail guide, doesn't help. "This is the gentlest horse in the stables. You won't have any problem with her. She's the one we put all our beginners on."

Not helping. "I understand. I'm not getting on."

Raine comes back around and stops in front of us. "I can't believe you! I even bought you cowboy boots so you can ride safely."

"Don't worry. I'll still wear them." And I will. "I'm just not going to wear them on top of a horse."

"Whatever. I'm going riding. I'll be back in an hour or so." Raine turns her horse around and catches up with the group heading for the trail ride.

"There's a lounge in the stables near the office. Right next to the tack room if you want to wait for your girlfriend in there."

I look at Shirley. "She's not my girlfriend." I don't tell her Raine is my wife. I'm mad. Taking it out on Shirley is the only option I have. I don't say anything else and leave Shirley holding the reins to the gentlest horse in the stables.

In the lounge, there's a pot of coffee already brewed so I help myself. It's thick and bitter. I set my styrofoam cup down next to the pot and walk over to a wall lined with brochures of activities. I pick up one that reads Ohio on it. I flip through the pages. I might check this farm out when we get back. The rest are around Ocean City. I pick another one with a group of horses on the front. They're standing on a beach. Some are in the water. Some are on land. I read the inside. Assateague Island National Park. I fold both brochures and put them in my pocket.

It's not long before Raine comes back. "Let's go."

I can tell she's still upset with me. She won't even look me in the eyes. We walk out past all the horses that just returned from the ride. "Thank you, Shirley."

I don't like that I'm following her and being treated like a school boy who's been scolded by his mother. I'm not about to chase her to ask for forgiveness either. I have a better idea.

"Assateague Island, Dev?" Raine is flipping the brochure I gave her as soon as we get in the van. I still struggle a little with driving on the wrong side of the road, but I don't let Raine know. She's still complaining about me not riding. I want her to know I don't hate horses. I just don't want to ride one. Everything I say comes out wrong. It doesn't help being forced to drive fifteen m.p.h. in a thirty-five m.p.h. zone. Every time there's a turn in the road, the car in front of us brakes. I decide to pass. There is nothing like the satisfaction of blowing them away as I go.

"Dev! Don't! Wait!" Raine's voice echoes in my ears. I see her reach out at nothing in my peripheral vision. I can also tell she's pressing the imaginary brake on the floor board in front of her seat.

"What the hell is wrong with you?"

"You can't pass like that!"

I can see she's ready to cry, so I lower my voice and try to speak nicer. I'm not sure I'm doing a good job of it. "Like what?"

"A double yellow line in the center?"

"So?"

"It means you can't pass. You can't pass on a curve like that."

"Raine, they were going fifteen m.p.h. What did you expect me to do?"

Now she's crying. I pull into the first spot I come to. It's right in front of the ocean. I can't stand to see her cry. I remove my seatbelt and turn to face her. I hate the distance between our seats. I reach out to hold her hand and push the hair from her face, but she pulls away from me.

"We're okay. I'm sorry."

She's really crying now.

"Raine, what is it?" She won't say anything. Won't turn to face me. I get out of the van, come over to her side, and open the door. I coax her out. "Let's walk the beach."

"No." She leans against the door.

"Tell me what it is."

"You were driving too fast. We could've been killed."

My chest tightens. Shit. Prem was killed in car accident. Road rage is what they said. I pull her close to me and wrap my arms around her. I rub her back. There's nothing I can say except the only thing I can. "Raine, honey. I'm sorry." I'm not sure how long we stand together, but I let her cry until she finishes. "How about you drive the rest of the way? What do you think?"

She nods her head. "Okay." I hand her the key and get in on the passenger side. I reset the GPS.

Assateague National Park isn't much farther down the road. We walk along the marshlands of the island. Before we get too far inland, I realize cowboy boots are probably not the best footwear on this terrain. Raine's riding boots aren't any better. We decide to sit on a rock cluster near the path we're following.

Raine is quiet and I'm having trouble finding things to talk about. "I don't understand it. The brochure says horses."

"Be patient. They're wild." At least her voice is normal again. Her eyes are still red. My gut twists. I hate myself for making her upset. I move closer to her and rest my hand on the rock behind her. She doesn't move away so that's a good sign. Then we see them.

"Oh, my God!" I can't think of any words to describe them. I watch them running together through the marsh in the distance. Wondrous is a good word. And extraordinary. Ethereal. Perfect. They're not large like the one Raine wanted me to ride. A cross between a pony and a horse, maybe? "I've never seen anything like them."

"Neither have I. I've seen wild horses on TV, but it doesn't compare to seeing them in person. Like this."

Raine leans into me now. I move my hand from the rock to her shoulder. Having her back in my arms, like this, makes me happy. I realize for the first time since knowing her that I will do everything in my power to make sure nothing and no one ever hurts her again.

CHAPTER SIXTEEN

I miss this. Really miss it. We're gone a week and I know. Minivan life is not for me. I floor the pedal of my Maserati until I hit eighty-five m.p.h.—as soon as I pass the sign that says I can go sixty-five on I-90 W. I don't care what the speed limit is. At four a.m. in the morning, no one is on the road anyway. I have my radar detector on. I'm not worried. I drive almost an hour when my phone rings. It's Naz. I answer it using the bluetooth. "What's up?"

"You're taking me to dinner."

"I'm what?"

"You're taking me to dinner and it's my choice. You can bring Raine if you want."

"And why am I doing this?"

"Pria is done. I just got off the phone with her lawyer. It's settled. We're gonna release a joint statement, and she's checking herself into a hospital for treatment."

"What is this joint statement?"

"Don't worry. You're gonna look like a saint."

I can't wait to let Raine know the good news.

As soon as I'm back home, I run upstairs to tell her. I'm not sure where she is. I passed my mom holding Prem in the family room. I look at my watch. Nine o'clock. Tufan should be at school already. I come back downstairs. Coffee. A full pot. I pour myself a cup. Pooja walks in and pours one for herself.

"Do you know where Raine is? I have some good news."

She looks at the clock above the sink. "Probably at work."

"What do you mean work?"

"I think that's where she went. She was dressed the way she used to when she went to her job sites."

I'm not happy. I know she's been evading me, but I'm sure I was clear enough on the subject. I hear the backdoor slam. It's Naz.

She walks in. I hear her talking with my mom in the family room. I decide to wait until she makes her way into the kitchen because I'm trying to push down the anger I have right now. Raine doesn't need to work, and I hate she's decided to go back without talking with me first.

"Hi, Mom." Naz comes in and kisses Pooja on the cheek.

"Do you want some coffee?" I move out of the way so Pooja can grab a cup from the cabinet and pour one for Naz.

"Thanks." Naz throws her purse on the chair and sits down. "What's got you in a bunch, cuz?"

"What?"

"I would think you would be happy the whole mess with Pria is about to go away. Clearly something else is digging its talons in now."

"It's nothing."

Pooja gives it away. "Raine went to work this morning."

"Ah. I take it you're not keen on her going back to work?" Naz adds cream to her coffee.

"What do you think? She doesn't need to work. I don't even need to work."

"Let me tell you something about American girls."

I pull out a chair and join my aunt and Naz at the table. "Enlighten me."

"Many of us don't want to sit at home and play housewife. Especially at twenty-five. And especially someone like Raine whose job is not in the office but on a job site. I can't imagine she will ever be content just staying at home."

"I have to agree with Naz, Devaj." Pooja places her hand on mine. "All the time she was with my boy, she worked. Prem allowed this. I can't say I like it either, but times are not what they used to be, and we are not in India. Even in India, things are changing. We should be proud to have an intelligent, resourceful woman in our family."

In my gut, I know what they're telling me is the truth. I don't like it. I want my wife home. With my children. With me.

· · ❧ · ·

I HANG MY KEYS ON THE hook by the door and kick my shoes off in the coat room. It's been a long day at the construction site going over the plans with Jimmy. Everything is quiet in the house. The first thing I need to do is nurse Prem. I'm leaking just thinking about it. I stop at the kitchen to put the milk I pumped at noon in the freezer. I close the freezer door and scream. Blue screams, Prem starts to cry. Blue is standing right next to the freezer door as soon as I closed it, holding Prem. "Oh my God, Blue. You scared the crap out of me."

"I'm sorry. He just woke up from his nap, and I heard you come home, so I thought he should be the first person you see."

She isn't wrong. "Of course he is, come here little one." He's still crying, but he's slowing down. As soon as I have him in my arms, he settles. I missed him so much all day. I take him upstairs where it's quiet and where it can be just the two of us. I decorated his room in a teddy bear theme with Winnie the Pooh wall decals. I even have an antique picture of a little boy saying his prayers holding a teddy bear. My grams gave that to me not long before she died. I think it goes well in here. At least while he's a baby. Prem still sleeps in a bassinet close to my bed at night, but I like coming in here to nurse him where it's quiet. He takes his naps in here during the day.

We're not alone for long because Dev walks in. He sits on the stool in front of the green antique rocking chair that also belonged to my grams. His face is serious. I know he wants to tell me something. I'm so tired from today, and Prem is perfectly content, so I just rock and wait.

"Where were you today?"

"I had to go to the job site this morning. It looks like I might have to go one or two more times this week. The rest I can do from home."

"We haven't discussed you working. Don't you think it would have been nice of you to tell me you were going back to work?"

"Dev, I'm not sure what you're upset about. You weren't even home when I got up. Maybe I should be asking where you were?"

"I went for a drive because I couldn't sleep."

"Okay. Well I started back to work and you know I did. You've seen me working from home. I told you I'm not a woman who can stay home. I have to do something."

"You do have something to do. You have Prem and Tufan. Raine, you don't need to work."

"I know. You told me. But I need to, and I want to. I can't be just a housewife. And besides, Pooja and Blue are happy to help."

"I know they are. I want something better for you."

"Dev, I'm not ready to be that woman. Please, can't you understand? I want to work."

"And what about Tufan and Prem?"

"I'm not working sixty hours a week. You make it sound like I'm never home."

"Well you weren't home today."

"One day. Really? I went in the office for one day after how many months at home?"

"Fine. So how many days are you going in to your office?"

"Right now it looks like only one or two days a week. The rest I can do from home."

Dev scrubs his face with his hands, takes a deep breath, and stands up. "I hope you're hungry. We're going out to dinner with Naz to celebrate."

"Celebrate what?"

"She settled with Pria. No more lies leaked to the papers."

"What about what's already been done?"

"Naz is handling it."

"Where are we going?"

"I guess Naz will let us know when she gets here. She should be here in about a half hour."

"Can't we push it a little later? I just got home. I'd like some time with the kids."

"See? It wouldn't be an issue if you were home. And not working."

"Dev, that is not fair."

"Yeah, well. Let's leave it for now."

Dev walks out before I can think of anything to say. I really don't want to leave it for later. I don't think there's anything further to discuss.

I hear Naz downstairs, so it looks like I don't even have a half hour. I look down at Prem. He's perfect, content, and loopy from a full belly. I'm not moving from this spot until I am good and ready.

• • ❧ • •

NAZ LEANS FORWARD FROM the backseat of my truck and looks at Dev and then me. "I can't remember the last time I've been to the Macaroni Grill."

"Yeah? Do they serve anything else besides macaroni?" Dev's question is answered by silence.

I shake my head. "I can't believe you just asked that."

"What? It's a logical question. I've never been there. I have no idea what it's like."

Naz reaches all the way to the dashboard to turn on the radio. "You'll like it. They do have a lot of pasta dishes, but you can get steak too or chicken. They have all kinds of things. Raine, maybe they'll have an opera singer tonight."

Dev talks to Naz through the rearview mirror. "I'm sorry, what? They have opera singers there?"

"Sometimes. They walk around the restaurant and sing. Sometimes they'll stop at your table."

I forgot about the opera singer. "I love opera."

Now Dev looks at me. Looks at the road. Looks at me. "How come I don't know that about you?"

I smile because I can tell he's about to tease me. Everyone teases me when they find out I like opera. I don't answer.

Naz answers for me. "Yeah. Dialah and I were a little surprised too. She convinced us to see Phantom of the Opera a couple years ago. I wasn't expecting to love it as much as I did. Wait till she does her opera voice."

"Opera voice? You sing opera?"

"Not exactly. It's just this thing I do sometimes."

"Let's hear it."

"Um, no. I have to be in the right mood."

"C'mon. What's it gonna take?"

Naz rescues me again. "That's what so funny about it. You never know. She just belts it when she feels like it. It's pretty funny."

"Wow. I can't wait to hear it."

I can't tell if Dev is serious or not, but I do know he's probably not going to give up on it anytime soon. I try and change the subject and turn it back on him. "You're telling me you've never seen an opera? You're in entertainment. How is this possible?"

"I didn't say I've never seen an opera. It's just not the first thing I would choose. That's all."

I guess I get that. "Well, it's not like they sing non-stop. They just sing a song or two if you happen to be there when they have a singer on staff."

"Ah. Well we're here so we're about to find out."

It's been a long day, so I'm glad we don't have to wait for a table. The hostess seats us, and the first thing I do is start drawing on the table.

"Raine, what are you doing?" Dev looks embarrassed.

I start writing the words to one of my favorite songs.

Naz saves him. "It's all right. That's also a thing here. They have paper on the tables, and you can write on them. Watch. The waiters do it too to keep track of your wine. It's the honor system. They have house wines. You mark down every glass you drink."

"So people can drink as many glasses as they want and mark down what they want?"

"Dev. That's why it's the honor system."

"Right. So they must compensate their losses on the price of their food."

Naz stops the direction the conversation is going. "Let's just order. I'm having the chicken under a brick."

"That sounds good, Naz." I read through the menu. I can never decide fast enough. Dev's having the chicken marsala. I really want the chicken under a brick, but I can't come to Macaroni Grill and not have pasta. I just can't. I go with the pasta milano.

Bread, chianti, and "Nessun Dorma". Dev sits back and rests his hand on my chair. I can tell he's into it when the singer hits the final notes. He claps the loudest when the piece is completed.

"See? It's amazing isn't it."

"I didn't say it wasn't."

"You didn't seem to be a fan."

"I guess it depends on the song and who's singing it." He winks at me.

Naz drinks the rest of the chianti in her glass and reaches for the last piece of bread. "I agree. I don't enjoy all of it. But that song. That song gets me every time."

The waiter brings our dinner. As soon as it's placed in front of us, it starts. First, queasy. Then, lightheaded. I hate it. I look around to see where the restrooms are. All the way across the dining room. I push my chair back.

"Raine, what's wrong?" Dev puts his hand on mine. I wipe my forehead. Beads of sweat fill my hairline. "I feel sick."

"You don't look well." Dev looks at Naz. "Can you take care of this? Get it to go?"

"Sure."

"C'mon, Raine. I'll take you out. Maybe some fresh air will help."

• • ◦✥◦ • •

RAINE'S TEARS MEAN nothing to me now. Not after what she's done.

"Why won't you believe me?"

I stare at her, standing in front of me wiping her mouth after the latest round of heaves into the toilet bowl. She has no idea it's not possible. "I'm not going to stand here and listen to more lies."

I walk down the hall to Tufan's room. He's asleep. Good. I don't want our mess to cause him any more pain. Only now I'm not sure how we can avoid it. I'm not staying with a woman who cheats on me. I'm not going to be raising any man's child other than Prem's. I can't understand how she could do this to me. I thought we were in love, thought she loved me. I believed her. All I know right now is I can't stay here. I run down the stairs, grab my coat and keys, and I'm out the door. I don't know where. Anywhere, but here.

"Dev!" Raine is calling out to me from the upstairs bedroom window. "Please don't leave. We need to talk."

I know there isn't anything to talk about. I get in my Maserati and do the only thing that has ever been true to me. Speed.

I shift gears as fast as I can. I don't care about anyone driving around me. I pass them if they aren't going fast enough. I don't care if there's a double yellow line. I don't care if you can't turn right on red. It's a stupid law anyway. I don't care about anyone or anything.

I didn't make it on the highway fast enough because red and blue lights flash behind me before I hit the entrance ramp. A second of consideration makes me pull over. What I really want to do is speed ahead, get on the highway, and make him pursue me if he wants me that bad.

I see the officer coming up the side of my car through the driver side mirror. I roll the window down. "Good evening, sir. I pulled you over because your plates are expired. You were also driving erratic, and I clocked you at fifty m.p.h. in a twenty-five."

I look up at her. I'm not sure how to respond. The last thing I expect is a redheaded female cop "clocking" me. "Whatever. I'm sure we can work it out." I reach in my back pocket for my license. Her flashlight is aimed right at my eyes and I can't see.

"I need you to keep your hands where I can see them."

I put one hand over my eyes so I can see her.

"I said put your hands on the wheel."

"I will if you can get that light out of my eyes. I can't see anything."

"Please step out the car." She opens my door for me and pulls at my sleeve.

"What the hell? I haven't done anything. Do you want to see my license or not?"

"I said get out of the car."

Another cruiser pulls up behind us with his lights also flashing. Every car that passes has their face turned on me. I get out. "Turn around and put your hands on your car."

"Is this really necessary?"

The officer from the second cruiser joins us. "Do you have a problem with the request? If you do, we can always cuff you and take you to the station."

"Cuff me? Really?" I start to laugh because it's ridiculous. After the night I've had, I can't help it.

"All right. It won't be funny for long." He grabs one wrist and twists me around. I feel a tight clasp replace his grip, and before I can react, I feel my other hand in the same tight pinch.

A tow truck pulls up at the same time my head is shoved into the back of the second cruiser. I can see the redhead talking into her shoulder when I'm driven down the road. I have no idea what just happened.

"This is ridiculous. I need to call my lawyer."

"Yes, you do."

"What does that mean?"

He doesn't answer me, but in about ten minutes, I get dragged out of the backseat and hauled into the police station side of Lakewood City Hall. As soon as we walk in the building, I tell the officer behind the desk I want to call my lawyer. Another one pats me down from top to bottom and in between then removes the handcuffs.

"You'll be given an opportunity soon enough. We have reports to complete first."

"I don't give a shit about any paperwork." I massage my wrists. I'm ready to punch. Anyone. I hate being treated like this. I've never been treated like this. "Do you know who I am?" is on the tip of my tongue. I swallow more words.

They try to hold my hand over a screen. I realize what's about to be done, and I pull my hand back. "No! Absolutely not. Not until I speak with my lawyer." I'm not about to be fingerprinted here until I speak with Naz. The last thing I need right now is to have an issue with immigration.

The officer lets go of my wrist. "Have a seat." He points to a wall of chairs on the opposite side of the room.

"I want to call my lawyer."

"Please have a seat."

I don't move right away. I know I have no choice. I sit where I'm directed and wait. And wait.

Two hours pass before I'm allowed to call Naz. Another hour passes before I actually see her.

"Come on. We can leave."

"Just like that?"

"Don't argue."

"I sit here for three, almost four hours, and I want to know why. Because I was speeding?"

"No. It's a combination."

"A combination of what?"

"Let's go. We can talk about it in the car."

I don't want to talk about it in the car. I want to talk about it now. I walk next to Naz through the hall and out the side door. Not the door I came in. I get in her car and wait. "Well?"

Naz puts her seatbelt on. "They said in addition to speeding there was erratic driving, which I've no doubt is true." She pulls out onto Detroit Avenue.

"Really? You believe them? Over family."

"Come on, Dev. Are you gonna argue with me on this?"

"Fine. I can't believe they arrested me for speeding."

"No, I said multiple charges. Your license plate is expired. Resisting arrest and attempted bribery."

"More lies. I did not resist them and I did not bribe them."

"We'll go over it together later. It's late."

"Take me to your house."

"Why would I take you to my house?"

"I'd rather not get into it."

"If you want to crash at my house, you're gonna have to."

"Raine's pregnant."

"That much I know. Macaroni Grill. Remember?"

"The baby's not mine."

CHAPTER SEVENTEEN

"You and Dev are putting me in a difficult situation."

I'm not sure how asking if I can stay with Naz puts her in a difficult situation. I'm the one leaving everything important to me.

Naz continues in her counselor voice. "Look. I think you should stay put. You have Tufan to think about. And Prem."

"But Naz. That's why I asked you. You're family."

"That's not the solution. This is Prem's house. Your house. You can't just uproot Tufan from the only stable thing he's ever known."

"Naz, I can't stay here. With him. He thinks I cheated on him."

"Did you?"

"No! Of course not. I can't believe you have to ask me that."

"I had to. I can't help you if you don't tell me the truth."

"Naz, I didn't cheat. I haven't been with anyone but him since Prem. I can't get him to tell me why he thinks I cheated on him."

"Look. Dev stayed at my house last night. He can stay with me for a while until you get things figured out. But you need to work it out. For Tufan. For Prem. For yourself. All right?"

"Are you sure it's all right?"

"It's not up to me. I'm doing this for Tufan and Prem. I want you two to get things fixed."

My chest tightens in a familiar reaction to loss and fear. I don't know what to do. I'm stuck, alone in a family that consistently thinks I betray them in one way or another. First, Pooja. Now, Dev. I wonder if I should even trust Naz anymore. After all, she's a Shukla too. I twist my hair between my fingers and inspect the ends. I kick the side of the kitchen chair I'm sitting in.

"Raine?"

I look up at Naz. Her expression is serious. "I'll do my best. Like I said. I don't know why he thinks I cheated on him."

Naz sighs. "I'm sorry you keep dealing with stubborn men."

"Prem wasn't stubborn."

"True. My mom on the other hand..." Naz covers my hand with hers. "I miss my brother too."

The knot in my throat tells me I'm about to cry even though I try not to.

"Does my mom and Blue know about the baby yet?"

"I don't think so."

Once again, I feel like I'm losing everyone I care about. Why does this keep happening?

Naz puts her hat on, wraps her scarf around her neck, and puts on her gloves. "You two need to talk. I need to leave anyway."

I turn around and see Dev leaning against the counter. I'm not sure how long he's been standing there. I didn't even hear him come in. I'm having a hard time catching my breath. I stand up to walk with Naz to the door. I hang there a minute because I'm nervous about how the conversation with Dev is going to be.

I walk back in but take a seat at the dining room table instead of the kitchen. I can still see Dev leaning on the counter from where I'm sitting.

"Why'd you do it?" His voice is low and broken.

It breaks my heart. "I didn't."

He shakes his head and pinches the bridge of his nose. "Please stop lying, Raine. Please, stop."

"I'm not." My voice cracks when I speak. "I don't understand why you think this baby isn't yours."

"I know it isn't."

"Dev. Do I need to educate you on the birds and the bees?" This aggravates me. Frustrates me. Angers me.

"I promise you that is the one thing I'm quite clear about."

I have no idea what he means. "I counted my days, but it's not one hundred percent accurate."

"You're not even taking birth control pills?"

"It is birth control. It's called the Fertility Awareness Method. I've always been regular in my cycles. I can't take birth control pills. I don't like the side effects." From where I'm sitting, I can see his head is still bowed looking at the floor. "If you were so concerned, you could've used something too, you know."

"That's just it. I did."

No way. I'm not stupid. "I may be naive in some things, but I do know when a man is wearing a condom."

"I wasn't."

I've had it. I go into the kitchen ready to let him have it. His solemn face stops me. He won't even look at me. I speak to him softer than I want to. "Why are you so sure this baby isn't yours?"

"Because my birth control is one hundred percent."

Oh my God. I start to cry because I don't know what to say or do. I know I haven't been with anyone else. "Why didn't you tell me you had a vasectomy?"

"Raine, I didn't have a vasectomy."

My sobs are harder because now I'm really confused. "I don't understand. I just don't understand."

"I can't have children. Mumps. I'm sterile."

Now I lose composure. Dev stands there with his head bowed to the floor. I lay mine down on the table and cry. I don't know what else to do.

· · ⚜ · ·

"TONI, THAT'S GREAT news! It couldn't have come at a better time."

"You know I have your back."

I don't believe that for a minute. Right now, she's come through for me. Tomorrow? Who knows. "When do they want me to start?"

"Disney wants you in Florida by the end of the month."

"That, I can do. January is arctic."

"Not a fan of the polar vortex, I see."

"Polar what?"

"Vortex. Never mind. You'll love Florida. It'll remind you of home."

"Great. You'll send the papers to Naz to look over, right?"

"Already done. Should be in her inbox now."

"And Toni. I don't need to remind you that I don't want another repeat of the last job. Everything is run by Naz first from now on."

"Always."

Toni closes the video conference before I can say anything else. I don't care. I'll let her have that one. I'm confident she got the message.

I write Naz a note and paste it on her fridge so she knows I'm heading over to talk with Raine. I want to visit with Tufan and Prem. I'm worried a little for Tufan. Prem is still a baby. I don't think my absence is going to harm him at this point.

The drive is quick because Naz lives in Lakewood too. Not far from the house. Edgewater park area. I can see why Naz likes it. It reminds me of my house in India because her condo is on the shores of Lake Erie. She has a lakefront view from her penthouse at the Winton Place.

I pull in the driveway and park in my spot next to Raine's truck. Tufan should be home from school. I walk in. Tufan is playing Roblox on the flat screen. I connected the LCD to the Internet last week. I want to make sure he has everything a boy can want at his age.

"Uncle Dev!"

Tufan stops where he's at and runs right into my legs. I remember the first time I saw him at Cleveland Hopkins Airport. He did the same thing. I miss him so much since I've been at Naz's. I'm going to miss him so much more while

I'm in Florida. I hope he'll understand when he finds out I'm going to be in the next Star Wars movie. I bend down to pick him up. He's getting big, but I can still hold him tight against me for the biggest bear hug his five-year-old body can take.

"Dev, why didn't you tell us you were coming?" My mom comes in and kisses my cheek. I never thought I would miss having her around. I do.

"I can only stay a few minutes. I wanted to talk with Raine if she's here."

"She's not back from work yet. She should be home soon."

"Really? Her truck's outside. How did she get there?"

"Went with the boss himself today. They were scheduled to do surveys from the air somewhere south of here."

"Hmm." I wonder how many times that has happened since I've been gone. Then I wonder if it happened while I was here. I still haven't got the truth from her yet. "Well, I guess I can tell you then. I'll tell Raine when she gets here. Where's Pooja?"

"Upstairs with Prem. Come on inside. Sit down. Tell us."

"Tell us, Uncle Dev. Are you coming home yet?"

I sit down and prop Tufan on my knee. "No, buddy. Not yet." I feel like I'm lying to him and I hate it. I know I have no plans of coming home. "I've been cast in a movie by Disney."

Tufan shoves off my lap and starts jumping up and down. "Yay! What movie? Is it animated? Is it with puppets?"

I start to laugh. Blue reaches out to Tufan to get him to settle down. He doesn't. He starts spinning around in the middle of the room. "Tell us. Tell us."

"All right. It's a role in the next Star Wars movie."

Tufan stops. "Star Wars? Uncle Dev. Han Solo is dead."

I laugh more because I have never thought of myself as Han Solo. "There's a whole lot of other characters besides Han Solo, you know."

"I know. I just think Chewy needs to have another owner."

Now I'm really trying hard not to laugh. "You might be right, but I have a feeling Chewy has other plans."

Tufan sits back down and starts playing around with the controls for getting his Roblox working again.

My mom is taking her about-to-mother-me stance. "Are you sure it's a good idea to leave now?"

I think it's a great time to leave, but I don't tell her that. "This is a role of a lifetime. I'd be crazy not to take it."

I hear Raine's voice outside and a door slam shut. My mom and I both look at the door. Raine walks in a minute later. She kicks her shoes off and takes off her coat. "Anybody home?" She stops as soon as she turns around and sees me. "Hi." Her voice is soft.

I miss her. She looks good. Really good.

My mom breaks the silence between us. "Come and join us."

"I will in a few minutes. Just let me check on Prem." She leaves. I want to follow her up, but I feel more like a guest now instead of her husband. I decide to ignore what I'm feeling, and I follow her up to our room. What used to be our room.

"Can I come in?"

"Sure."

I close the door behind me. "I'm going to be leaving."

She starts to change her clothes. "I thought you already did."

"I mean I'm going to Florida for a few months to shoot a movie."

"Oh." She stops unbuttoning her shirt and goes into the bathroom to finish. I can hear her crying. It doesn't make me happy to know I hurt her. I still can't forgive her.

· · ❧ · ·

"THAT'S ALL HE SAID?" Dialah puts her arms around me. "He deserves a kick in the butt. I can't believe he's related to Naz."

I pat Dialah's hand on my shoulder. "Don't be too hard him."

"How can you say that? The man accuses you of cheating on him, moves out, and then tells you he's going to Florida for a few months."

"It's his job."

"I can't believe you're defending him."

"I'm not defending him."

Dialah doesn't have to say anything. Her tight lips tell me exactly what she wants to say.

"Okay. So I'm defending him. But I still love him. He's still my husband, and I worry about Tufan and Prem."

"You need to take care of yourself first. You can't take care of anyone if you don't."

"I know."

"How has work been treating you?"

"Work is great. It's what gets me up in the mornings."

"Have you told them you're expecting again?"

"Uh, no. And I'm not until I have no choice. They made me stop working the minute they found out about Prem. I'm determined to stop when I'm ready this time."

"You might not have a choice. Baby bump's got a way of spoiling the surprise."

"I know. I plan to tell them when I have to and not before."

"Why don't you go to Florida with him."

"What? Dialah, he doesn't want me."

Dialah tightens her lips again and breathes in deep.

"What is it? I know you have something to say so just say it."

"I don't know how."

"Dialah, we've known each other for years. You've never had a problem before. Just say it."

"Tell me the truth. Because we have known each other for years. Did you have sex with anyone besides Dev?"

"No! I can't believe you even asked me that."

"See? I knew you would be upset."

"I'm not upset." But I am. Even my best friend is questioning my integrity. My faithfulness to my husband. "I need to leave."

"Hold on. Stop."

I'm not listening. I start to put on my boots.

"Raine. Let me finish."

"You have finished. What else is there to say?"

"You know you didn't cheat. That baby didn't get there by itself. You know it's Dev's. He's obviously not sterile. Make him prove it."

I stop putting my boots on. I sit back in my chair. She's one hundred percent right. "Wow. I've been so focused on how hurt I've been I missed the obvious."

"Good. Get yourself down to Florida and make him see what a fool he is."

As soon as I'm home I find Blue and Pooja, tell them what I've decided, and what I'm going to do. Go and get my man. Blue has a better idea.

.. ❧ ..

"NO."

"Devaj, you're being unreasonable."

I'm not about take advice about my virility from my mother. I'm this close to the x in the corner of the monitor. I decide to click on the microphone button instead. More perks of video conferencing. Having complete control over a conversation with my mother. Her lips are moving. I can tell what she's saying without hearing. I watch and wait. When I see the repeated pattern of my name, I click the microphone button again.

"Devaj! Are you listening to me?"

"Yes."

"Why aren't you answering me?"

"Because I've already told you my answer."

"Fine. Raine will be there this weekend."

"Wait. What do you mean? Raine is coming here?"

"Yes. You're being unreasonable. I tell you what you should do and you refuse."

"And what does she expect from me?"

"Probably the same thing I'm asking you to do. Prove you're not that baby's father."

Raine coming here is not a good idea right now. I'm right in the middle of filming. I can't have personal life interfere with my craft. It just won't work. "She can't come now."

"Why not?"

"It's not a good time."

"Well, if you don't want her down there, you know what you need to do."

I take all the breath I can into my lungs. I hate when she does this to me. I hate when she backs me in a corner. I hate how she always gets what she wants. "All right. What exactly do I need to do?"

"See a specialist. I'll have Naz send you some names. Naz tells me Cleveland Clinic has a hospital down there. I'd go there. Keeps everything in one place."

"You've talked to Naz about this?"

"Why wouldn't I? She is your lawyer, isn't she?"

"Yes, but what does that have to do with anything?"

"Devaj. You and Raine can't continue living separately. It's not good for you. It's not good for her, and it's not good for the kids. This has to be settled one way or the other."

How is it I'm constantly faced with ultimatums by my own mother. "I think I can decide what is good for me."

"I don't think you can. Raine swears that child is yours. I believe her."

My own mother doesn't support me. "Of course you do. Far be it for you to ever support your own son."

"Not when he's being unreasonable. You go see the doctor, and then we'll know who's right and who's wrong."

I can hear Aunt Pooja in the background whispering something unclear. My mom shakes her head and waves behind her back. Great. It's a family affair. I'm surprised they don't have Prem in the monitor shaking his finger at me and smiling. Or even Tufan. Thinking about them makes me remember how much I miss them. I don't want to separate from them. I don't want to separate from Raine.

"Okay. I'm going to do what you're asking. But when the tests come back, just remember you're the one who asked for it."

I'm not sure I can face my life without her in it.

CHAPTER EIGHTEEN

"Come in. Have a seat."

"Thank you for meeting me so early." I look around the room while Dr. Wagar takes a seat across from me. "I appreciate you being able to accommodate my schedule."

"Not a problem. We got the tests back." He's even smiling about it. "It's good news."

"I could use some."

"It's not impossible for you to father children. Tests show you have a very low sperm count, which is a common side effect for adults who have contracted mumps."

"It's not impossible" are the only words I hear. Everything else is background noise. What have I done? More important, what am I going to do now?

I stand up to leave as soon as Dr. Wagar finishes explaining his diagnosis. I shake his hand and walk out. I need to get in touch with Raine. The words in the letters I've written, never meaning to send, flood my brain. What I need to say can't be said in a letter or over the phone. It needs to be said in person.

At the production site, I can barely focus while I'm in hair and make-up. A woman I haven't seen before is assigned to do my make-up. I close my eyes while Stephanie brushes cream on my face. She moves progressively around me. At one point she straddles the chair I'm sitting in while she's talking about something I'm sure I don't care about.

"Are you going?"

I open my eyes to see Stephanie leaning forward in front of me with a brush and mirror in her hands. Bursting cleavage is the first thing I see. I've no doubt it's on purpose. I'm used to it. I can't help it. I look. "I'm sorry, what?" I look up at Stephanie's face. Crooked teeth smile back.

"Will you be at the party tonight? After wrap?"

I know what she's talking about, but at this moment the only person I want to spend any time with is Raine. I miss her mop of red hair and perfect white teeth. I miss Tufan. I miss Prem. I miss holding her, and I miss Raine holding Prem.

"No. I won't be there. I have somewhere else I need to be."

· · ❧ · ·

"HOW IS SHE?" I FINALLY ask Naz the question I've wanted to ask from the minute I got the results from Dr. Wagar.

"Why don't you go see for yourself."

"Come on, Naz. Tell me how she is. Even my mom won't tell me anything more than 'good' or 'fine' or something like that when I call." I punch the throw pillow sitting next to me on the couch. "I want to know what she's been doing. Has she been seeing anyone?"

"Dev, look. You need to talk to Raine yourself. I'm not getting in the middle of it. Stop pulling the embroidery on that. You're gonna ruin it."

I put the pillow down, lean back, and rest both arms along the back of the couch. "But you're her lawyer. You're always in the middle of it."

Naz throws a pillow from her other couch across the room, but I duck before it can hit me in the head. "Hey! Be careful. You're gonna ruin the embroidery."

"There isn't any on that one."

"So, has she been seeing someone?"

"What do you think? I swear men can be so stupid."

"Excuse me?"

"Do you really think there's gonna be much action with a baby bump the size of watermelon?"

"I doubt she's the size of a watermelon, yet. She's only what? Five months?"

I haven't spoken to her for months so I really don't know what to expect.

"Dev, just go see her."

"Does she know?"

"Know what?"

"About my test results. I told my mom. I don't know if she told Raine."

"I don't know either. My guess is no. Raine hasn't told me anything. Dev, go. See your family."

I can't even drive myself there. I'm having the Maserati shipped because I didn't want to wait any longer than I had to, so I took the earliest flight available. Now, I'm here. I don't know why it's so hard to go home. My home.

I stand up and toss the throw pillow back at Naz. It hits its mark. "Hey!"

I don't stay to hear anything else and walk outside on the veranda of Naz's condo and stare at Lake Erie. It envelops me. Just like the ocean in front of my house in India. I know what I have to do. I just need to make up my mind and do it.

Naz drops me off in front of Raine's house on her way to meet up with Dialah. It's weird even thinking of it as my house. Not after what I've done to her. I look at my watch before walking up the drive to the front door. It's a quarter to eight. Hopefully she's home on a Friday night. I stop at the foot of the stairs leading to the front porch and wonder if I should go to the backdoor instead. I start to turn around when I hear the suction sound of the front door as it opens. Then comes the snap of the screen door.

"Uncle Dev!" Tufan yells my name over his shoulder before he runs out onto the porch, jumping from the steps into the best bear hug I've had in months. I've missed this.

I watch the door to see who comes out next.

"Devaj!" My mom covers her mouth with both hands. She walks down the stairs holding her blue sari up from the ground. She wraps her arms around both me and Tufan while pulling me down to kiss my cheek. "Why didn't you tell us you were coming?"

"I wasn't sure if it would be okay."

"What is this? Of course it would be okay. This is our home. Your home. I'm so happy you're here. Come. Let's go in." She pulls on my sleeve.

I'm still carrying Tufan. I can tell he's grown. Not only his weight, but his legs knock right above my knees.

"Let me tell Raine you're here."

"She probably already knows now." I give Tufan's hair a toss and put him down as soon as we're standing on the porch. I take a deep breath and follow them in. The next person I see walking down the hall toward me is Aunt Pooja.

"Devaj! Welcome home, nephew. It's so good to see you. Come here and give me a hug."

Another bear hug. Aunt Pooja hugs me tighter than I ever remember her hugging me. I'm overwhelmed to find everyone glad to see me. I look around. I don't see Raine anywhere.

"She's upstairs with Prem. Why don't you go on up and surprise her?"

I'm not sure that's a good idea. But my mom and Aunt Pooja both insist, so I do. I don't remember the stairs ever creaking this much.

• • ◦❧◦ • •

HOW MANY TIMES HAVE I asked Pooja not to come upstairs until Prem is sound asleep for the night. As soon as I hear the crick-crack of the stairs, I know I'll have to start all over. Prem's eyes are wide open, and he sits up to see who it is.

"Shh...shh...shh... It's nobody." I look at the closed door that's still open a slit. "See?"

We wait a few seconds. Prem stares at the door. He looks back at me. He questions me with his baby sounds that almost form words and points to the door.

"Nope. No one's there. It's bedtime. Sleepy time." He curls himself in my lap while I lay his head against my heart. He puts his palm flat against my round belly. I start to rock him again. I know he's probably done nursing for tonight because he was almost asleep before he sat up to see who was at the door. I cradle his head with my hand and kiss the top of his curly head of hair. Just like Tufan's. His eyelids rock shut. I can tell he's ready to be moved to his crib by the dead weight of his body. He exhales one deep cleansing breath, and his hand drops to his side. He's out. I stand up and carefully position him on his back and tuck his blanket tight around him. I have to be careful when opening the door. I'm afraid the slightest sound might wake him. It doesn't.

I can see the light in my room through the half-open door. I go in to shut it off.

"Crap! Dev!" I stomp the floor and cover my mouth. I might have peed myself. Again. "You scared me to death."

Dev reaches out to me, but I shake it off.

He moves back one step. "I'm sorry, Raine."

I push by him and beeline for the bathroom. Yep. I peed myself. I can hear him talking through the door.

"I didn't know what to do. I saw you with Prem, and I was trying to be quiet."

I clean myself up and wash my hands. "You didn't have to be that quiet."

"I didn't want to scare you. So I came in here."

I wipe my hands on the towel and come out. "Why didn't you let anyone know you were coming?"

"I didn't know if I'd be welcome."

"Dev. Come on. Of course, you're welcome."

"Did my mom tell you?"

"Tell me what?" Dev sits down on the love seat. The same love seat we used to cuddle together on. The same love seat where he would kiss me non-stop for forty-five minutes at a time. The same love seat where my babies might have been made. That love seat.

I want to sit next to him, but I don't. I lean against the dresser. Dev sits back and scrunches his forehead with the heal of his palms. I'm not going to make it easy for him. I have heard the news, but he needs to tell me himself.

"Raine, can you sit here next to me? Please?"

I wait a few seconds before I do. He takes my hand in his and holds it there between us. I watch while his thumb designs circles on mine.

"I'm sorry."

I don't say anything. I wait for him to continue.

"I never should have reacted the way I did. I never should have doubted you. I'm an idiot."

"Yes, you are."

He doesn't say anything, just smiles and nods his agreement.

"But you're my idiot." I've missed him too much. More minutes pass while we sit together and tangle our fingers some more.

"Can you forgive me?"

I can tell he's looking at me. I know I'm letting him off too easy. I can't help it. "I forgive you." The babies are moving so I move our entwined hands to my belly.

Dev's hand covers only a quarter of my stomach. "I don't think I will ever get used to feeling that."

"You? Try being me. The only time I don't feel them is when they're sleeping."

Dev lays his head on top of my stomach. "Wait." He sits up. "Them?"

. . ∽ . .

"I THOUGHT BLUE TOLD you."

"My mom wouldn't even tell me if she told you my test results." I can tell Raine enjoys knowing my mom is on her side of this. I don't blame her. "Do you know the gender?"

"Not yet. They're in there tight, and they haven't been in a position we can tell yet."

Two babies. Not one, two. How did I go from not being able to father one to having two at the same time? I slide my fingers through my hair.

"Are you doing all right there?"

I'm not sure. I'm still getting used to the idea of being able to father children. I don't know what to say. All I can do is watch her watching me.

"Don't worry. I was speechless too when I found out."

"When did you find out?"

"At the last ultrasound. You can come with me to the next one if you want."

Raine gets up and walks down the hall. I stay where I'm at because I think I'm in shock. I see her bend over the banister. All I see is one foot. I get up to check on her. "What are you doing?"

She turns around. Her mouth is covered with her forefinger against her lips. "Shh...I thought I heard something."

I stand where I am and listen. All I hear is the TV. "What are they watching?"

Raine pulls me back in our room. "I don't know. I don't recognize the show. I'm sure I heard Tufan up here though. I think your mom or Pooja took him back down stairs."

"You're probably right."

"Let's go downstairs for a while." I watch Raine pick her way down each step in a zig-zag. I don't want to go downstairs. I want to stay up here in our room alone. With Raine.

I take two steps down and the third step creaks. Raine stops and looks at me over her shoulder. "You have to step the way I step to avoid the creaks. It wakes up Prem."

"Okay." I do the zig-zag step on each edge going down until I'm right behind her.

She's listening to see if Prem wakes up. "I think we're good."

I start to laugh a little. "My mom and Pooja go up and down the stairs like this?"

"We all do." I can't help laughing a little louder.

"Shh... Trust me, you don't want to know what Prem is like when he's sleepy. He fights it and it takes forever to get him to sleep."

The truth is, I really would like him to wake up. I've missed him and I can't wait to start getting to know him better.

We reach the family room where my mom, Pooja, and Tufan are huddled together on the couch. They're watching another Indian movie.

"Raine, Uncle Dev! Come and watch with us." Tufan runs to my side, grabs my hand, and pulls me to the couch.

Raine falls into the recliner. Pooja and my mom make room for me on the couch and Tufan plops into my lap. All we need now is popcorn.

CHAPTER NINETEEN

Two babies. I look at the women sitting with us in the waiting room. I wonder if there are any others carrying two babies. I see Raine across the room checking in. She comes over and sits down next to me. "I'm not going to make it."

"What's wrong?"

"Look at how many are here before me. I'm never gonna make it."

"Tell me what you need me to do."

Raine exhales. It reminds me of when we did Lamaze with Prem. I wonder if we'll need to take it again.

"Nothing. There's nothing anyone can do for me."

I'm still not sure what the problem is. I know if I ask, I'm going to get blasted, so I don't say anything. A nurse comes out and calls the name of the woman sitting across from us.

"Oh God. Four more. I have to wait for four more. I don't think I can take it."

"Raine, honey. They gotta have more than one technician. It might not be as long as you think."

Raine is not pleased. She rips open a Parent magazine and stares at me while flipping pages. I don't think I'll be commenting any more.

Next, Raine goes up to the window again. I can't hear what she's saying, but I know it's not good. She comes back and sits down. "They won't let me go to the bathroom."

"What? That's ridiculous. How can they refuse a pregnant woman? What the heck's the matter with them?" I can tell Raine is uncomfortable. She's ready to cry. "I'll get the key myself."

"No." Raine grabs a hold of my arm. "Just sit down." She props her head on her hand and links her arm with mine.

"I don't understand. Do you need to use the restroom or what?"

"I do."

"Okay, then." I start to stand up again, and Raine pulls me back.

"Don't. They're running behind. It doesn't usually take this long."

"That's not the point. You should be allowed to use the bathroom."

Raine smiles. "Dev, it's all right. I understand why they can't. I had to drink thirty-two ounces of water before the test so they can get a clear picture."

"So they're making you hold it?"

The nurse opens the door to call the next person. "Raine O'Shea-Shukla?"

I'm completely annoyed at them for making her wait. I walk through the halls to the exam room with Raine, preparing my words for the first person who talks to me.

The nurse helps Raine prepare for the exam. I hold her arm to steady her while she adjusts herself on the table.

The technician comes in, and I'm ready to pounce. "Good afternoon. I'm so sorry it's taken this long. I promise to be as fast as I can. I know you must be ready to burst."

Raine smiles. Her face is calm and expectant. I can tell she's excited to see what the monitor reveals. So am I. I hold Raine's hand while the technician squirts a clear gel on her stomach. The minute I hear the whoosh...whoosh everything else melts away.

Two babies. Two heartbeats. Still no idea if they're boys, girls, or one of each. I don't care. My heart is so full of joy and happiness I can't speak two words together all the way home.

It's clear to me what I need to do. I have Raine's forgiveness. Now I need to earn it.

· · ໖ · ·

"KEEP YOUR HEAD STRAIGHT."

Naz is pulling so hard on my hair I can't help letting it pivot when she pulls.

"I can't. You're pulling too hard and I have to pee."

Naz stops pulling and walks around in front of me holding the brush in her hand with both hands on her hips. "What does one have to do with the other?"

"You try carrying twenty pounds of baby on your bladder while your best friend pulls your hair out."

"I think you're over exaggerating just a bit. Go. Hurry up."

I don't wait even two seconds. I don't hurry up either. I don't understand why I have to get dressed up like we we're going to a wedding. It's only dinner.

Naz knocks on the door. "Did you drown?"

"What? Ew! No. I'll be out in a minute." I wash my hands and stare at myself in the mirror. I've gained so much weight with this pregnancy. My cheeks fan out like one of those lizards I've seen on National Geographic. Or was it the Discovery Channel? It doesn't matter because I'm sure I may be the missing link. I open the door in time to see Naz's fist raised and ready to knock again.

"I'm ready. Let's go."

"No, we need to do your make-up."

"I already did my make-up. I don't need any more."

"Just a little. Come on."

I stop and plant myself where I stand. "No. I'm not putting any more on. I'm ready."

Naz folds her hands on top of her chest.

"I'm not changing my mind. I'm hungry. I'm tired. If we don't leave now, I'm not going."

"Please? I just want to do a little touch-up."

"Have you met me when I'm pregnant?"

"Actually, I have."

"Okay. Have you met me carrying twins?"

Naz laughs and tosses the brush across the room. It lands on target but then plops to the floor in front of the dresser. "You win. Just don't be complaining to me later."

"I doubt it will be a problem."

Pooja and Blue are dressed in two of the nicest saris I've seen. I wonder if they're new. I walk over to Tufan who's also dressed up in his best suit. Little Prem is squirming in his car seat. Blue must have dressed him. He's wearing a baby bow-tie. I'm not going to tell her it's going to last all of twenty minutes tops. "Where's Dev?"

"He's going to meet us there." I look at them all waiting for me to say something. I'm not sure what is up with them. But they're acting a little strange.

Naz picks up Prem in his car seat and walks out the door. I grab the keys to my truck and we all pile in. It's a good thing Dev is meeting us because we don't all fit in my truck. Naz buckles Prem in the back seat. Everyone is in except Naz.

"Don't worry. I'm driving too. Follow me."

"I think I know where the Pomeroy House is."

"We're not going there."

"What?"

"Just follow me."

I'm not happy. I was looking forward to Surf and Turf. I yell at Naz walking down the driveway. "Do I need to remind you, I'm pregnant?"

"Not gonna work this time, hon." Naz waves at me while she's walking away. She gets in her car, pulls out, and waits in the street.

I have no choice. I look at everyone in the car. No one says anything. "Do you guys know where we're going?"

Nothing. I put my truck in gear and back out. We're heading toward North Olmsted. When we turn onto Great Northern Blvd, I'm sure I know. "It's Macaroni Grill."

"Nope."

"Tufan!" Pooja and Blue say it in unison. I look at them in the rearview mirror. They won't make eye contact. We pass Macaroni Grill. I look at Tufan. I know I can get him to tell me if I push. I don't. We're heading into Columbia Station. We reach the park with a gazebo on the left. Naz turns left. I'm really confused now.

The park is decorated with string lights including a white tent not far from the gazebo.

. . ✿ . .

"SHE'S HERE."

Dialah's cue causes my stomach to drop to my feet. I put my bended knee in Shirley's clasped hands for a leg up. I almost make it. Whinny makes a lateral move. Dialah holds the reins tight to steady the horse. I don't know if I can do this. I've only had a few lessons. I'm still uncomfortable on the back of an animal with a mind of its own. Riding without a saddle makes it worse.

Shirley clasps her hands again for another try. "Just like I showed you at your last lesson. Hold onto the mane when you pull yourself up. You can do this."

"It feels wrong. I can't believe that doesn't hurt her."

"It doesn't. It's the best way to keep her from moving back because you're pulling her toward you while you're mounting."

I try again. It works. I'm straddled across a horse. Never have I imagined myself doing this. I want this for Raine. For my babies. For my family. I want to do it right this time. Lessons at Shirley's North Royalton farm help, but I still struggle.

Dialah comes up next to me. "I'm really proud of you for doing this."

"Proud?"

"Yes. I know how hard it must be. I love horses, but I would never be able to ride bareback."

I'm not sure why, but Dialah acknowledging this to me calms the overdrive in my nerves. Now I wait until Dialah tells me everyone is in place.

"It's time." Dialah nods to the DJ to start the music.

Overdrive turns into turbo. Bold, Italian lyrics blast over the sound system. Will she recognize the song? Like the song? I can't move. It doesn't matter because Shirley slaps Whinny on the rump. I grip the reins tightly. Whinny stops. Shirley comes to my side and loosens my grip. "Remember what I said. Loose. You need slack so she's not getting mixed signals."

I give Whinny her verbal command. "Walk." She doesn't move. I squeeze my leg, applying firm pressure with one leg against Whinny's side. I hear another slap on Whinny's rump and we're walking.

I'm focused on keeping my hand right where Shirley put it. My other hand is holding tight on Whinny's mane. The path is straight. Straight for the gazebo. Raine is standing on the stairs. The rest of the family are standing behind her. Whinny picks her way to the stairs of the gazebo. Forget turbo. More like Nitro Boost.

· · ⌘ · ·

TUFAN TAKES OFF OUT of the truck and beelines straight for the gazebo. He's still running around inside it when we get there.

"Tufan, settle down." Blue helps Pooja lift Prem's stroller up the stairs, so we're all standing inside. Prem is fidgeting and wants out.

"This is nice, but I thought we were going for dinner."

Music starts. Everyone around me stops and looks up. Opera? Too contemporary. I can tell it's Italian. I recognize the melody. I've never heard this version before. It's beautiful and immediately speaks to my heart. "Ti'amore. Si. Ti'amore. Cuando ti'amore." I'm focused on the song. What is the name of it? I know it. I try to understand the words. I'm trying to identify the singer.

Then I see him. A man on a white horse riding in my direction. Tufan is silent by my side. Even Prem is quiet. The closer the horse and rider get, answers to my questions begin to form in my head.

Dev. Riding bareback. No saddle. Just a blanket.

Tufan takes my hand and squeezes. "Just like in the movies."

Blue pulls him back. "Shh. This is the traditional way a groom collects his bride."

Dev reaches the edge of the stairs. As soon as the lyrics become English, I recognize it. "Nights in white satin. Never reaching the end. Letters I've written, never meaning to send."

Dev sings the last lines of the song along with Rhydian. "And I love you. Yes. I love you! Oh, how I love you. Yes, I love you. How I love you. I love you!"

Dev stretches out to me. Blue pushes me forward. "Go, child." I can't express anything I'm feeling. My emotions are raw and overflowing. Naz and Dialah help me onto the horse with Dev. I'm sitting sideways in his lap. I barely fit. The last place I should be right now is riding on top of a horse. Dialah is walking on one side and Naz is on the other, so I feel safe enough even though I'm uncomfortable. Dev reins us around back in the direction of the tent.

"This is for you. For us. For our family."

"I don't understand."

"I'm sorry for everything. For not believing you."

"You didn't know."

"It doesn't matter. I want this to be a new start for us."

We reach the tent where Dialah and Naz are waiting. Blue, Pooja, and Tufan are almost where we are.

"I don't know what to say."

"You don't have to say anything." Dev kisses me. The babies kick in my belly. I put Dev's hand there so he can feel them too.

"I'm never getting used to that."

Naz and Dialah help me down.

A woman wearing a black cowboy hat and tuxedo walks up to take the reins. I've seen her before.

"Congratulations!"

"Thank you." Where do I know her from? I watch for a second while she walks the horse behind a stage on one side of the tent.

Dev answers the question for me. "Shirley."

I look at Dev. "What?"

"Ocean City. She's the guide from Ocean City."

I look back to find her, but she and the horse are gone.

"She has family in North Royalton."

"How do you know this?"

"I called her for riding lessons."

No way. "*You* called her?"

Dev smiles his smile that melts my heart. "Well, I had Toni arrange it."

"I see. Now I understand." I can't help kissing Dev again. This time it lasts a little longer. I don't want it to stop, and I can tell he doesn't either.

"You two, there's plenty of time for that later." Dialah.

Dev pulls back from me first. "I don't want to wait until later."

Me either. But we do. Dev takes my hand and guides me through the inside.

The sides of the tent are rolled down. The walls are white like the top except for clear windows with painted grilles. I'm glad because it's a little chilly. White lights are strung in an **x** from one corner to the other. It's decorated with towers of colorful flowers. Every form of daisy I've ever seen intermixed with heather and fern. Peach and lavender roses decorate the table in the front.

People I haven't seen in a long time come up to congratulate us. Jimmy and his wife, Alicia, are here. I haven't seen Alicia in years. Dev even invited some of the laborers I've worked with. Naz is happy. I watch her direct people as they come in. Sonny is on the side, giving instructions for the buffet spread out along the sides of the tent. I'm looking forward to another India Gardens meal, and it doesn't disappoint.

The lights on the stage change. A spotlight shows in the center. A man holding a violin walks out on stage. He's dressed in black leather pants, white shirt, and leather jacket.

Naz takes the microphone. "I'd like to say a few words to the bride and groom." She makes it short and sweet and introduces the band, featuring violinist Darek Garver.

Darek raises his bow and points to Dev and me. "This is for you. Dev and Raine Shukla."

It's the theme from Star Wars. Played on a violin. I'm speechless, amazed, and glued to the performance. I've never heard anything like it. I look down the length of the table. Dialah is sitting near the end. I can't even get her attention. I throw a balled-up napkin over everyone's head. It hits the mark.

Dialah leans back in her chair and mouths, "What?"

I wave for her to come down by me. She drags her chair and sits behind me. "Where did he come from?"

I lean into Dev. "Do you know him?"

"Who? Darek? We met at a concert in India. Toni booked…"

"Right. Toni."

Dialah leans forward in between us so she can hear. I've never seen her interested in anyone before. Not this much, anyway.

The next song they play is by Journey. Dev stands up and holds out his hand. I take it while he leads me to the dance floor. It's a classic and another one of my karaoke songs. The words touch my heart. Dev sings in my ear. "I'm forever yours, faithfully."

Dev kisses me. I feel his heart so close to mine. And I know our joy will fill the earth and will last till the end of time. He chose me.

CHAPTER TWENTY

"No way. No how." Raine's familiar words echo behind the music.

I wanted this time around to be different. I wanted it to be an expression of change. I wanted it to be willing acceptance. I wanted us to face our fears together and overcome them. It's not going the way I planned.

The reception is slowing down. Only a few couples are left dancing together. The band is packing up. The last song is playing. An oldie, but goodie. Enrique Iglesias. Naz already left to take Blue and Pooja home with the boys. I see Darek and Dialah standing together near the stage. He's positioning his violin on her shoulder from behind showing her how to play.

Raine stops dancing with me and physically moves my chin to face her.

I look at the woman I'm married to. I don't understand her refusal.

"I'm five months pregnant, Dev. You know how I feel about flying. How can you expect me to just get on a plane and go to India?" She looks down at the bump between us.

I like her pregnant. Pregnant with my babies. "Raine, it's only for a few weeks. We'll be back soon enough." She isn't saying anything. "I cleared it with Dr. Hill." Her eyes widen. I know she's at least considering it. I think.

I pull her back in my arms, molding her body close to mine, and I speak softly next to her ear. "I chartered a plane to take us. All of us. As a family."

I still can't tell if she likes the idea or hates it. She rests her head on my shoulder. Holding me. Swaying with me. Saying nothing. I just want to hold her. Doesn't she know? "I can be your hero. Better than in the movies."

"I know you can." She tangles her fingers in the hair at the nape of my neck.

"I would never let anything happen to you." I kiss the top of her head.

"I know."

I brush my fingers down the side of her arm. "And I will stand by you forever." I can tell she's smiling now. Her hair tickles my cheek. "Am I in too deep?"

"Maybe." Her words are lost to the sound, but her voice vibrates against my chest.

I just want to hold her like this. "Do you think I've lost my mind?"

"Probably."

I can't help teasing her more with the truth in the words of this song. "Would you save my soul tonight?"

"Absolutely."

I cradle her close and kiss the dimple at the corner of her mouth. The one that belongs to me. "You know you can take my breath away."

"I do."

Her mouth is so close. I touch her lips with mine. I don't care about India. She's here. With me. Tonight and forever. I can kiss away her pain. And I do.

BOLLYWOOD BARGAIN

. . ⚓ . .

THREE HOURS IN A TRUCK driving down I-71. Four with the stops I need. That's how long it takes to get to Hocking Hills State Park where Dev booked a cabin. Probably Toni. I don't care. It's better than hours on a plane. Even if we are the only people on it. We needed somewhere close, kind of close anyway. I love Dev for trying to help me with my flying phobia, but I'm much happier with this road trip. I'm not ready to deal with flying.

I reach across the back of the seat so I can play with the hair at the nape of his neck. He smiles at me and puts his hand on my knee. The GPS announces our destination is five hundred feet ahead on the right. Dev pulls in and parks near the entrance. The cabin is brand new. It doesn't look like any cabin I've seen before. More like a luxury tiny house. It's small, but there's an outdoor pool and a hot tub on one side and a fire pit with two lounging chairs on the other. Definitely built for two. I look at Dev.

"Are you coming?" He's already grabbed our one suitcase from the back of the truck. His free hand is reaching out to me.

I take it and we walk up the path to the door. Dev unlocks it and starts to let me go in first. Before I step in, he holds me back and sets the suitcase down. "Wait."

"No." I know exactly what he's thinking. "No."

Dev doesn't listen. In seconds, I find myself in his arms. I hang on tight around his neck because I can tell he's struggling. My one hundred thirty-five pounds is now close to one seventy. He walks us in and sets me down in the middle of the living room.

"See?" He's still holding me as I slide down the front of him.

The entire layout is on one floor. The vaulted ceiling has two rotating fans hanging down the center. There's a fireplace against one wall. It's stone and I can't believe how large it is. Majestic. It's the only word I can think of to describe it. I can see the bedroom through the door on one side of the fireplace.

"A Tardis." I can't help it. It's the first thing I think of when I walk in. "You know. Bigger on the inside."

Dev shakes his head. "You watch too much TV." I grab the first thing I see and toss it at him.

"You missed." He walks across the room with our suitcase and flings the throw pillow back at me in the process.

I move out of the way just in time. "You don't seem to mind when it's you I'm watching."

I can hear him opening the suitcase in the other room. I walk to the large picture window in the back of the house. The view of the sunset is spectacular. I hear Dev come up behind me. I turn around and see another spectacular view. The chiseled abs I've come to love.

He hands me my purple, two-piece bathing suit. My purple, two-piece *maternity* bathing suit. The one I removed twice from the suitcase before we left. "I'm not putting that on."

"Come on."

"No. I told you before we left I'm not wearing it.".

"Fine with me. Hot tubs are more fun in the buff anyway."

I can't believe him sometimes. "I'm not getting in the hot tub in the buff either." I don't tell him how grossed out I am just thinking about how many people probably do go in naked. In the same hot tub. In the same water. Ew! I can't stand the thought.

"Okay. Wear your clothes then."

"What? No way. No how."

Dev encircles me. I lay my head on his chest. It's so comfortable in his embrace. Safe. I love this man. I take my bathing suit from his hands. "Fine. I'll be out in a minute." He kisses me. I don't want him to stop, but he does.

The bathroom is almost as large as the bedroom. I've never seen a shower as large as this one. It's a walk-in shower room with glass doors on each end. I check my look in the mirror over the double sink. A mistake. Now I don't want to leave this room.

"Raine!" Dev calls me from the pool. "You're gonna love this. The stars at night."

I'm absolutely certain I'm not gonna love it. I wrap my oversize bath towel around my shoulders. It doesn't cover me the way I want. I readjust it around the top of my chest. My belly is still popping out between the slit in the front. I want to cry. I throw it on the bed and shuffle through the suitcase. Dev's beach towel. I pull it out and wrap it around myself. It fits. Now I do start to cry.

"Raine, what is it?" Dev walks through the bedroom door and comes over to where I'm standing. My throat is tight, and I can't talk because I'm trying to stop crying and I can't.

"Hey, hey...shh...shh..."

I'm not a baby and I want to tell him so, but I still can't form words. Dev pulls me into the hug I love and just holds me until I'm able to stop.

"I'm sorry."

"You have nothing to be sorry about. What happened?"

I pull back to show him. "This happened." I circle around to give him the full picture.

"Raine, you're beautiful. That's all I see."

"Dev. I can't even use an oversized bath towel anymore. In case you haven't noticed, the only thing that fits is your beach towel. A beach towel, Dev." I can feel the tears start to build again.

"Hey. I don't care if the only thing that fits is a bedsheet."

I know he can't be serious. "A bedsheet? If that ever happens, two words. Gastric bypass."

Dev starts to laugh.

"I'm serious."

"I know you are." He puts my hair behind my ear. "I seriously doubt it will ever come to that."

"I already feel that big."

"But you're not. Come on. I want you to see."

I follow him out. It's been a long time since I've seen a sky like this. Laced with stars. Pitch black surrounds us. The only light is from the fire Dev already has flaming hot in the fire pit and one light in the house. Dev drags the two lounge chairs together so we can sit closer together. Dev holds his phone up to the sky.

"What are you doing?"

"Looking at the constellations."

"On your phone?"

"Try it." Dev moves closer to me so I can see his phone with him.

"What am I looking at?"

"It's an app. You hold it up to the sky like this, and it tells you what stars and constellations you're looking at."

"Wow. Just, wow." I've always loved the stars and astronomy. I take Dev's phone and hold it up in different directions.

"Wait." Dev moves my hand while I'm still holding the phone. "There. It's the Milky Way." He points into the blackness and circles a long section of sky.

"I've never seen the Milky Way before." I give the phone back to Dev and lean back in my chair. Dev takes my hand in his, both of us looking up at the vast, dark emptiness full of lighted pinholes. Spectacular.

Dev whispers close to my ear. "How about a swim under the stars?"

I turn to face him. This time, I lean in to kiss him. He cups my face in his hand and caresses my cheek with his thumb. "I've never been kissed under the Milky Way."

Dev smiles. "You do know it's there even if you can't see it, right?"

"Okay. I've never been kissed under the visible Milky Way."

"How about taking a swim under the visible Milky Way?"

I pretend to think a minute. "Why not?"

Dev helps me get up from the lounge chair. I kiss him again. I'm sure swimming isn't the only thing that will happen for the first time under the visible Milky Way.

• • ⌘ • •

"I DON'T THINK IT'S a good idea."

I can tell Raine is afraid. I hold her hand while we walk around the bike path and pavilion at Hocking Hills State Park. "The Park Ranger tells me there's a waterfall that is not difficult to get to and also Dead Man's Cave has an easy trail."

"I know. But he also said there are some places that need caution."

The last thing I want to do is put Raine in any kind of danger. Maybe coming here wasn't the best idea. I watch as an elderly man begins his descent down the stairs. He uses his cane to steady himself on each step. Raine is watching him too. "If you don't want to, it's all right."

We start to walk back to the car.

"Let's do it. As long as I can have my water from the car."

"Wait here." I run ahead to grab two water bottles and throw them into a small backpack I sling over my shoulder. Raine is waiting for me at the trail entrance. "Ready?"

"Let's do this."

She holds onto the rail and takes my hand in her other while we climb down. It's not as difficult as I first imagined. It's a regular wooden staircase built into the side of a rock formation. When we get to the bottom, there are wooden bridges in two different directions. It smells almost like a hothouse. It's damp and green.

"Dev, it's stunning. Like a fairy garden."

I have no idea what a fairy garden looks like. It reminds me of a jungle in the Amazon. I've never been to the Amazon, but I know this has to be something like it. Raine walks across the wooden bridge to the left, holding onto the rope railings as she goes. I walk faster to catch up.

"The Park Ranger was right. It's not so bad."

"Raine, hold up. I don't want you to lose your footing." I'm starting to think this was a bad idea. The trail is dirt and stone in places. It runs along a stream. I don't like the slippery feel under my feet.

"Dev, who would have guessed a hidden gem like this can be found in the middle of Ohio?"

I'm holding her hand tighter now. Another wooden bridge crosses over a hole where the stream empties into and circles down like a whirlpool. I can't say I've never seen anything more intriguing, but Raine is right. This place is a hidden gem. We follow the trail to the edge of towering black rocks. There is a small ledge where people pass to get to the other side of the trail. I can't find any other way to continue forward except by following the ledge. I don't like it. There's no railing and it's only about a foot across. "I think we should go back."

"What? No. I can cross that."

"Raine, no. I don't think we should."

She looks around. We watch people crossing. Little children, young and old. Raine looks at me. I know she wants to keep going.

"Fine. I'll go first and you follow me." I take one of her hands and place it on my hip. She grabs onto my other side, and I step up slow to begin to cross.

"It really makes me mad to see that."

I have no idea what she's talking about.

"This place is true nature, and people leave their empty Starbucks cups laying around. Do you think we should pick it up and throw it out?"

"No. Leave it. You might lose your balance." I can tell she's not thrilled with the idea. "I'll get it on the way back if it's still there." We reach the end of the ledge where there are three rock steps. I take a careful step for each one. We can hear people laughing up ahead. We walk around a couple large trees and boulders. Now I would believe we were in the Amazon if I didn't know exactly where we are.

Raine walks around me. "Amazing! I'm going too." She walks straight into the clear pool of water surrounding the slim line of a waterfall in the center. Little ones splash water at each other. Raine splashes too. "Come on!"

I know it's not a good idea. I smile from the edge. People are laughing and playing. One couple is standing directly under the falls. If I wasn't so worried about Raine right now, that's exactly where we would be too.

"I can't take my parents anywhere." A young girl standing next to me laughs with her friends.

"Those are your parents?"

She rolls her eyes. "Yes."

"They're just having some fun." I smile and walk straight into the water after Raine.

.. ❧ ..

DEV PLOWS THROUGH THE water in my direction. I can't wait for him to reach me. I love it when he gets a look in his eyes that says, "Devour."

He grabs me from behind and wraps his arms around my waist. My large waist. He buries his face in my neck. I turn around and his lips find mine. I don't want him to stop, but right here and right now is not the place.

I pull back and splash him. He splashes me back, and I head straight for the waterfall. I decide it's our turn. The couple there before left the spot and moved closer to the edge to play with the kids splashing around. I let the water fall against my back. A perfect massage. I twist side to side to allow the water to hit each shoulder blade.

Dev joins me. "Better than the hot tub?"

"No comparison." I let the water flow on top of my head like a shower. I know I'm going to regret the tangles later, but I don't care. It's divine.

"You know we're not allowed to be in here."

I stop to wring some of the water from my wet locks. "What?"

"Apparently, it's not good for the flora and fauna."

"Dev, we need to get out. The last thing I want to do is get in trouble by a Park Ranger."

I start to walk out of the pool, and Dev holds me back. "Hold on, now. They'll just ask us to get out."

"I don't care. This place is untouched. I don't want to contribute to ruining it."

"Come on. Let's go see Dead Man's Cave." Dev lets me go and follows me out of the pool. Just in time. A Ranger appears from behind one of the boulders and blows a whistle

273

motioning for everyone to come out. I'm so embarrassed. The Ranger stares at both of us. It's clear he knows. Dev places my hands on his hips and drags me back up to the narrow ledge. I want the Starbucks cup still calling me to grab it and throw it out. Dev doesn't let me.

"Stay here." I watch him climb back up to the ledge, grab the cup, and put it in his back pack.

"Thank you."

He holds my hand all the way to the wooden bridges at the bottom of the steps where we came in. "Are you sure you want to keep going?"

"I feel good. Let's keep going. I want to see the famous Dead Man's Cave." I don't tell him the calves in my legs are starting to burn.

"All right." Dev takes my hand and we cross over the wooden bridge in the opposite direction. We cross over another strategically placed manmade cement bridge. It's wide enough on top that people can cross going in both directions, but it doesn't have rails. It's not high, but I feel off balance when we cross.

"Check this out." I follow Dev's line of sight ahead. It's a tunnel carved into a rock mass. There's only room to go one direction so people have to wait on each other to make sure it's clear before entering.

"I'm not sure I want to go through."

"If you want to go back, we can."

I look through the entrance to see through to the other side. It's not as long as I imagined. I watch the elderly man with the cane picking his way through the tunnel. I take a deep breath. "No. Let's go. I do want to see the cave."

Dev waits until it's clear and motions for me to go first. "I think you can go first on this. It's a straight line."

"No, I'd rather you go first."

He puts my hands in their place on his hips and goes in. It's only about ten feet long. Not bad. On the other side it's wide open. The cave is to the right. No way I'm going to climb it. A steep set of stairs line one side of the rock mass. Another set of stairs line the other side. The cave is at the top in the center.

"I'm not sure this is a good idea."

"I agree."

"Let's see what's a little farther down the trail."

I don't move from where I'm standing. The only thing ahead of us is another set of stairs. A lot of them. "I don't want to stop, but I know I need to."

Dev comes closer to me and puts me on a boulder. He pulls out one of the bottles of water. "Have some."

Maybe that's what's wrong. I drink half the bottle. Dev sits down next to me and puts his arm around me. "How about we head back? Get some steaks to grill? Relax under the Milky Way later?"

One look is all I need. Devour.

. . ⌘ . .

STEAKS ON THE GRILL, relaxing by the pool. That's where we should be right now. Not hiking through a mid-Ohio jungle. What was I thinking? I can't wait to get Raine through the trails, up the stairs, and back to the cabin in the woods. Safe, happy, and in my arms. Raine calling it a Tardis makes me smile. It's true. The cabin does look bigger on the inside. Her face is pale, and I can see droplets of sweat along her forehead and upper lip. As soon as we're back through the tunnel I guide Raine to a group of rocks near the cement bridge. "Let's take a minute and rest."

"Yeah. I think that's a good idea." She wipes her forehead with the back of her hand and swipes her upper lip after.

"How do you feel?"

"Tired."

I think she's more than tired. I hate myself for agreeing to hike down here. Raine sips more water. I want to carry her the rest of the way out, but I know I won't make it. I don't want to take a chance of hurting her if I fall. "So. You really think this place looks like a fairy garden?"

Raine spews out the water she sipped right after a Park Ranger walks by. The water just misses his back. She's laughing at my question, but I'm not sure why.

"The expression on your face."

"What's so funny about it?"

"I don't know, you looked like you got a whiff of something that smells bad."

"It kinda does. Don't you think?"

"It smells damp to me."

"You're probably right. So, are you going to answer me?"

Raine is kicking stones with her foot. "About what?"

I shake and wobble my head to clear it of any form of expression. I do my best deadpan impression. "The fairy garden."

She slaps my arm. "That sounds creepy."

"Okay. Forget the fairy garden. Tell me something about yourself I don't know."

She turns her face and stares at me sideways. Her lips tip up at the corners. I'm not sure if she's about to start laughing again or not. She takes all of her hair and pulls it over one shoulder and starts braiding it.

"Hmm." She looks around. "When I was little, I cried when they paved the dirt road to my Gram's house in West Virginia."

I don't expect that kind of answer. "Where did that come from?"

"From the deepest recesses of my childhood." She's giggling when she says it. "Places like this remind of a different time in my life. When things were simple. And pure. I hate it when something so beautiful and untouched gets ruined by people. Like that Starbucks cup."

"I can see that. You prefer dirt roads to paved roads."

"What? No." She slaps me on the arm again. I hold it and pretend it hurts. "To me, it meant more people would be invading our little secret hideaway in the hills."

"When I'm finally able to get you to India, there are still plenty of little hideaways you can only get to by a dirt road."

"Really? I thought India was mostly flatlands and dry.

"Some places are. Northern India has a section of the Himalayas. I would love for you to see Shimla."

"When I think of the Himalayas, it sounds so far away."

"It is. But since you like hideaways in the mountains..." Raine stands up before I can finish my sentence. "Are you rested enough?"

"I think so."

We walk single file with me in the front until we reach the cement bridge. People keep coming across. I know there's room for both directions, but I want to be safe and try to cross when it's just Raine and me. I walk us up the three cement blocks and across the platform. On the last block down it happens. One unsteady step onto one slippery stone. One slip and one down. Raine makes two.

CHAPTER TWENTY-ONE

"I'm fine. The babies are fine." Blue, Pooja, and Tufan surround us as soon as I put the truck in park. Pooja and Blue both help me down from the truck. I reach in the back and grab the crutches.

"Are you sure?"

"I'm sure. The doctors kept me overnight to make sure. It's not uncommon for women to fall when they start getting bigger. It's a balance thing."

Both ladies walk with me to the other side of the truck. Dev already got out and is leaning against the side. I hand him the crutches. He places one under each arm. Blue and Pooja look at each other. "Devaj? We thought..." Blue immediately gives her son a hug and pulls him down to kiss his cheek then holds his face between her hands. "Does it hurt?"

"No. Not right now. It's only a sprain."

Blue hugs him again. Dev's face from over Blue's shoulder screams help.

The baby kicks hard, and I press in on my side.

Pooja touches my elbow. "Raine?"

I put Pooja's hand on my belly, hoping for another kick. There it is. Blue turns around and joins us. Both ladies are holding my belly, waiting. I watch Dev swing by behind them. He doesn't get far before they see him struggling up the stairs. I tried. I let them help him inside while I lug the suitcase from the back of the truck. Now it's me standing at the bottom of the stairs looking up. I'm not an invalid. I'm just pregnant. I take one step at a time. I can't wait to see Prem and Tufan. I'll have to wait until Tufan gets out of school. I leave the suitcase at the door. I can hear them in the family room. Dev's sitting on the couch holding Prem. Blue sits next to him.

"There's my baby boy!"

Prem hears my voice, points in my direction, and squeals. I'm sure everyone can hear my heart beat. It feels like it's going to leap out of my chest. I hug my baby so close, and he nestles his cheek against my heart. He's latched himself so tight he feels like a part of me.

"Sit down." Pooja helps me to the recliner. "Have you eaten?"

"Not yet."

"Good, I'll start dinner. You two relax."

Prem is sprawled across my chest on his tummy. Each hand clutches the cloth of my shirt on each side. I massage his back. I try to move him to adjust his weight on my chest. He whines his complaint and grabs on tighter to my clothes. Stuck to me like glue. "Mommy loves you so much."

Prem gurgles his response in sad baby mumbles. I continue to talk to him and soothe him. He missed me. I missed him too.

Dev holds his hand out to me. I take it. "You're a good mother."

"You're a good father."

"I don't know about that. I never should have let you go down that trail."

"Dev, please. It was my choice. And I'm fine. You're the one who got hurt."

"This is nothing compared to what could have happened to you." He shakes his head. "Raine. You could have lost them."

"Dev, I think you're over reacting just a little. It was one step, and I landed on top of you. Not hard rocks. Thank you very much."

"Doesn't matter. From now on, I'm not letting you out of my sight. Someone needs to be with you wherever you go."

"Uh, I don't think so. I'm not a child. I can take care of myself."

"Raine, please don't go against me on this."

"Against you? It's more like you going against me. Plenty of women have a minor fall when they're pregnant. It happens."

Dev stands up and then falls back in pain. "Shit." He stands up again. This time on one foot and hops to his crutches. "I'm not going to argue with you. I need you to do what I'm asking. That's all."

"It doesn't sound to me like you are asking."

Dev puts an arm over each crutch and hobbles out of the room and down the hall. I hear Blue's voice and then the familiar snap of the front porch screen door.

Blue comes in next. "What's going on?"

"Nothing." Discussing my marital problems with my mother-in-law? No.

"Are you sure, dear?"

Nope. Not going there. "Positive."

Blue sits for a few minutes silently, and I know she wants to continue the discussion anyway. I don't say anything.

"Prem. My nephew Prem. He was an Indian man, but an Indian man raised here in the U.S."

She's not telling me anything I don't already know. I'm determined to stay quiet. I rub little Prem's back. The tight grip on my shirt has loosened, and he's sound asleep on top of me.

"Let me explain how things are with Indian men."

I'm afraid of where this conversation is headed. I need to stop her before she starts. "Blue, I appreciate what you're trying to do. But some things stay between Dev and me."

I try to close the recliner with Prem sleeping on top of me. It doesn't work. I need a nap.

"Please. Let me ask you one question, and then I promise I will leave it alone if you don't want me talk to you more about it."

I relax back into my reclining position. "Go ahead." This is a mistake.

"Would you like to know how I've been able to enjoy a career for most of my life? You see how my son feels about his wife working. I can promise you the majority of men feel this way, including Dev's father. I've no doubt there will be other things you might have differences of opinion on. Do you want to learn my secrets?"

Afternoon naps are overrated.

. . ❧ . .

"TONI, THAT'S GREAT! When does it start?" I cover my left ear so I can hear Toni. It doesn't help. I put my iPhone on speaker then hold it close to my right ear. "Tell me again. I can't hear you."

"I said July 25th."

"Raine will be close to delivery by then. How long will I be away?"

"That's just it. You won't need to go anywhere."

"I don't understand."

"Dev. They're shooting in Cleveland."

"No way. Here? How did you make that happen?"

"I didn't. Scenes from previous films were shot in Cleveland. The production company wants scenes from this movie in the same place. It's perfect, right?"

"You have no idea." I hang up the phone and push the swing with my good foot. Wait till Tufan hears the news.

"Uncle Dev!" Tufan runs up the street calling my name. Pooja straggles behind. He climbs the steps two at a time and slams into me. The swing hits the rail behind it.

"Slow down, buddy! How was school?"

"It was okay. I'm glad you're home. Everyone missed you." He hugs me tight around my neck.

"They did?"

"Yes. Prem wouldn't stop crying every night. He's been so crabby. I couldn't even get him to laugh."

I hug him again. "I'm glad to be home too." I want to tell him my good news, but I need to talk to Raine first.

"What happened to your foot?"

"It's nothing. I twisted my ankle a little. It'll be good as new in a couple weeks."

Tufan inspects my foot, surveys the crutches, and looks back at me.

"They didn't put a cast on it?"

"No. It's only sprained."

He looks at my foot again. "Oh. Does it hurt?"

"Not right now, it doesn't. Only when I walk on it."

"Oh. Can I try your crutches?"

"I don't think they'll fit. You might have to grow a little more."

"Oh."

"How about we go inside and see what the others are doing?"

Tufan shrugs his shoulders. "Okay."

"Can you help me up?" I reach out and let him pull me to my feet. I pretend I need more help than I do. Tufan hands me each crutch. I'm not looking forward to the next few weeks on crutches.

Pooja catches up and follows us in. Tufan runs straight for the family room to find Raine. My mom meets us at the door. "Shh. She's asleep."

I peek around her. No doubt. Lifeless. Except for Prem's limp body molded on top hers, rising with each breath she takes. My news about Krrish joining forces with The Avengers will have to wait.

· · ໑ · ·

I CAN FEEL THE WEIGHT on my chest lift. A cool, soft balance replaces the void from my feet to my neck. I can hear whispers around me, but I don't want to move. Dense sleep is still pressing me down. I welcome it to stay. The whispers fade until soft murmurs of new voices echo behind the dark curtain keeping my eyes closed. The voices are louder. Are those light sabers? I open my eyes.

Tufan lifts his head up. "She's awake."

Dev twists his head in my direction. He's lying on his back on the couch with Tufan tucked in the side between him and the back of the couch. "Playing catch up?"

I yawn. "I'm not sure. Probably." I close the recliner so I can sit up. I move the blanket to the side. "So, Tufan. Did you take good care of Honey while we were gone?"

"Yes." His eyes are fixed on the flat screen.

"Not even a hug?"

Tufan flashes me a look while he's climbing over Dev to get off the couch. "This is an important part." He keeps watching while he walks over to me and climbs in my lap.

I watch with him. It might be an important part, but it's the part I hate the most. Han Solo is standing on the bridge with his son, Kylo Ren. "I hate this part."

Tufan looks at me as soon as Han Solo falls over the side. "Raine. It's pretend."

His little face is serious. He reminds me of his father. I hold him close. "I know it's pretend."

It's the first time I've thought of Prem without crying. It's the first time I've thought of Prem, and I believe everything's going to be okay. It's the first time I've thought of Prem since... I'm not sure when.

Tufan pulls back from my embrace. "Can we tell her now?"

I look at one and then the other. "Tell me what?"

Dev sits up and tries to get comfortable. Tufan hops off my lap and pulls a footstool in front of him. "Thanks, buddy."

"Tell her, Uncle Dev! Tell her."

Dev clears his throat. "I was going to wait until later or tomorrow, but I guess now is okay too."

Dev's hesitation makes me nervous. I'm afraid I'm not going to like what he has to tell me.

"Uncle Dev's joining The Avengers!" Dev throws a couch pillow at Tufan. It hits him in the side of the head. "What? You were taking too long!" Tufan throws it back. Dev swerves and it misses.

"Is it true?"

"Yes. I talked to Toni earlier today."

He's leaving. Again. I know I need to get used to this. I can't hold back the tears forming in my eyes.

"Raine, what is it?" Dev tries to stand up on one leg, but after one hop, he falls back into the couch cushions.

Tufan hobbles over on his knees and holds my hand. "Don't cry, Raine. This is good news. Tell her Uncle."

"Can you give us a minute? Play with Honey for a bit? Maybe Naniji needs some help with Prem?"

"Okay." Tufan stands up still caressing my hand with his. "Don't cry. It's good news. You'll see."

"I'll be okay. Don't worry."

Dev tries to stand up again. This time he manages to reach the stool and pull it in front of me before sitting on it. He places one hand on the side of each of my thighs.

"Tell me. What is it?"

I look down at my lap. I'm nervous about looking at him. Dev pulls my chin up, so I'm looking straight into his eyes. The concern I see on his face calms me. Strengthens me. "I thought you would be here for the babies when they're born." The tears start to fall.

"Raine..." He pulls me into his arms. "I'm going to be here."

I'm sobbing so hard that his words are garbled. I sit back so I can see his face. "I don't understand."

"They're going to shoot the scenes in Cleveland. I don't know all the details yet. There may be a couple weeks in Pittsburgh, that's only two hours away." Dev cups my face between his hands. "If I have to go there before the babies are born, I'll have a plane on standby so I can get back here in time." He kisses my forehead. "I promise."

Dev wipes my tears with his thumbs. I'm holding onto his wrists. He pulls me closer to kiss my lips. "I promise you, I'll be here."

I kiss him back. I don't let him stop. I want him to know how much I need him. How much I want him. I wrap my arms around his neck. His hands slide down the sides of my body all the way along the side of my thighs.

"I love you." The breath from his words tickle my lips.

"I love you too."

· · ❧ · ·

"WHY NOT?"

"Because there will be nothing for you to do."

"Please? Please? Please?"

Where is Raine? She's much better at consistency when Tufan begs. "We're only doing a reading today."

"So. Please, can I come?"

"I promise to take you on a day when you'll see something fun."

"But Uncle..."

Aunt Pooja steps in. "Come on, Tufan. Let's walk to the park."

"I don't want to go to the park."

"It'll be fun."

"No, it won't. There's no one to play with."

"Prem will be with us."

Tufan sulks in the chair. "Naniji, Prem can't slide down the slide with me. He can't swing with me. He can't cross the jungle gym with me or climb the spider web."

"Tufan. I will help you slide down the slide with Prem. And I'm sure there will be other children you can play with."

"No, there won't."

"We'll see. Come on." Pooja waits at the door, holding Prem in her arms. Tufan slides off the seat and walks in slow motion to the door with his head sunk low.

I want to take him with me. I always wanted to go on set with my dad. He didn't take me until I was a teenager. I promised myself I would never say no to my kids.

My mom walks through the hall, wiping her hands on a dishtowel. "Do you know when you'll be home?"

Raine waddles in. She's big. I will never tell her, but she is.

"No, but probably not too late."

"I'll make something easy to warm up, then. Just in case." She nods at Raine and smiles. "You two have a good day."

Raine looks at me. "Ready?"

I can't understand why Raine insists on dropping me off. "You don't have to take me."

"Yes, I do. You can't drive the Maserati downtown."

"That's not a reason. Of course, I can drive the Maserati."

"Trust me. Not a good idea."

I still don't understand why, but I've learned to let small things stay small. I reach out to help her with her bag. It's not a bag. It's a small suitcase. "What's in this? Do you really need all this?"

"Yes. Let's go." She grabs her keys from the hook by the door. I have no choice but to waddle out with her.

Raine drives down Lake Avenue to the Shoreway along the edge of Lake Erie. In ten minutes, we're in downtown Cleveland. Traffic is light. Raine pulls into an open lot on the square in front of Tower City. "You don't have to park. Just drop me off."

Raine ignores me. Pays for the parking ticket and parks. I watch her methodic movements. I open the door to get out of the truck while she ruffles through her bag. She comes around the back of the truck to meet me. She has her MacBook and leather binder in her arms.

"You're walking me in?"

"Not exactly."

I stop and wait for her to catch up. I wait because I'm not sure if she's going to continue with her explanation. She passes me and keeps going right to the crosswalk in time for the orange hand to flash *Don't Cross*. I meet her at the corner and wait. "Are you going to tell me?"

"Let's get a tea at the food court before we head up."

Now I know it's something.

. . ❧ . .

THE LAST THING I NEED right now is tea. Maybe someone will have herbal tea. I shouldn't have listened to Blue. I should have told Dev before we got here. Now I'm so nervous, I don't know if I can tell him without it turning into a serious argument. I can't remember what herbs I need to stay away from. Dr. Hill told me because some of them might induce labor. I can't remember what she told me. No herbal tea for me today.

Before we reach the food court, Dev pulls the side of my shirt. "Raine. Hold up. I want to talk." He walks me to a bench at the edge of the fountain with water dancing to the music. I decide I'm just going to tell him.

"Project Manager?"

At least he's not yelling. "Yes. For the construction department."

Dev sits silent. "How?"

"Um. I do have a strong background in construction and project management."

"I know that." I can tell he's struggling, but I wait. "You're pregnant."

Of course. Of all the reasons he might object, it's always the *you're pregnant*. "You do know it's against the law to discriminate against women because they're pregnant."

"Raine, that's not the point. I'm surprised. It doesn't matter what the law says. I know it's considered. It has to be."

"Well, let's say they didn't know I was pregnant."

"You didn't interview with them?"

"Not personally." I know I'm not going to get away with leaving out details so I continue. "Toni worked it out."

"Toni?" Dev folds his arms across his chest. "Explain."

"Blue spoke with her."

"Blue?" Dev stands up and turns his back to me. He presses two fingers across his eyebrows at the same time. He's not happy.

I wait until he wants me to continue. I look at my watch. We're going to be late. "Look. Your mom knows how important it is for me to work."

"Raine, you don't need to work."

"Dev. I know you think so. Let me ask you this. Do you think your mother needed to work?"

"That's not the point."

"Actually, it is the point. Your family business is entertainment."

"So?"

"Why can't we continue the family business together?"

Dev stares at me and doesn't say anything, hands still folded across his chest. He looks at his watch then takes my hand. We walk past the elevators toward the hall connecting Tower City to the Renaissance Hotel without saying another word.

．．❧．．

I CAN'T SPEAK. I HAVE nothing to say. Raine is right. Entertainment is my family business. Mom worked and still does in some capacity. She has a reputation in the industry. Dad and Mom worked together for years. How did Toni even pitch this? I find out as soon as we walk in. The Ambassador Ballroom. Where everything starts.

"Dev!"

"Toni?" Toni air kisses each of my cheeks and does the same to Raine. "What are you doing here?"

"Are you serious?" She steps back and folds her arms across her chest. "An Indian superhero joins The Avengers. I can't miss this." She turns to Raine. "Are you ready?"

"Yep. I have it all here." Raine holds up the leather binder.

"All right, then." Toni begins to walk Raine across the room.

"Wait." I slide in between them. "Can one of you tell me what's going on?"

Toni looks at Raine. "You didn't tell him?"

"I haven't had a chance."

I can't believe her answer. We live in the same house. We drove here together. I'm not sure how many chances are required. "Now is fine."

I wait for one of them to start talking. They both start at once. I hold up my hand, and they both stop. "Raine, how about you tell me? Toni, can you give us a minute?"

Toni looks at her watch. "You two work this out. Raine, I'll be over in that corner where the Construction Department is gathering. Meet me there. All right?" Toni doesn't wait for a response.

I look at Raine. "Well?"

"It's simple. We have papers to sign."

"What kind of papers?"

"Employment papers. An employment contract."

"And Toni needs to be here for that?"

"The agreement is more than just a standard agreement."

"Naz should be here. Not Toni."

"Naz has already reviewed it."

I don't need this. Not today. Not on the first day. "Naz is involved? Why not include my mother too? Make it a family affair." As soon as I say it, I know. I walk away. If I don't, I'll reveal a side of myself I hate.

"Dev, wait. Please. Let me explain."

I stop because that's exactly what I want. An explanation. I wait. My insides are at war. I can see the stress in her face, and I don't want that for her. Especially now. It's not good for our babies. It's not good for her. It's why I don't want her to work. My sense of protection wins the war. I take her hand, and we walk from the middle of the room to a couple of chairs paired off to the side. "Tell me. I'm listening."

"I did talk with your mother. Listen. Don't be mad. She saw us struggling."

"Struggling? Is that what you call it?"

"Yes. It's what I call it. Now, listen. She only wanted to help. I didn't believe it either at first, but I do now."

"Go on."

"She told me how your father felt the same way about her working. They came to a compromise. They would work together."

"I know all this."

"Okay. Here's something you may not know. It's why Toni is here."

"I'm still listening."

"She and Naz worked together to come up with appropriate employment contracts, so I can work in the construction department of movies you film."

I'm not sure I understand completely. "So, you're saying wherever I go to film, you're required to come with me to work on the set?"

"Not required. Well, maybe. Yes."

"Is it maybe or yes?"

"Yes. If I, we, want to."

"No. I don't like it."

"Why not? I've told you. I am not a person who can sit at home and be a housewife. This is a good solution. Tell me why so I can understand."

"What if the production company doesn't want a wife in tow?"

"That's what I am to you? A tow?"

Shit. "I didn't mean it like that."

"How, then?"

I reach out to her and she turns away. "I only meant to say I'm afraid it might limit my role choices. You've been a supervisor. You have to know what I'm talking about. What if you had a choice between a laborer who requires certain accommodations and one who doesn't. Which one would you choose?"

She turns back around. Her green eyes study my face. "It would depend on what accommodations are required. And if it's an ADA request... Well it can get complicated."

"See?" I pull her around to face me, and she lets me hold her hands in mine. "I don't want to make things complicated for them."

She's staring at our hands entwined together. Still thinking. "It's why Toni is involved. Toni told us when she pitched it, they loved the idea. Something about helping the talent have a good work and life balance. They agreed it's important for creativity. Dev, I don't want things to be harder for you."

She's not wrong. I do feel more creative and energetic when life off the set is good. A food cart rolls by in front of us. "Mimosas. Are you hungry? Do you want something to drink?"

She shakes her head. "I think you do."

I walk over and fill one plate with food and ask for two glasses with plain orange juice. I set the plate down on another chair beside us and hand Raine her mimosa sans champagne.

"Listen, Raine. The truth is, I don't know if it will be harder for me. I guess we can try it out and see how it works. I want you to be happy. I do."

She takes one sip then leans over and kisses the corner of my mouth. I can see the smile in her eyes.

"I don't think you have anything to worry about. You are an alien with extraordinary ability."

I kiss her back. I can't wait until later when I can show her more of my extraordinary abilities.

EPILOGUE

I can feel the warmth of Dev's body standing behind me. My absolute favorite place to stand on our yacht is the bow. Right at the tip. I lean forward against the rail. Dev hands me a cup of steamed hot tea. I miss my green tea latte from Starbucks, but Dev brews a decent competitor. He wraps his arms around my waist.

"I promise you this. One day you're going to see yourself carved into the front of this ship forever, captured as its figurehead."

The wind is blowing, but the sea is calm. Dev holds onto the rail in front of me to keep us steady as the ship bobs up and down. He kisses my neck. I sip my tea and turn around. He holds us safely in place. "Where are the girls?"

"The Aunts." Dev kisses my cheek.

"Prem?"

"Still asleep." Dev kisses the corner of my mouth.

"Tufan?"

"Helping." Dev's kisses move to the center and claim my mouth.

I will never get used to how he makes me feel. He stops and takes the cup from my hand. "We can't have a repeat of yesterday."

"You don't enjoy having hot tea spilled down the front of your sweater?"

IREANNE CHAMBERS

"Umm, no."

Dev helps me down from my perch. He piles the pillows to the side so we can relax together on the couch. The sunrise is brilliant orange and red against light blue. I never get tired of watching the sunrise at sea. Familiar colors but always different. Always unique.

Dev hands me my tea and cradles me in his embrace to enjoy it together. "Cappy tells me we'll reach Dublin by noon."

"Cappy?"

"Don't ask."

"I'm sorry, but I have to know. When did Captain Jack become Cappy?"

"Prem. I took him to the bridge. Instead of Captain, he called him Cappy. It caught on. The crew calls him Cappy. The Aunts call him Cappy. Cappy Jack."

"Cute. What does he think of it?"

"Are you kidding me? He loves it."

"I'm glad. We can't have an unhappy Captain." I sip more of my tea.

"Are you excited?"

"Is it obvious? I've always wanted to trace my ancestry. I can't wait to get there."

"Naz and Toni are meeting us in Dublin. I'm not sure where yet. Toni will let us know once we make port."

"How long do we have before you have to be on set in London?"

"Last I spoke with Toni, it was a month. And don't you mean until *we* have to be onset?"

"Of course. I'm so excited about this one."

298

Dev plays with my hair. The door to the living room slides open. Tufan joins us on deck and climbs onto the couch between us. "Are we there yet?"

"Not yet, buddy. Why don't you tell Mommy what you've been working on in school?"

"I'm just learning about different kinds of stories. You know, fairytales."

"Tell Mom what happened in your last online meeting with your class."

Tufan rolls his eyes. "It's not that funny."

"Maybe not. Tell Mommy anyway."

Tufan takes a deep breath. "All I did was tell the teacher about Daddy making a fairytale movie."

"A fairytale movie?" I shoot a silent question to Dev over Tufan's head.

"When I told the teacher the name of the movie, she wouldn't believe me. She kept trying to tell me I was wrong. I had to make Daddy tell her I was right. She wouldn't just believe me."

I'm still confused about why Tufan thinks it's a fairytale, so I ask him.

He gives me another eye roll. "Because nobody dresses in those kinds of clothes and it's nonsense."

I'm still not catching on. "How do you know it's nonsense?"

"Mommy. The title? *Nonsense* & Sensibility?"

"*Pfft.*" I shake my head. "No. No. No. This is serious."

I smile when I look over at Dev. He gives me a don't-look-at-me shrug. "First, Daddy is playing in a sequel to Bride & Prejudice. Do you remember that movie?"

"Of course, I do." Tufan tosses a throw pillow in the air and catches it. I'm sure it might end up overboard, but I decide we can risk losing another one. This conversation is too important as far as I'm concerned.

"It's a modern day version of a Jane Austin classic called Pride & Prejudice." I continue to explain to Tufan how Nonsense & Sensibility is a satire of Jane Austin's Sense & Sensibility. "You see? They're not fairytales. They're classics."

After I'm finished, Tufan says nothing. He gives the pillow one more toss, bites his lower lip, and looks at Dev. I can tell he's considering what to say next.

"The Hobbit is a classic."

I inhale a deep breath. "Maybe Daddy can explain it better." I think I'll stick to construction. Pooja and Blue each bring one of the girls outside with us. Prem is toddling next to Pooja, hanging on tight to her fingers. He runs straight for me as soon as I hold out my arms to him.

"How is everyone this morning?"

Blue smiles at the bundle in her arms. "The girls just finished breakfast." Blue hands little Blue to Dev. Pooja hands me a fussy little Pooja as soon as I have Prem propped in my lap on my side.

My little bundle settles down as soon as I put my cheek to hers. I never believed it possible to have this much joy in my life. Dev leans over Tufan and kisses me. I can see the coast of Dublin in the distance. I look around at my family and I know. This is one. One of those fixed moments in time I want to remember. I look at my babies. All of them. I make a silent prayer for all their wishes to come true. May their hearts always be joyful and their songs to always be sung.

May they stay forever young. May we always stay forever young.

THE END.

If you enjoyed reading **Bollywood Bargain**, please consider giving it a review.

. . ❧ . .

READ MORE BOOKS FROM **IreAnne Chambers**:
Majestic Estates Series:
Storm Chasers of Wentworth Hall.
Folly at Sausmarez Manor
Mystery at Harlaxton House
Wolfe of Toddington Peaks
Regency's British Empire Series:
Aphrodite Mine
Isle of My Man
Pirate be Mine
Aliens of Extraordinary Ability Series:
Bollywood Bargain
Seasons Bliss Series:
Countess who Kissed a Count
One Man and a Babe
Timeless Twists
Nightingale Songs
Find all books by IreAnne at:
www.IreAnneChambers.com
Join the The Cozy News for New Releases.

ABOUT THE AUTHOR

IreAnne Chambers' books contain the spirit and tone of the traditional Regency with the promise of mystery, adventure, and mishap weaved in to create happy-ever-afters with plenty of fun and surprises along the way.

IreAnne looked to her Scottish and Irish heritage and discovered the name Eireann (Erin). Eire means Ireland in Gaelic and IreAnne was born.

IreAnne also enjoys writing poetry and song lyrics, but her love for the Regency romances of Jane Austen, filled with dashing heroes and feisty heroines, spurs her desire to write Fun, Cozy, Historicals, and Then Some...

As novelist and Nobel Prize winner Toni Morrison said, "If there's a book you really want to read, but it hasn't been written yet, then you must write it." IreAnne does just that.

Follow **IreAnne** here:

BookBub

Amazon

Goodreads

Instagram

Facebook

Pinterest

Twitter

Don't miss out!

Visit the website below and you can sign up to receive emails whenever IreAnne Chambers publishes a new book. There's no charge and no obligation.

https://books2read.com/r/B-A-FKKH-TAZCB

BOOKS 2 READ

Connecting independent readers to independent writers.